The Fat Chef

Fredrik Nath

FINGERPRESS LTD
LONDON

The Fat Chef

ISBN (pbk): 978-1-908824-31-8

Published by Fingerpress Ltd

Production Editor: Matt Stephens
Production Manager: Michelle Stephens
Copy Editor: Madeleine Horobin
Editorial Assistant: Artica Ham

www.fingerpress.co.uk

For Nicola

The Fat Chef

Chapter 1

ANNA—The name of a French potato dish created by Adolphe Dugléré, to accompany roast meat and poultry.
— Larousse Gastronomique

I

Paris, 14th June 1940.

Raoul, the Executive Head Chef, was a large roly-poly kind of man. He stood on the grey stone flags outside the Hotel Metro, shoulder to shoulder with Marek the Head Chef, and Philippe the Maître d'Hôtel, as they watched the German column passing by in its triumph. He wore a white chef's tunic buttoned to the neck and grey, fine-checked trousers. In his right hand he gripped a long soup ladle as if it were some kind of cudgel with which he could keep the evil of the invading forces away. It gave him a ridiculous feeling of security in a world where now there was none. He had grabbed it as he left his kitchens even though he knew it was more a statement than a weapon. He tapped the bowl against his left hand.

There was a faint, familiar smell of Paris mornings in his nostrils and he wrinkled his nose in recognition. Because of his size his companions were too far apart to converse, but he could make himself heard by leaning over to speak to either in turn. The hotel staff crowding around them under the arches maintained their stony silence. There was no reason for anyone to cheer. France had accepted defeat and now the Germans came. It was as if a depression of mood had descended upon anyone French; as if a mass-mourning was in progress.

Some of the kitchen staff stood watching the passing column too, though others had their backs turned in protest. Raoul regarded their faces and could envisage the lost hope as if it drifted away into the dust of the summer's day. He felt his heart harden as the troops filed past. He was French and his pride in that remained, sharing everyone's dismay and feelings of hopelessness.

Natalie, a demi-sous chef, stood facing him and dabbed at her eyes with a white lace handkerchief. Raoul watched her. His heart softened and he wanted to put one of his big, rotund arms around her. He had known her for so many years but never given voice to his admiration, and now that she worked in his hotel kitchens it would have been improper. So Raoul never expressed his feelings for her and she seemed oblivious.

Even George the concierge had tears in his eyes; he wore that puckered facial contortion only a crying man can portray. Some of the crowd lining the Rue de Rivoli bore expressions of curiosity, others like George showed obvious distress. Many of them had relatives or husbands in the now dispersed army, spread across France, going home, or else escaped to England with the departing Rosbifs. Raoul could feel the despair of defeat in the air like an acrid smoke from an untended fire.

2

Dust rose in a cloud above the armoured cars, the tanks and the marching infantry as they passed by, heading towards the Arc de Triomphe. Drums sounded the marching beat, and in the distance a band played some meaningless German tune, wasted on the ears of the defeated French. Raoul wondered what would happen now. Would life continue as it always had before? Would they destroy Paris? Surely, even the Germans would not raze the city as rumours had hinted for the last week. He leaned forward and put a placatory hand on the shoulder of one of the waitresses.

'Don't worry, Collette. Business as usual. We will rise above all this politics. You'll see.'

She looked up at him. Young, blonde and pretty, her make-up laden tears streaked her cheeks and her moist eyes seemed to beg reassurance.

Raoul's broad cherubic face above the generous double chin showed only empathy. He realised she was too distressed to reply, so he patted her shoulder and turned to George.

'A bad day for France. A bad day for Hotel le Metro too, I think.'

George looked up at Raoul; he wrinkled his forehead, and his small moustache twitched as he said, 'I really thought the Maginot line would hold them.'

'So did we all, my friend. Maybe they will go home once Pétain makes peace.'

'Yes. Peace.'

The approach of a group of soldiers detached from the column, marching towards the crowd, interrupted them. In front was an officer in a green SS uniform. He was of medium height and thin, all angles and points. Raoul disliked him at

3

once. There was a mean look in the man's expression as if he bore a grudge against everyone before him. He had hazel eyes and an angular chin. A wisp of dark brown hair poked out above his left ear from under his black peaked cap.

'You there,' he said, pointing at Raoul.

'Me?'

'You, the fat one. Who is in charge here?'

'The manager, Monsieur Robert. He is inside.'

'Well get him.'

'I am the Head Chef. I will send someone.'

'No. I want you to go. You look like you need the exercise. Go.'

'I am not in your army. I do not take orders. If you wish to speak to Monsieur Robert please come inside and the concierge will telephone him from the lobby.'

George sniggered, but covered his mouth with his hand and turned away. He was a small man, with a generous moustache and black, bushy eyebrows. His dark red uniform was a little too long in the sleeves, but smart enough. He always reminded Raoul of Groucho Marx.

The green-uniformed German removed his white leather gloves and approached through the spectating staff who stepped out of his way like the Red Sea parting before Moses. Raoul stood still. He towered above the German and remained unwilling to give ground.

'I am Hauptsturmführer Schiller,' the German said. 'I am in charge of logistics and I am here to commandeer this hotel for the Third Reich. You and all your staff will do as I say if you wish to remain working in the hotel. Is that clear? Now get out of my way or I will have you removed.'

4

Raoul stepped aside and the thin man brushed past him, crossing the red carpet and entering the arched doorway to the old hotel's lobby. Raoul could smell 4711 cologne and sweat as the man swept by. He wrinkled his nose again.

They smell like perfumed pigs and have worse manners.

The assembled staff began to disperse leaving Raoul and Philippe alone outside looking at the smiling soldiers filing past. A drummer drilling a tattoo on a snare drum smiled straight at them as he passed. Raoul felt more like striding forward to strike him with his ladle. He gritted his teeth.

'What happens now?' Philippe said.

'Now? It seems we will be cooking for German soldiers. I hope they like escargot and garlic, but I doubt it, my friend.'

'Why not? The beauty of your cuisine is not changed by the customer, only its contents.'

'All the same, there will be changes, but we must persevere and bend in the wind of change.'

'I've never seen you bend Raoul. Maybe if you lost a little weight…'

Raoul laughed out loud. 'No. The Tour Eiffel does not bend either, and it is still standing. They will try to change us though. I'm certain of it.'

'We can only hope the war ends soon.'

'Maybe it will last fifty years. Who knows?'

'I hope not. My son is in England.'

'Let us pray it does not. Meanwhile, we must do what we can to keep France, like our hotel, as French as we can. It would be a shame to have German food on our tables.'

'Or Germans sitting at them.'

'Yes, but that is the only thing we cannot control now.'

They turned and mounted the steps. Raoul's heart felt as heavy as a German dumpling as he crossed the lobby, but his nature was one of optimism and he still had hope. It was a hope the Germans would soon leave and life could go on as it had done for two centuries in the Hotel Metro.

2

Bergerac, Late Summer 1917.
The boy's fist landed with a slapping sound as it struck Raoul on the chest. There was pain, but it was dull and reached his brain a long time after it landed. After all, it needed time to travel through his bulk. He would have run away but his rotund legs made it hard to gather speed, so he sat down in the mud instead, anticipating the arrival of a booted foot. Resigned to the inevitable, he placed his hands behind him, podgy fingers spread out like sausages providing a firm base, his arms two thick tent poles propping him up.

It had been like this for a long time. The older boys teased him, made him cry, and sometimes beat him. At times his body bore livid testament to the abuse, with large bruises and welts carried home but hidden from his parents. He knew they would have been upset had they known. They often told him that his was a family of large people. Both of them were large too and he wondered at times whether they had also weathered the abuse of ignorant peers when they were fifteen-years-old like him. The endless cycle of teasing, pushing and punching, ground on in his daily life, though he was used to it now.

But today was different. Today, the expected boot-blows did not arrive and he watched with surprise as a big boy stepped between him and his persecutors. Raoul had seen this fellow before, but did not know his name. He felt as if their lives were in parallel since they had both grown up in Bergerac without ever speaking. Today the parallel lines converged and overlapped. Today Raoul's life changed, and for the better.

'Leave him alone, can't you?' the big boy said.

'Sticking up for Fatty are you?'

'Just leave him alone, he doesn't do any harm.'

'He's stupid and fat and you're a Jew. Thought you didn't like pork, but seems I was wrong. You make a good couple,' the boy who had hit Raoul said.

'Pick on him again and you'll get hurt. I mean it. Now go.'

The speaker was a little older than Raoul, tall and well built. He stood with his back to the victim, his fists raised like a real pugilist. He had a shock of wavy, brown hair and a large hooked nose, and as he frowned at his opponents Raoul thought he looked grim. In the day's fading light, he looked enormous too against the red and grey, cloud-layered sky, as if he towered above the fat boy looking up at him from the ground. For long moments there was silence apart from the sound of the wave splashes of the Dordogne River flowing past. A glimmer of envy took Raoul. He wished he could be like this dark courageous fellow, though he knew inside he could not.

The two other boys moved off laughing and gesticulating at Raoul's protector as the big fellow turned, leaning forward to offer Raoul a hand. Pulling the plump boy up, he said, 'I'm Pierre Dreyfus.'

'Raoul Verney. Thanks for helping me.'

'It doesn't mean we're friends.'

'No, of course.'

'And don't expect me to do that all the time. Why don't you defend yourself?'

'I'm no good at fighting. Usually, once they've hit me a few times, they get fed up and go away. I don't mind. I'm wearing armour.

Raoul slapped his plump tummy and smiled. Pierre smiled too.

'Yes, guess that layer of rubber comes in useful.'

Their eyes met and the humour of the moment erupted into laughter.

'No. Really. Why did you help me?' Raoul said.

'I just don't like people picking on others.'

'It doesn't bother me any more.'

'It should bother you. Have you no self-esteem? No pride? I wouldn't let anyone treat me like that.'

'You would if you were my size Pierre. Bet no one picks on you anyway. You look tough.'

'They try.'

'They do? Why?'

'Didn't you hear what they said?'

'About you being a Jew?'

'Yes.'

'They pick on you for that?'

'Yes.'

'But you fight them.'

'Yes. I have pride. It doesn't happen often but when it does, I give as good as I get, so mostly they leave me alone.'

'Perhaps you will be a great fighter one day.'

'No. I'll be a farmer like my father. I live on a farm on the south side.'

'I'm going to be a chef. My papa is a cook, but he says I should be a proper chef in a restaurant. He wants me to go to a college in a couple of years to learn how to do that.'

'You cook?'

'Yes.'

'You can cook fish?'

'Yes.'

'Then come fishing tomorrow with me and Auguste and we'll find out if you can cook.'

They walked in silence to the place where, across the bridge, the southern road branches, the lower road stretching away across the flat, verdant farmlands of the Dordogne valley, the other following the river. They parted there, and Raoul never forgot Pierre's advice. He determined he would never give in to bullies again, whoever they were and whatever it took.

Chapter 2

BÉCHAMEL—A hot sauce made by combining hot flavoured or seasoned milk with a roux.
– Larousse Gastronomique

I

The kitchens were hot and steamy despite their size. Scrupulous in their hygiene, the kitchens of Le Metro occupied as much space as the dining room. Ten benches for food preparation and three sink areas stood occupied by kitchen staff. There were head chefs, sous-chefs, demi-sous-chefs, kitchen cleaners, washers up and porters. There were managers, under managers and separate staff for room service, all of whom were subservient to Raoul when it came to the food, its quality, and its contents. Yet no one disliked him. He was a jovial man who listened to his staff and although he ran a tight ship he gained respect for his ability, his humour and his fairness. And he still cooked when the mood took him. He ate too, in quantities that had become a byword.

On that Tuesday morning, preparation was the word of the day. The entire floor buzzed with movement and activity.

Despite the bustle of the kitchen no one spoke much. They carried a burden. The weight of the defeat—the affliction of occupation—it was as heavy and as ponderous as an epidemic of plague. To Raoul it was as if each saucepan, each frying pan, had a layer of burnt-in grease that flavoured everything; that made life a drudge. They had lost their freedom and gained an occupying force of Germans and were powerless in the Nazi grasp.

Raoul was overseeing the pastry chef making mille-feuilles. They discussed the flakiness of the pastry as if life could carry on as normal, though both knew it had changed. It was as if, as they talked, each of them thought about something else, but neither of them wanted to express those thoughts; neither of them wanted to face the truth. Raoul was sampling one of the cream-layered desserts when George tapped him on the shoulder.

'Excuse me Raoul. That German fellow wants everyone upstairs.'

'German fellow?' Raoul said, wiping his cream-bedecked mouth on his sleeve.

'Yes the one in the officer's uniform. He wants everyone upstairs in the foyer.'

'But what about the guests?'

'He's already got rid of most of them. The Hotel is now to be occupied by German soldiers only.'

'Rubbish. How will the Hotel be paid? If we have no guests, then we have no money. Ridiculous, I will speak to him.'

'It may be unwise. He has sent away two of the concierges and several of the cleaners.'

'Sent away? Where?'

'I don't know. They were Jewish and he said they can't work here any more.'

'We'll see about that.'

'It's no use. Monsieur Robert has tried but it's no use. Can I tell them everyone will come up now?'

'Yes, George. Tell them. Damned soldiers; no common sense. If we are all upstairs, who will prepare the food?'

Raoul took down a ladle from its hook above the preparation table. He banged it on a large cast iron frying pan hanging over his head. His staff greeted the evacuation orders with muted puzzlement and hushed whispers that spread throughout the kitchen like butter melting in a pan. Raoul led the way and they ended standing in an orderly formation as if they were posing for a group photograph at the foot of the galleried stairs in the foyer of the hotel. Their curious faces looked up towards the stairs, where Schiller stood next to Monsieur Robert. Raoul stood at the head of his staff a pace in front of them. He was about to climb the stairs when Schiller opened up.

'You will all know that the Führer's victorious forces are now in charge of your country. It is his wish that the transition should be smooth and peaceful. We do not want any trouble, and I wish to reassure you that most of you will be allowed to continue working in the same roles you have occupied here even though this hotel is now commandeered for the use of the military.'

A soft murmur spread at the word "most". The implication was clear.

'We require that all Jews among you will declare themselves and register with the local police. In due course, you will need to wear an identification badge. There is no place for Jews, Blacks or Asians in this hotel any longer, by military order. I have a list here of all the names of the staff and each of you will be questioned about your origins in due course. It is only a formality and you have nothing to fear.'

'Excuse me,' Raoul's voice boomed from below.

Schiller looked down at him. He fixed Raoul with a look of distaste. 'Yes?'

'How do you expect me to dispense with the three out of four of my kitchen porters who are from Senegal? I cannot run a kitchen with only one porter.'

'Then you will have to do some carrying yourself. You may find the exercise beneficial. It is not appropriate for people of such races to work in a German hotel. They cannot be trusted. If that is all?'

Schiller, now greeted with stony silence, raised his right arm, 'Heil Hitler,' he said, his voice peremptory and curt.

Raoul moved onto the first step, but a small hand tugged at his sleeve. He glanced to his right and noticed whom it was holding him back.

'Natalie, these people are unreasonable.'

'Nothing will be served by you getting yourself arrested. We all have to obey. They have all the power now.'

'But it's ridiculous. How do I find replacements? So many people have left Paris; there will be no one to work in the kitchens.'

'Please, don't cause trouble. You don't know what you are doing.'

Raoul shrugged. 'Standards will slip and it's their own

fault.'

There was no one at the head of the stairs now and he had lost his opportunity. It would wait. There would be plenty of time for him to remonstrate; he excelled at that. The thought of capitulating to this little German stick-man rankled and he could not understand why they singled out Jews and Blacks, it was foolish. Many of his best workers fitted that description. Perhaps his people would not cooperate and the Germans would give up. Yes, they would give up once they discovered how impractical their demands were.

2

Raoul stared out of the window at the Tuileries Gardens, green and ornate. The large late-summer raindrops pattered on the shutters and the sill outside as he stood in front of the desk in Monsieur Robert's office. Outside, the morning was dull and grey and the weather matched the feelings in Raoul's mind as he listened to Schiller, who seemed to think that by occupying the manager's seat, he could dictate how Raoul was to run his kitchen. Monsieur Robert stood fiddling with his tie as he stood by the window. Raoul smiled towards him. He wondered whether he was trying to reassure his hotel manager or himself.

'So,' Schiller said.

'So?'

'You have worked here for how long?'

'Four years.'

'You know all the kitchen workers?'

14

'Yes.'

'You can identify which ones are not French?'

'Not French? You mean?'

'Jews and the like.'

'I'm sorry. I wouldn't be able to recognise one of your "Jews" if I was speaking to him. They are like anyone else. As long as they work hard, I have no way of knowing what their religion or politics might be. Religion is not one of the topics we discuss in the kitchen.'

'Silence,' Schiller banged a flat hand on the blotter in front of him. 'Ever since we came here, ever since the fall of Paris when we took over this hotel, you have been obstinate and difficult with every little adjustment of the running of the kitchens.'

'No.'

'No?'

'No. You can't blame me because you sacked three of my porters, removed the pastry chef, and expect business as usual. This is a hotel. It is not the army. We need our trained staff.'

'And the food?'

'My food is a delight for anyone,' Raoul sniffed and shifted from one foot to the other. He knew Schiller saw him as troublesome and he knew not to overstep the mark. He also knew he was not expendable. Schiller on the other hand, needed the hotel to run well.

He is a man after promotion as anyone can see. Keeping the General Staff happy is everything to the man, the slimy little toad. Just try to get a replacement top chef to work under Nazi rule. Try it.

Schiller had the air of a man who could be vindictive and

15

Raoul knew quite well the fellow would take it out on his kitchen staff. He felt like the lord of a castle who in defeat must look after his people, however low their status.

'I think you need to be a little more… international… in your approach.'

'International? What do you mean?'

'Some German dishes would go down well, I think.'

'What? Sauerkraut?'

Schiller lost his temper. He jumped to his feet. It was not what Raoul had said: it was his intonation and the smirk on his lips. The German raced around the desk as Raoul watched. Schiller raised his right arm and slapped the chef backhanded across the face. The blow was hard enough to draw blood from the big man's lower lip. Raoul thought maybe he needed his armour of blubber on his face now, but he also knew the loser in the fight was Schiller, as long as he did not react. He stood still. He even smiled. He knew it had to be infuriating to the German.

Monsieur Robert said, 'Hauptsturmführer Schiller. You told me your directive was to treat French people with dignity and politeness. Is this how the occupying allies behave? You want me to complain to General Lammerding?'

Schiller turned on the manager. 'I will have order in this hotel. General staff of the High Command will stay here. They will be treated like the conquerors they are, you hear?'

As if remembering where he was, the German stopped shouting as he stepped back around the desk. He smoothed his tunic as he sat down, and looked up with anxious brown eyes. 'I will personally interview every member of the staff here. I will not tolerate Jews, foreigners or communists. It is a matter of security.'

Raoul said nothing. Their eyes met.

Schiller said, 'Get out.'

Through the blood trickling from his lower lip and down his chin, Raoul smiled. 'You want German dishes, do you? I'll give you some. I have no objection to some German food as long as I can get the supplies. Will it be a problem?'

'Of course not. Leave a list of supplies with my adjutant officer and I will sign for it. Don't forget,' Schiller said, calm now, 'I will start the interviews in the morning. Seven o'clock.'

'So I cancel breakfast?'

'What?'

'I will have to cancel breakfast unless you do it one at a time and leave the rest of the morning-staff working.'

Schiller waved Raoul away. It was as if the man had tired of fighting, becoming exhausted over the conflict which seemed as if it was transmitted somehow from the battlefield to the hotel.

Leaving, Raoul still smiled. His swelling lower lip stung and he licked it with his plump, fleshy tongue. The discomfort did not stop him smiling. The man was absurd. There was no German food to match the dishes he cooked, but if they wanted to play those games, he would be pleased to comply.

Chapter 3

CONFIT—A piece of pork, goose, duck or turkey cooked in its own fat and stored in a pot, covered in the same fat to preserve it.
– Larousse Gastronomique

I

Raoul felt unsteady sitting draped over a stool in the kitchen. Around him, the kitchen buzzed. Lunch preparation was in full swing and apart from shouting an occasional instruction, he was at ease. This was his world, his empire. No one had more sway than he in his underground cavern where, like some subterranean Greek god, he issued orders and people obeyed without question. Running a kitchen as big as this, it had to be so. Raoul understood that. He knew efficiency and effectiveness ran hand in hand and he knew he was very good at what he did. Although in the kitchen he was a king who oozed confidence and stability, in his personal life he was a mild man. Apart from his unrequited feelings for his demi-sous chef, there had been no women in his life, and Natalie could hardly count as a "woman in his life"—he knew that. It made him shy and awkward with women in social interactions, but he hid it well. He had a sense of humour and an inimitable air of bonhomie.

Natalie sat in front of him holding a damp cloth with which she dabbed at his cut lip, clucking like a tiny dark hen. She had tied her dark-brown hair back into the nape of her neck, and she wore the demi-sous chefs' uniform, all grey cotton and secured with a black belt. Her brown eyes were sharp and clear and her high cheekbones and narrow chin gave her lower face a faint triangular appearance. Raoul looked at that familiar face in front of him and the sight warmed his heart. How could he be angry when confronted by this tiny, angular angel?

He knew he still saw her as she once had been, when he cooked the fish her brother had caught and the four friends sat by the Dordogne eating trout and laughing around the open fire on long summer evenings. She had always been much smaller than he was but she always seemed to be the one who occupied his gaze.

'He hit you. You, the Executive Head Chef too,' she said.

'It is nothing. Work as usual, cher Natalie.'

'You caused trouble?'

'No. I teased the man but he is humourless.'

'Don't provoke these people.'

'Or what?'

'They are evil and they have power now. People are disappearing because of them. They get a green card and have to report to the police then they never come back. My friend Marcel's father went when they summoned him and he has not come back.'

'Maybe they send them away somewhere. It is not my

business. All I know is they are like pigs at a trough. Not much good for anything but bacon.'

Raoul chuckled and Natalie frowned. 'Pierre has been made to register at the prefecture. He wrote to me last week.'

'Even your brother Pierre? How is he?'

'He is well enough but finds it hard even to feed Monique.'

'I am so sorry to hear that. Perhaps I can send him some food. The Germans have promised we will be unrestricted as long as we serve some German recipes. There is no rationing for the German officers here. There could be plenty left over.'

'How can it be delivered? I can't go and anyway the Germans might intercept the parcel.'

'I have a grateful customer who works on the railway. I'm sure he can help. Leave it to me. I owe your brother much.'

'Oh?'

'He protected me when we were boys. He never told you?'

'He didn't say it that way, but I'm sure you are right. Can we really send some food?'

'Naturally. I will make some enquiries.'

'Raoul, I'm afraid.'

'My dear Natalie. I won't let any harm come to you. We are old friends. Relax yourself, you will be safe here at the Metro.'

'You don't understand what is happening. Raoul, they are locking up all the Jews.'

'So?'

'I'm Jewish. I will have to register; then they will know where I am and can get me anytime.'

'I keep telling you. I won't let them harm you.'

She raised her hand in a gesture of frustration.

'You really don't understand any of this do you? The Germans hate us Jews. They've already incarcerated all the German Jews, burned synagogues, killed people. They will do the same here, and you? You sit here making beautiful food for them as if none of it is happening. I don't understand you.'

She walked away and Raoul cocked his head to one side as he watched her cross the clean bright tiles. He began to wonder if she was right. Either way, he felt he would be able to protect her. Perhaps he would intercede with Schiller. He knew Schiller hated him but he also knew the man was enough of a realist to know Raoul would be hard to replace. He had been relying on that before and now he realised he had to keep capitulating to keep this slim finger-hold on his position.

Raoul knew he could tame any man with good food. What was it Napoleon had said? An army marches on its stomach. Yes, he would make these Germans march. He determined to make their stomachs large and round and heavy. If they marched anywhere, it would be with heavy, greasy German food in their bellies. Even Schiller, the gangling soldier, must have a heart in his stomach like all other men.

Monsieur Robert interrupted his musing. He was a man of middle years, receding hair, and a small moustache. His black suit always seemed to Raoul to be immaculate; pressed and clean, it fitted his frame like a chameleon's skin. He was a man to blend in and cause no trouble to anyone, but his efficiency and knowledge of the hotel made him superb at his job. He placed a hand on Raoul's shoulder. As their eyes met, he noticed the manager had tears in his eyes.

'Henri, what is wrong?'

'Wrong? Nothing.

'Your eyes, you're crying.'

'Don't be silly. It's the onions, your sous chef is preparing them over there.'

Raoul blinked and realised he was mistaken. He laughed with embarrassment. 'These days, nothing would surprise me,' he said. 'We are experiencing terrible things down here, you know.'

'Did he hurt you?'

'Who the sous chef?'

'Stop it.'

'No. Cut my lip that's all. It is fine now. I made him lose his temper. He's a stupid man and reacts badly to my teasing. I will behave better next time. Really, I promise.'

'It seems to me you are oblivious to the desperate times we are in. These Germans, they can have any of us shot out of hand. We have to do as they say. There is no other way.'

'Hah. I will not be bullied by them. Yes, I will give them their German Sauerkraut shit. I will make them so unwell they will keep the doctor out all night. Wait and see.'

'No. Please. If you made them all ill, they would have you removed. I can't afford for that to happen. Who could replace you, my friend?'

'I was joking. Relax. I know how to do my job. I won't cause any more trouble. I know they will take it out on my staff, so I am here. I will do what I do best. I will create a German menu. You want me to bring it to you?'

'Yes, Raoul, please do that. He wants to do the interviews tomorrow. Perhaps then we can talk over coffee.'

'My friend, it will be a pleasure. He wants to remove anyone who is Jewish, does he?'

'Yes.'

'Ridiculous, this stupid war. I don't believe it.'

'They did it in Germany. There are hardly any Jews there. There is too much anti-Semitism in Europe anyway.'

'You are Jewish?' Raoul said.

'Me? No. I just think they start with Jews then move on to another group. Next time it may be Frenchmen. It won't stop with the Jews.'

'Everyone is so pessimistic. Maybe we will get some kind of peace and return to normal.'

'With the franc devalued? The nation will be …be… impoverished.'

Monsieur Robert waved a hand in the air as if he was wafting away some evil spirit with a psalter. Shaking his head from side to side, he made his way to the kitchen entrance and Raoul began prowling the restaurant to make sure the tables were laid to his satisfaction then he walked to his office, adjoining the foyer. He had menus to plan and Germans to "poison" with filthy German food.

2

They were fishing. At least the older boys were fishing. Raoul stood watching as Pierre baited his hook. The spring sunshine illuminated him and a fresh breeze stirred the brown flowing river as Raoul stood on the grass observing his companions. It was the first time he had done this, because he had never had a chance to fish. Auguste, Pierre's friend had his line in the water. He had sunk his weighted worm deep, explaining how the fish lurked at the bottom of the river when it was spring and came up to take flies only when the river warmed up in the summer. Auguste was a stocky lad, but not of Raoul's dimensions. No one would describe Raoul as stocky. He was more used to "fat" or "gross".

Every time he stood up the others shouted and made him sit.

Pierre tried to explain, 'Raoul. Don't you understand that the deeper they are, the more of the bank they can see. You are our cook. We are the fishermen. You are the cook. The sitting cook. Understand?'

'Yes Pierre.'

'Good. There are big trout in these pools. You brought something to cook them with?'

'I have a skillet my father lent me. I have to make a fire. I'll need to get wood and some stones.'

'Well?'

Raoul stood up.

'Sit down will you?' Pierre said.

Raoul sat down. 'But how do I collect wood and sit down at the same time?'

'Only your body is fat. Your brains, which are normal, should tell you the answer.'

Pierre smiled. It was a good-humoured remark and Raoul smiled back. He knew what his new friend was saying. He turned and crawled to the edge of the bank higher up. Out of sight of the anglers he began to gather kindling and tree branches. Julien, his father had told him what to do.

24

'Cook over charcoal. Don't let the flames burn the fish. Here. Take this.'

It was a mixture of herbs: dill, and rosemary.

'Gut them—you know how to do that. Then put the butter inside, with the herbs and plenty of salt. Finish with the lemon juice.'

'Yes, papa.'

'You need some vegetables?'

'No, papa.'

'Huh. It is not a meal. It is an orgy.'

'What is an orgy?'

'You'll see, you silly boy.'

Puzzled, Raoul packed the bag his father gave him. As he set off down the road he could feel his father's stare. He glanced over his shoulder and saw the plump face grinning. He loved his father and somehow understood how Julien wanted Raoul to have a successful day. It was the essence of their family. Food mattered. It was to be years before Raoul understood how a passion for food and striving for its perfection could drive a man's ambition. Since coming to the Metro, it was his obsession.

Chapter 4

DU BARRY—Name given to a variety of dishes containing cauliflower.
— Larousse Gastronomique

I

Schiller stood in Raoul's office in front of the Head Chef's desk. There were no windows and a fan kept Raoul cool although outside it was a gentle spring morning. He always felt hot.

'Look, Verney. I'm sorry I lost my temper. I have a job to do. Sometimes it is not pleasant but it is a form of pressure. You understand?'

'Yes?' Raoul said, his face expressionless.

'All I want is to do my job. I am sorry for the sackings. You surely understand it is only my duty.'

'Yes?'

Schiller slumped down in the chair opposite the fat chef. He drew out a tin of military-issue cigarettes. Raoul thought he could not be a happy man. It was as if he wished to unburden himself. His face showed lines of strain and he looked older to Raoul somehow.

'Would you mind not smoking in here?'

'What?'

'I would be grateful if you didn't smoke. The odour gets into my clothes and it is hard to be certain of flavours and aromas then. I'm sure you understand my duty as a chef is to keep fit for my duties.'

Raoul smiled as he spoke. His voice had the pleasantness of a politician. Schiller looked him in the eyes. Doubt seemed to obscure his gaze, like a gossamer veil between them. Raoul shifted in his chair and thrummed his fingers on the blotter before him.

'Truthfully,' Raoul said, 'it really does make a difference. A fine wine cannot be appreciated with smoke fumes in one's nostrils.'

Schiller grunted and put his cigarettes away. He leaned forwards.

'This hotel is changing. Some of your staff will have to go. As long as they register with the police, the Reich will look after them in the manner to which they are entitled. They are not really human you know.'

'I'm sure the "Reich" has it all worked out, but my problem is the number of workers I have at my disposal. Of the hundred or so kitchen staff here, you have removed almost a third. You want German food for your Generals. Without my staff, it will be hard to give you what you want. Can you not overlook their religion?'

'Religion?'

'Yes. Who really cares whether they are Jewish or not?'

'It is not a simple matter of religious beliefs: it is eugenics. I

27

thought you knew that. It is about race. It is a matter of human and sub-human. I am amazed you do not understand. They were responsible for the First War and their machinations helped to create this one. They scheme and they plot with their filthy lives, their obscene faces. It isn't religion at all.'

'You really believe that?'

'Of course. It is well-established. We Germans are Aryans; the true master race. Inside us are the seeds of supermen. The Führer is even now planning to free Europe of all Jews, blacks and sub-human species.'

'And we French?'

'Why, you are our noble allies in this world-wide conflict. No different from the Spanish and the Italians, who support us in their way. Of course, they are not of the same quality as we Germans but not everyone can be racially pure. I think the Führer must understand that.'

'The Russians then?'

'We are at peace with them as long as they do nothing to offend or threaten us, but they are communists and that in the long run cannot be merged with Third Reich ideologies.'

Raoul stood up and gestured towards the door.

'I'm afraid I have to plan my menus now. I don't mean to be impolite but you understand I'm sure…'

'Menus. Of course. What are you planning?'

'Mehlsuppe. My only problem is obtaining the marjoram. It's in short supply.'

'Marjoram? I will see what I can do. General Müller is partial to celebration soups; he remarked upon it at dinner.'

'That would be good. Now, if you don't mind…?'

'Yes, of course. We have an understanding? No more of your… your obstinacy. With cooperation, I am sure we will get on.'

'Yes. Cooperation.'

Schiller gave the Reich salute and walked out. Raoul crossed the office and shut the door. A slow smile flickered upon his lips as he returned to the desk. He thought he had Schiller figured out now. There must have been some pressure on him to make him behave in this way. Perhaps Monsieur Robert really had complained to the General? What was all this nonsense about Jews anyway? It had almost seemed as if Schiller was seeking approval, or at least some kind of understanding from him. Perhaps if he caused Schiller enough trouble, he could get the man removed.

He was still smiling and picturing the scene. Schiller with his head hung low, General Lammerding pointing to the hotel entrance with a stern look on his face. Yes. That would be a very satisfactory outcome. He needed to ensure things went wrong for him. But how?

An ally among the General staff would be a good idea. Not Lammerding. He was soon to leave anyway. Perhaps Müller. Here was a man who was fond of his food and wine. Maybe a trip downstairs for a complimentary tour of the cellars and a bottle of Chateau Lafite?

You can't waste the '29, but maybe the '27, which is getting a little past its drink-up date and was never a great vintage anyway. Then a Sauerbraten. Yes. That's it. War through flattery and bribery. They point a gun, you point a ladle.

He began to feel empowered. It was the first time he had experienced this since Paris fell to the enemy. Everything happening so far had been utterly depressing and even Raoul had felt his humour waning at times. If he could turn them against each other in some way, then he would do so.

But how?

2

At three o'clock in the afternoon, the Rue de Rivoli was quiet. A few cars passed by in the summer sunshine. The Seine, brown and untroubled, flowed by as if nothing was amiss, yet as Raoul and Natalie walked, taking a shortcut through the Tuileries Gardens, he felt as if everything was progressing to his satisfaction. The hotel kitchens were running well and that evening he had an appointment with General Müller, to discuss wine. He intended to take him down to the wine cellar and lubricate the wheels of bribery and corruption with fine Bordeaux—not his wheels, but the General's.

They turned left into the Place de la Concorde, and as they walked past the Fontaine des Fleuves Raoul reached out an arm and placed it around Natalie's shoulder. A momentary squeeze. She took his plump fleshy hand in hers and looked up at him.

'I wanted to thank you.'

'Whatever for?'

'The food you sent. Pierre wrote to me and said it was a lifesaver. Well, all except the pate.'

'It was off?'

'No. It contained pork.'

'Ah. Stupid of me. I should have realised. He was not angry, was he?'

'No. He gave it to a priest.'

'Oh?'

'Yes, Père Bernard. He said he was a friend of Auguste's.'

'Yes, he went to church a lot. I never understood their friendship.'

'There is not much friendship now between them. Auguste persuaded him to register with the police, and since then he has been so restricted he cannot earn money or get food except between three and five o'clock.'

'It's ridiculous, to treat people in this way. You have registered too?'

'No.'

'No?'

'I was hoping to get away without it. If they don't know I'm Jewish, what can they do? I am only a statistic. As long as I work and earn my living, who would know?' Who would talk?'

'Maybe you are right. They will never know. What happened when Schiller interviewed you?'

'I lied. How would he know?'

'With a name like Dreyfus? He hasn't threatened you?'

'No.'

'Tell me if there are any problems. I will always help you.'

She stopped, and turning looked up at his face.

'Since I came to Paris you have been my saviour. Without your help I don't know what I would have done.'

On tiptoes, she craned her neck and kissed him on the cheek, one hand resting on the back of his wide neck. He wanted to take her in his arms but dared not. He was not a woman's man. Who would ever want a man as gross and flabby as he?

He patted her on the back and they resumed their stroll. Their pace had slowed as if neither of them wanted the little journey to end. Crossing the Pont de la Concorde they leaned over the railings, looking at the brown swirling water below. The day was warm and balmy and Nicole wore a yellow flowery dress. Raoul glanced sideways at her, admiring how well she looked out of her uniform.

'You know, Marek thinks the war will continue for many years.'

'He might be right. I hope not. Whatever happens, I won't be safe in France until the Germans leave, even then there may be French Nazis in control.'

'Natalie, Natalie. You are too pessimistic. Why would anyone want to hurt you? They are not even aware you are Jewish.'

'I don't know. I don't understand it really. But we have experienced prejudice since the beginning of history. It is a Jewish burden. Maybe you can't understand.'

'I understand the fact of it, but not the reasons. Enough of this miserable talk. You can make me a cup of coffee when we arrive.'

She smiled and he continued to bask in her company as they rounded the corner with the iron railings into the Rue Chevert and crossed the road to her small tenement apartment. They climbed the narrow stairs and Raoul felt the doorframe tight as he entered; it brushed against his jacket on both sides.

Settling himself on the sofa, he waited until she reappeared with a coffee pot and two demitasse cups.

'You know it's not real coffee don't you?'

He smiled. 'For you I would drink nettle tea.'

He looked around at the familiar room as she poured the chicory. A small oval rug in reds and greys lay under his feet and the low table where she poured the coffee looked scarred and pitted from long use. The mantel held a clock permanently displaying six-thirty as if both the minute and the second hand had, like France, given up the fight and both rested, pointing downwards. A picture in a silver frame stood next to the clock. Raoul knew that picture. It was a relic. It was history in the making for him. He stood in the centre of the three boys. Auguste to the left and Pierre to the right. Raoul's bulk kept them far apart and it always made him smile. He made them look like skinny little people in the photograph. He even recalled how Natalie had to step back to get them all into the frame.

His eyes drifted to take in the open window to his right. It looked out on an alleyway, faced by a red brick wall and there was a café opposite, below to the left. The awning was green and stained as if it had long been neglected like Natalie's window boxes, which contained last year's brown and withered flowers. The green-painted shutters flapped when the wind blew but he imagined Natalie never shut them. She was hardly ever here with the long hours she worked. His fault perhaps, but he enjoyed her being at the Metro when she worked, for it gave him pleasure even to see her washing up.

He sighed as he took the cup from her and made an involuntary grimace as he swallowed the bitter brew.

'Why don't you bring back some coffee from the hotel,

Natalie? There are few enough perks.'

'I would be sacked. If everyone did that, there would be no coffee for the Germans. Monsieur Robert would be in trouble then, so would you.'

'I'll bring you some next time I walk with you. No one questions me.'

'I think if you gave Schiller any excuse he would have you thrown out or worse.'

'Him? He's nothing. I am going to persuade General Müller to put him under a bit of pressure. We'll see what happens then.'

'You promised not to cause any more trouble. If they want to, there are six of us whom they might question more closely. Schiller is SS and he has ties with the SD.'

'Where do you hear all these things?'

'My friend, Marcel Maujean. I met him when I arrived.'

'Oh.'

'What do you mean "Oh"?'

'Nothing. He's your boyfriend?'

'No. He has a girlfriend already. Her father owns a shop down there.'

She pointed to the window and Raoul was glad she looked away since he did not want her to see his frown.

'He works?'

'He's a student. He hates the Germans more than anyone I know. At times, I think he would kill every one of them. He offered to help me escape and says he knows people who can help.'

'You want to leave?'

'No Raoul.' She reached out and touched the back of his

hand.

'I cannot let you down after you have done so much for me.'

Raoul began to flush. He said, 'I must go. I need to change my clothes before I meet the General tonight.'

'You'll be careful? I mean, you won't cause trouble.'

He smiled but said nothing. He was determined to cause as much trouble for Schiller as he could and General Müller was only the start. As he went down the stairs, he wondered what it was about the man he detested so much. Intolerance? Dislike of French food?

No. The skinny little rat-bag is so steeped in bigotry it oozes from every pore and I know that's why I hate him. He's a bully.

Chapter 5

ENTRÈE—Today the entrée is usually the main course of a meal, but in a full French menu, it is the third course, following the hors d'oeuvre (or soup) and the fish course and preceding the roast.
– Larousse Gastronomique

I

Boot-leather soles tapped behind him as Raoul descended the concrete stairs. The hotel, built more than two hundred years before, possessed extensive underground cellars where there was storage both for wine and for a variety of foodstuffs. The illumination was from bare electric bulbs hung from the rough walls and ceilings, connected by exposed wires, since there was no way or indeed necessity to cover the bulbs with shades.

They turned left at the bottom of the stairs where a barred gate blocked the way. Raoul extracted a key from his waistcoat pocket, opened the door, and indicated for General Müller to enter. Müller was a grey-haired man in his fifties, he moved fast and looked athletic for his age, though there was the beginnings of a pot beneath his military tunic. He was a

Francophile and Raoul liked the way the man showed interest in food and wine, as if he had arrived to learn instead of convert the French nation to German culture.

'You first,' the General said, 'I can't squeeze past your generous frame, Raoul.'

Raoul smiled and continued to lead the way to a long room with a high-arched ceiling, wooden wine racks lining the walls and at the far end a small wooden door, locked and secure.

'Above us is the Rue de Rivoli,' Raoul explained.

'Yes, Raoul. There must be a reason you abducted a General of the Third Reich whose stomach is rumbling even as we speak, but I cannot guess what it could be. I have seen wine cellars before.'

'Not like this General.'

Raoul made his way forward from the door. 'Here to the right are the more usual Bordeaux wines. They are stacked by appellation, growth, and then year.'

He moved on, deeper into the long room.

'Here are the Bourgogne wines. You know Romanée-Conti? We have cases of it. The Rhone wines are opulent and big over here. This Hermitage is one of the best in the country.' He gestured to his left.

'But of course, none of these wines can compare to the six First Growths.'

Raoul stopped at a barrel set out in the walkway. Two tasting glasses and an opened bottle of claret stood upon it. Müller stepped forward and picked it up.

'Lafite,' he said, his voice low and husky as if now, confronted with this wine, he was feeling like a priest who picks up a saintly relic.

'Yes. You know a hundred years ago they thought Lafite was too weak so they mixed it with Hermitage to add body.'

'They did?'

'Perhaps we could try the mixture? It would be a very unusual experience for us both.'

'Don't you dare. It would be as tactful as telling Himmler his mother was Jewish.'

The echoed sounds of their mirth reverberated in the dome of the cellar. Raoul poured two glasses, each one a third full.

'It has been open for two hours.' He handed one glass to Müller. He was beginning to like this man despite himself. He watched as Müller took the glass with respect. He swirled the wine in the glass and sniffed.

'Raoul,' he said, 'the colour is a little yellow. Is that how it is supposed to look?'

'Yes, Lafite is often like that—when it is drinking.'

'The nose is strange. I get odours of petroleum as well as faint mature fruit.'

'You know your wines, General.'

'Call me Kurt. After this, how can I call you anything but a friend?'

Raoul clinked his glass against the General's. 'Santé,' he said.

'Prost,' Müller said and they drank, swirling the wine in their mouths. Raoul had to admit, it was a wonderful wine, though he knew he preferred the '29.

'Tell me Raoul, why did you single me out for this tasting? You want something?'

'Me? No. I just realised you like my country. This wine is

among the best we have to offer. Anyone who appreciates it is worthwhile.'

'Wouldn't anyone?'

'Well, no.'

'You mean?'

'Some of the officers here in the hotel have no respect for my country and its wonderful food. I know you have such respect, which is why it is a pleasure to cook for you.'

'Officers? What officers?'

'Oh, I can't mention names, it would be like betraying someone I don't even know. Come, let us try this mixed with a Hermitage. An experiment. Centuries old, this experiment.'

'No. Please. I am enjoying this. It is true, I love your country, I love the food, and I love the women. Such women. So feminine, compared to the ones at home. Raoul, if you met my wife…'

'It is a pleasure I have not had. She is perhaps coming to Paris?'

Müller choked on his wine and began that particular splutter and cough which will come to a man who inhales his drink. Raoul patted him hard on the back.

'I'm sorry. I said something?'

Müller looked up. Calmed now, he cleared his throat. 'You have the very devil in you Raoul. Never mention my wife when I am enjoying myself. It is like sacrilege to a priest. Particularly, when I'm drinking a wonderful Lafite and thinking of French women.'

They looked at each other. Then laughter came and for Raoul it was as if it hid the war away behind a barrel nearby, ready to emerge, but for this one moment in time, invisible.

The mirth they shared surprised him too. It was genuine. They were two human beings, not German or French, simply wine lovers, sharing a holy creation of angelic stature, poured from an old, dusty, green glass bottle.

Presently, Müller said, 'What were you saying about my men not liking France?'

'Not France but French things. It upsets me still not to serve French food. Schiller insists we serve German food.'

'You think I came all this way to taste the same food I had at home? Schiller said this?'

'You are a good interrogator General. I didn't mean to say his name. Please don't say anything.'

'Why not?'

'He will be upset… And my staff…'

'Only a moron would come here, to the Metro, and demand the menus change to everyday German food. Even the Führer drinks French wine and eats French food. If you change it all as Schiller wants, the General staff, when they stay, will be furious. I'm afraid I will have to say something.'

'But if you tell him I told you…'

'No, no no. Don't worry Raoul.' Müller waved an unsteady hand. 'Your secret is safe with me. Leave it to me.'

'I wish I had not said anything now. You seem to have a knack of getting things out of me, without me even knowing it. We could maybe open a Bourgogne?'

'Which one?'

'Maybe Romanée Conti would be too rich after the Bordeaux.'

Raoul stood up and appearing unsteady removed a bottle from a wine rack.

'This one.'

He handed the bottle to Müller.

The German squinted at it. Although Raoul knew the General was not drunk, he had made him drink most of the bottle of Lafite, so he thought Müller was well on his way.

Müller frowned. 'Savigne-les-Beaune? I don't know this one.'

'A wine of beauty. All cloud-berries and spring forest fruit. They drink young unlike the Vosne Romanée's.'

Raoul pulled the cork, trapping the bottle between his generous thighs. Pouring two glasses, he said, 'You know Schiller sent the pastry chef away somewhere?'

'Where? On an errand?'

'No. To a camp.'

'Nothing I can do, I'm afraid. Once they are gone, they are gone. Jewish?'

'I don't know. Maybe he annoyed Schiller. That man has a temper. He hit me once, a while back.'

'He hit you? Where?'

'On the mouth and in Monsieur Robert's office.'

Müller smiled. 'He hurt you?'

Raoul waved an open hand in the air. 'Nothing to me. I am strong.'

Müller remained silent now, concentrating on the wine. Raoul continued to describe the bouquet and the finish and by the time they had consumed another bottle, he had to steady Müller as he stood up. He knew however he had sown seeds, nothing more. To his mind, it was imperative Müller should remember everything, so he knew he had to feed the General and not only water him with his wine.

2

Raoul brought out the sauerbraten himself. He had made the marinade the day before. Choosing the best white wine vinegar, and adding the peppercorns and bay leaves, he had smiled to himself. Determined this would be a feast for General Müller, he attended to every detail himself—to Marek's consternation. He even carved the sirloin of beef at the table and fussed over the sauce, insisting he pour it himself over General Müller's plate. Müller winked at him as he served. They both had a little secret from the wine cellar. The wine on the table was the '29 Lafite. Raoul felt as if it was justified. Müller seemed a true Francophile and he appeared enamoured of the hotel, of France, and of the wonderful wine Raoul provided.

'You've become a waiter now?' Marek said as Raoul re-entered the kitchen.

Marek, a man of medium height, had dark, greased, swept-back hair and brown sharp eyes reflecting his efficient nature. Like Raoul he wore the tunic of a chef, smart and starched.

'Stop it. You don't trust me? I know what I'm doing.'

'But why are you going to the tables? You never, never enter the restaurant when the food is out. You are in love with these German pigs all of a sudden?'

'Marek. Marek, why don't you see the panorama? General Müller likes us. He enjoys France and all we have to offer. He would be very useful as an ally. Maybe he will get Alphonse back.'

'You haven't heard?'

'Heard what?'

42

'They shot him.'

'What?'

'They shot him. Apparently, he and his brother were communicating with the Rosbifs. He had a radio hidden in his rooms. They took him out and shot the poor bastard.'

'I don't believe you. They shot him?'

'Raoul, wake up. We are not playing some interesting culinary game. This is war. Some of us have to fight to stay alive and fight for our country. I'm looking for a way, but all I can do until I find one, is be obstructive in a little way. And you? You wine and dine these animals. You know what they are doing? They mark everyone they don't like with a yellow star with "Juif" written on it. Wake up will you?'

Raoul frowned. He felt his heart race and a redness rise up his face. He grabbed Marek by the shoulder. It was a grip of iron.

'You don't fucking understand, do you? Müller is a pleasant man. He loves French food and wine. He will protect us from Schiller if we play the game. We need supporters and allies to get through this sea of shit we are in. We have unregistered Jews in the hotel, working in the kitchens. We need a quiet life for now. There is plenty of time to do other things, but just now we think of the people. You hear?'

'Put me down, will you?'

Raoul released the hapless chef and smoothed the creases he had made on Marek's white, bright tunic.

'Look I'm sorry I lost my temper. You've ever seen me so worked up?'

'No.'

'Then understand what I'm doing. We can't fight these

43

people. If we can get Schiller out, maybe his replacement will be more amenable.'

'Or maybe worse.'

'Perhaps. It is a risk I'm willing to take. I need Müller. We need him. If Sauerbraten is all it takes, that and a few bottles of wine, then it's worth it.'

'You are like Pétain. You think keeping these monsters happy is a key to our freedom. You know they've devalued the franc? Twenty francs to one filthy deutsche mark. You know what this means? A German soldier can order a bottle of Cheval Blanche and pay a twentieth of the real value. We have to fight somehow.'

'Think about it. We are fighting. I'm doing it with food and wine. You think I would be any use with a gun?'

'Why not?'

Raoul smiled as a sudden memory came to him. 'I can use a shotgun, but it won't help us. Be patient. Be patient with me, with the Metro and with our people. I have a feeling all France will rise up in the end against the invaders. Meanwhile, we play them against each other. Don't cause a problem until we know the outcome. Now let me get the Swartzwald's torte ready.'

Raoul stomped across the tiles. As he grated the chocolate over the cake, he felt he knew what he was doing and that he had nothing to lose. He cared no more for his life than he did for Schiller's military standing. He was determined to do the best he could and if it meant producing exquisite cuisine for these invading Huns, he would do that.

Chapter 6

FRICASSÉE—A preparation of chicken in a white sauce (veal and lamb may also be prepared in this way).
– Larousse Gastronomique

I

Summer rain began to fall as he stood on the doorstep of the apartment house. In his left hand he carried a bottle, and in his right he fumbled a key. Raoul was alone, though it was nothing unusual for him. He lived alone. In the last month, he had begun to feel it was a burden, this selfish existence. Working, coming home, reading, sleeping, and then the cycle beginning again, as if that was all life would ever hold for him. He sometimes wondered if there was a plump lady somewhere who would not find his rolls of blubber a source of disgust or amusement. The previous night as he drifted off to sleep he could still feel the gentle touch of Natalie's lips on his cheek. He wished the second it had lasted could have been minutes and in his dreams he had become the man he wanted to be. In that dream he had held her, leaned her backwards like a tango dancer and kissed her like a true man. That dream remained with him even to the next morning when he watched her carrying plates across the kitchen after breakfast. The thoughts were now becoming painful. He felt like a man who was only allowed a sip of a beautiful wine and some other person drank the entire bottle.

Raoul climbed the three steps and entered his apartment. When he had looked for accommodation he chose the top floor even though he found stairs difficult. They made him breathless and it always irritated him, but he felt compensated by the view from his window. He flicked on the light. The large room appeared before him and he took off his light jacket and hung it on the coat-stand by the door. The first thing he did was to open his bottle of wine. It was not a fine Burgundy, nor was it a wonderful first growth Bordeaux. It was a plain, fruity and gutsy Bergerac—the sort of wine he had grown up with, and one he loved more than even a Chateaux Malartic Lagravière. It was the tannin that transported him to the Dordogne. He sniffed the wine in the glass and placed it with the opened bottle on the dining table by the window. He looked around the room at the paintings. Country scenes and rustic farm pictures reminding him of home. That was his reason for buying them in the first place. Home.

He had adored his childhood and he missed his wonderful loving parents. He took a mouthful of wine and he pictured his mother as she lay on the bed in the hospital. He had held her hand and when her breathing finally ceased, he had cried into her palm as if such tears could express his feeling of loss, though he knew even then it could not. He realised the loss of her was not a moment but a decade-long drawn out part of his life, when he constantly wanted to pick up a telephone and tell her how he had achieved a Gold Medal at the Ritz or got his job at the Metro. But of course she was dead when he achieved in life, and he felt cheated of that pleasure. It was a pleasure fostered by her constant support and belief in him as a man and of course, as a chef. Without her encouragement and her ambition for him, he knew life would now be very different.

He drank another glass and pondered how he would make life difficult for Schiller. The man was a pain in the backside. Apart from the sackings and the forced registering of Jews, he had now the effrontery to dictate what food should be served. Hah. Müller would put him right. Raoul felt maybe he had obtained an ally and he thought back to the end of the evening, when Müller, a little drunk, had shaken his hand as an equal and embraced him.

It was true, some would have seen him as nothing more than a collaborator and a traitor to France but Raoul needed the hotel to function and he needed someone who would act as a buffer to his plans. He wanted rid of Schiller because he knew Schiller would be efficient at rooting out his Jewish staff. Another man might not have this Nazi's ability to sniff out Raoul's people. It reminded him of the tale he once read of a "Witch Smeller". They had used such a man in the ancient times, when they picked on poor and innocent victims and called them witches. The "Smeller" would sniff at them and proclaim they had the scent of the Devil and then they would burn them at the stake. He could almost see Schiller in his mind, dressed as a medieval peasant sniffing at Natalie. He laughed because he realised the mental picture was making him furious. It was pathetic. She loved him as a friend. He loved her like—well what did he love her like?

He had no right to covet her. He was not anyone to whom she would be attracted. He stood up. He looked down at his belly. Raoul wobbled his stomach. He hated himself then. All his life he had been big. Big in stature and big in girth. Of course the bullying stopped once Pierre took him under his wing, and he formed such a close bond with Auguste and Pierre that it shaped his self-esteem. He was a damned good cook and a loyal, reliable friend whom the two other lads came to admire. He knew this because they told him so often before he left to train as a chef in Lyon. He knew he owed them for that. They had propped him up when he lay on the proverbial ground and others kicked dust in his face.

He finished the bottle before he retired and dreams haunted him. Dreams of Natalie, where she reached for him and their lips met and he carried her off into a sunset, far away from war-torn France. The sun was shining and he could feel cool seas washing over his shoulders, Natalie's hand in his as they swam together. Then his alarm clock rang out a jarring clang, and it was all gone, like a bubble bursting in the chocolate fudge.

2

At the service entrance Raoul and a porter stood watching as the delivery came in. The sun shone off to the right, but it was not high enough to bring any significant heat. It cast long shadows away to the left, pointing towards the east end of the Rue de Rivoli where, even at this early hour, Raoul could identify the muted sound of trucks. The delivery truck backed up and the driver descended to the cobbled roadway beneath the arch. Seawater dripped from the back, and as the man lowered the tailgate Raoul could smell the fresh sea-shell smell of the fish in crates, organised and labelled for the prospective customers.

There was pleasure for him in this delivery. He intended to make bouillabaisse, and his fish stew was not like the ones from Provence or even Marseille, it was the particular way his father had taught him to make it, and he honoured him whenever he created the dish. The porter began humping the marked crates onto his barrow.

A voice, sharp and level, made Raoul turn around.

'What is this?' It was Schiller. He stood behind Raoul with a cane in his hand, tapping his boot. What he thought he looked like at six in the morning, acting like a drillmaster, had Raoul puzzled.

'A truck.'

'I know it's a truck. You think me stupid? What is it doing here?'

'Delivering fish.'

'That is not what I mean. It is obstructing the entrance. My orders are that all entrances must remain unobstructed at all times. I have told you this. It is a matter of security. You will have to ask him to move it at once.'

'My dear Hauptsturmführer. It will take only a few minutes to unload the fish. If I had more than one porter it would of course be quicker, but even this takes longer now. You know why that is, I think?'

Schiller poked Raoul in the chest with his black cane. Raoul backed away. He could feel his temper simmering and he did not want to spoil the broth by boiling over.

'Hauptsturmführer, it will take just as long to finish the unloading as it will to shut the tailgate and move the truck. He might as well…'

Schiller regarded Raoul with a frigid stare. His pale eyes narrowed.

'Who ordered fish anyway?'

'I ordered the fish.'

'You didn't tell me.'

'You see every manifest. You must have known?'

'Herrings?'

'What?'

'Herrings. For pickling?'

'No. I make a fish stew which is one of the best. You will enjoy it. It contains a variety of fish, depending of course upon what is available.'

'I don't like any other fish.'

'Then you will, I am sure, enjoy the Weiner schnitzel. General Müller asked especially for fish tonight. He is entertaining an actress.'

'Weiner schnitzel again? It is on the menu all the time. Can't you cook anything else? You're supposed to be a chef, not a school cook.'

Raoul felt himself flush. Even the bullies of his childhood had never managed to make him lose his temper, but he knew it was close. He smiled. It was his only defence. He could see his father's large frame and the big man's words came to him too. "They can call you anything at all my boy, it doesn't matter, as long as it isn't fillet mignon, because then they might eat you."

Still smiling, he said, 'Come Hauptsturmführer, let me cook you some breakfast. The truck will be gone in a couple of minutes.'

Raoul gestured the kitchen entrance and placed a placatory hand on Schiller's arm. The German leapt back as if Raoul were about to attack him. His face showed fear.

'I'm sorry, I didn't mean to startle you.'

'You didn't. How could you? Yes. Breakfast and make sure they stop outside without blocking the archway next time. It is a way for enemies to block a retreat.'

'You would retreat?'

Schiller said nothing. It was his turn to flush. Raoul walked to the kitchen door and gestured Schiller to follow him. Stepping inside, he clapped his hands and instructed one of the staff to bring a chair and a table for Schiller.

Minutes later, he left Schiller eating boiled eggs and smoked salmon with German sausage and cheese, and made his way up to the office. He felt happy to have controlled his temper. He was glad he had controlled Schiller too.

Chapter 7

GIROLLE—The French name for the chanterelle.
– Larousse Gastronomique

I

Raoul stood over the heated pan. He was using butter, not olive oil. He preferred to start dishes with butter because his father always did. It bubbled and melted. There was a fierce satisfaction for him in this dish—it was pure French. There were no German equivalents and it made him feel good.

He added the garlic and waited a moment for the pressed cloves to release their oil and flavour. He added the previously chopped onions and the leeks. Raoul watched as the mixture bubbled and steamed before him. The sight reminded him of days at home, in Bergerac. His father fussing, his mother watching. He recalled how his father scolded when he had not chopped the onions finely enough. He even recalled the clip behind the ear.

Next, he added the fennel and then waited until the onions were beginning to glaze. He did not want them browned. Stirring, he waited for ten minutes then picked up his tomatoes. There was guilt there. He knew fresh produce was in short supply and he understood how his fellow countrymen all over Paris, would struggle to get the right ingredients, but he loved his cooking. There is no love as pure as the love of food he said to himself, though it was scant compensation for his collaboration. The Germans obtained anything they wanted and he complied like a good collaborator. He hated his work then, and it tore him in two. He hated the politics, but loved his cooking. How could any good chef cook food to a lower standard than the best, as long as it was within his means and ability?

The orange zest and the fish-stock came next. Raoul wondered, when he was preparing the crevettes, whether it was worth the trouble to remove the intestines, but capitulated in the end. A good cook would never make a customer ill, even a German.

He added the rest of his ingredients, tomatoes, tomato puree, fennel seeds, fish trimmings and herbs. Mineral water and saffron came next. He boiled the stew for forty minutes. He felt irritated that he had to spend the time to skim the surface, but he had a seat by the cooker and he also had a book to read—The Count of Monte Christo, so he made no bones about it.

Straining the mixture he decanted it and added his fish. Monkfish, mussels, sea-bass, and red mullet all went in. He seasoned and tasted the dish. Thinking for a moment, he realised to his chagrin, he had not poured in the Pernod. Raoul struck his forehead with the palm of his hand. How could he be so careless? He measured a large glass of the yellow liquor and attacked the stew with it. He tasted again and this time knew the flavour was perfect. Bouillabaisse. The life-blood of France. He knew that although recipes varied from place to place, his was one that knocked the socks off any rival. He smelled the steam from the pot and he thought of his father. The old man would have been proud of his son.

Raoul was enjoying himself. He felt as if he had put some-thing of himself in this dish—his own individual stamp. He knew the diners would never forget this delicacy, and if they did they could only be Philistines and his food would be pearls before plump porkers. He smiled, imagining all the German military hierarchy bent over a huge trough—would they have curly tails too beneath those green uniform trousers? Probably.

Philippe, the Maître d'Hôtel, interrupted his thoughts. Raoul jumped when he heard his friend clear his throat be-hind him.

'Philippe, what are you doing here?'

'It is important I speak to you Raoul.'

Philippe was a broad, stocky man with short, brown hair, and most of the time a ready smile. He was not smiling now. His face was serious, his brow creased in a frown.

Raoul handed over to Marek, who seemed to object, but ignoring his head chef's grumbles he took Philippe by the arm and they walked towards the wine-cellar steps.

'In private?' he said.

'Yes.'

Extracting his key Raoul unlocked the heavy door and they both descended into the cool dark cellar. Switching on the lights, he turned to face his friend.

'Well?'

'We have a problem.'

54

'Yes?'

'They've arrested Rachelle Weismann. You know, that pretty little cleaner? She was only seventeen. Took her away in a truck. It was full of prisoners. I don't know where they've taken her, they won't tell me.'

'Why did they arrest her?'

'If they needed an excuse, it will be because she did not register when the other Jewish staff were ordered to. She's only a girl for God's sake. She probably just put it off and now she's gone.'

Frowning like Philippe, Raoul said, 'That's terrible. Perhaps they will let her go with a warning. You've talked to Schiller?'

'He's the bastard who arrested her. What's the point?'

'It won't help if I talk to him. He hates me. Perhaps Monsieur Robert can influence him?'

'He's tried.'

'Then all we can do is wait.'

'Yes. You know we have several others who have refused to go to the Prefecture?'

'Yes. I don't understand how the Germans, as foreigners, can find out who people's ancestors can be. It's a mystery.'

'Wake up Raoul. It's a nasty world out there beyond your kitchens. They're using Frenchmen in the administration to dig up everything about everybody. Worse still, they reward people for informing on others. Some even settle feuds with their neighbours by telling the Germans about minor indiscretions. Our country is being ripped open and we do nothing.'

'Well I'm sure that will be the end of it all. Let's just keep them sweet and feed them. We can't do anything about the arrests, you know that.'

'I've known you for what? Six years? I never thought you were a fool. Now…'

'Look. I'd love to destroy the German army, blow them up—all at once. I can't. Nor can you my friend. We have to wait for Pétain to get a peace settlement and then life will become tolerable. Think of the long term.'

Philippe struck him with his fist on the shoulder. To Raoul, it made no impression. He stood firm, like a mound of lardons in cold weather; like a rock battered by waves.

'Philippe, please. Listen to the voice of reason…'

Philippe stood his ground. He looked with furious eyes into Raoul's. He walked away into the cellars, stopped and then turned, coming back.

'Raoul. I can only assume you have become a man who collaborates with these German pigs; pigs who trough at out tables, shag our women and look down upon us all. Don't ever speak to me again. You bastard.'

Philippe pushed past the puzzled chef and made his way to the steps. Ascending he turned and said, 'You know, if you were a real Frenchman, you would poison them all instead.'

Raoul stood watching as Philippe disappeared through the door, leaving him alone in the wine cellar. He detected a faint yeasty smell combined with the aroma of the bouillabaisse, and the quiet enclosed him. The cellar was cool and silent. There was a sense of peace about the place. Raoul was not deaf to that. It was as if here he stood in an ancient museum, where holy relics lined the walls and he was the keeper, the man with the key.

Shaking his head he ascended each step with a plodding

reluctance to re-join the world of ordinary men; men with so little knowledge of the things that mattered most in life, the things he had learned about in his life. Yes, it was true. The love of food is innocent of all evil and it unites everyone. And wine? Wine was the lifeblood of France and he had the key to this little capillary. Maybe Philippe was right, but what could a fat chef do?

Nothing.

'Nothing,' he mumbled to himself, as he reached the last step and took deep heavy breaths. He waited until his breathing settled and opened the door.

2

The rain fell in buckets as Raoul and Natalie walked towards Rue Chevert. The packet of coffee felt heavy in Raoul's hand as he pulled her slim frame towards him to shelter her under his umbrella. He could feel the wetness of his trouser legs as they walked and he regretted setting off so late in the evening when the heavens were opening up, but Natalie insisted. He knew how enslaved he had become. He felt resigned to the idea that he would do anything for this tiny, sugar-plum fairy who walked so light and airy beside him in the rain. It was almost as if he imagined she could melt in the torrent as he manoeuvred the umbrella above her sweet head. The feel of her bony shoulder as he placed his plump arm around her aroused him, though it produced only feelings of embarrassment in case she should suspect his ardour.

Rounding the corner he could see, through the veil of

sloping rain, two men standing in her doorway. They were sheltering from the downpour. Their black suits, black leather coats and the hat each of them wore, made them look like gangsters in a Hollywood motion picture. He remarked as much to Natalie, who looked up and stopped, stock-still.

'Back. Raoul, come back.'

'Eh?' he said.

He became aware of her hand tugging at his sleeve and he acquiesced with reluctance. She pulled him back around the corner.

'They've come for me.'

'What?'

'The Germans. They've come for me.'

'Don't be silly. They are just passing businessmen, sheltering from the rain. Come, let me see you safely home.'

'Oh, Raoul. Don't you understand what is happening here? I didn't register like they said. They will take me away to a work camp or worse. I have to get away.'

She stood with her head beneath the umbrella and Raoul adjusted its position to protect her better, until he could feel the raindrops on his back.

'Away where? What are you talking about? Back to Bergerac?'

'I love you so much but you can be so stupid sometimes.'

'You what?'

'Stupid. You seem to ignore the obvious all the time. You cook wonderful food for these bastards and all the time they take people away, and who knows what happens to them? You want me to go away too?'

'No. You said…'

'What?'

'You said you loved me.'

'Yes. I love you. You know that.'

'You love me?'

'Dear Raoul. This is not the time. I have to get away.'

He said nothing. The revelation of her words fixed him to the spot. Raoul felt like a condemned man in prison whose lawyer had appeared with a pardon in his hands.

'Natalie. You mean that?'

'Yes, of course. They will take me away if I dare to go to my apartment.'

'No, not that. You love me?'

'You big silly oaf. You don't know that? All these years…'

He reached for her and she pushed him away.

'I'm in danger and all you can do is try to kiss me?'

'Natalie. Please.'

A man walking a bichon frise approached. He smiled and said in an apologetic tone, 'My wife's dog. I would have preferred a bigger protector to walk with in the night. Now there are so many Germans, I may need to get a tiger.'

He huddled in a thick raincoat of brown gabardine and doffed his hat as he passed, raindrops trickling from the brim. Raoul smiled back at the man. There were few bigger creatures than Raoul, and he knew it.

'Natalie?'

'What?'

'I will go and see who they are. You wait here in the doorway. If it isn't safe, I will come back.'

'Where will I go?'

'For the moment, that doorway. You can rely on me. I will

protect you. I love you too.'

'Raoul, this is not the time…'

'No. Be patient. It is like waiting for a soufflé to rise. It requires humility and patience. Relax yourself. I will protect you.'

Leaving Raoul with the umbrella, she flitted through the rain to the doorway of an apartment house behind them. There was a dubious look in her eyes as she watched him depart, and he noticed it, glancing over his shoulder. Approaching the two men, his galoshes splashing in the pooling rain, he made to enter the house and pass them on the steps, but the one to his left grabbed his arm. Raoul reversed down a step.

'You go where?' the man said.

'You are French?'

'What are you? Stupid?'

'Silly of me, I thought you might be German.'

'We are Special Brigade. Police.'

The man flashed a small wallet with a picture and some kind of official stamp. He put it away so fast in the rain, Raoul remained unsure of the man's name.

'I'm sorry, I didn't see it properly. Can I see it again please?'

'Shut up,' the second man said. A weasel-faced fellow with a tiny black moustache; he had a scowl on his face and kept his collar pulled up around his neck.

'You want what?' Raoul said.

'What are you doing here?' the first man said. He was clean-shaven, middle forties, Raoul guessed. The grey eyes were steel-hard.

'I'm visiting a friend.'

'Who?'

'Natalie Dreyfus, we work together.'

'You know her well?'

They stood on the steps looking down at Raoul, who looked up at them from under the umbrella. The rain was slackening now; it pattered away over Raoul's head and dripped from the policemen's hat-brims. He looked the man in the eyes.

'Yes. I know her well. We work in the same hotel. I brought her some coffee.'

Raoul gestured with his coffee-bearing hand.

'She's an unregistered Jew. Where is she?'

'I'm sorry. I don't understand the question.'

The man stepped down and shoved Raoul in the chest. He might as well have punched Mont Blanc; as useful as eating a meringue with a knife.

'Look there's no need for this. I'm a friend, visiting after work. I've done nothing wrong. Is it not obvious? If she isn't here, then I will go.'

'When did you last see her?'

'She was at the hotel and finished her shift at three this afternoon. I brought her some coffee.'

'Coffee?'

'Yes. There is nothing illegal about that, is there?'

'Give it to me,' the first fellow said.

'Why?'

'Evidence. Here, hand it over.'

Raoul complied. He wished he could cut them up and add them to his bouillabaisse.

'She isn't here. If you see her, it will be an offence not to report it, you hear?'

'Of course. If I see her…'

'Your name?'

'Raoul Verney. I'm Executive Head Chef at Le Metro.'

'Get out of here, you fat bastard.'

Raoul stepped back, down from the step on which he perched.

Waste of good coffee.

For the first time since the Germans occupied Paris, he realised what was happening. There was no going back now. He had to protect Natalie and she loved him. What could that mean? He rounded the corner and his head seemed to spin. She loved him. Did she mean it? Perhaps she had meant she loved him as a brother. Perhaps it was an innocent use of the word. But love? He knew he was in love, but was she?

Chapter 8

HAM—A leg of pork, cured in various ways.
– Larousse Gastronomique

I

They walked hand in hand. He wondered whether it had taken the Special Brigade of the Vichy police to unveil her feelings. He grasped her hand. It was small and thin, his was large and plump, but to Raoul the feel of her fingers clutching his was like a spoonful of salmon caviar, beautiful, soft, and cool. From time to time, as they walked he glanced down at her and she in turn looked up and smiled. He could not help but see it was a happy smile, as if now that her secret was unveiled it brought her relief and happiness. The rain began to peter out, and as they walked they stepped over puddles. On the bridge, despite the narrow brush with the SB, they dawdled, still hand in hand, still feeling their way in this new-found revel of affection.

Raoul dared not hope she meant it. As they looked down at the flowing circles of rain on the grey river, he chided himself. Surely a dream does not come true in real life. Not during a war? Not when so many lives were upturned and ended?

He saw no signs that she had not meant what she said. She never let go of his hand.

'Raoul?'

'Yes?'

'Where can I hide? They know your name, so your apartment is not safe. I have nowhere else to go. If I try to get to Pierre they'll catch me on the way, or I will endanger him and Monique.'

'I am more resourceful than you think. I can hide you at the hotel. I know every inch of the place, every little space. You are so small and thin, it will be easy. You may not be so comfortable all the time, but you will be safe. I will make certain of it.'

'But they will search.'

'No. Why would they suspect? To hide in a big hotel would make you invisible to them. Maybe you can still work in the kitchen. They never come there. I can teach you to make fricasse Espanol. We can...'

'You're day-dreaming. It is all so dangerous. If they found me, they would shoot you. You really want to take that risk?'

Raoul turned towards her.

'Risk? I would risk anything for you. I have always regarded you like this. If only I had not wasted so much time. I never imagined...'

He leaned forwards, pursing his lips. He dared not hope he would reach his target. When he did, it was electric: he felt a thrill such as he had never felt elsewhere in his life. Even the gold medal in Lyon was as nothing to him compared to the feel of her damp, cold lips against his. He grappled with her, unused to the sensation of another so close as she placed her arms around his neck. He knew any passing policeman or even a passing SD officer would interpret it as a humorous tableau. The big, plump fellow with the small skinny girl in his arms. He did not care. He had the one thing he had missed for all his adult life.

He had love.

2

The wet pavements of the Rue de Rivoli reflected the faint light spreading through the hotel's windows as Raoul and Natalie peered around the corner of the building. Raoul looked up and down the now deserted road. The Metro was quiet and no one seemed to be going in or out. A military vehicle approached in the distance; Raoul could hear the deep throaty growl of the engine and he pulled her back.

'Here. Hide behind me.'

It was no great feat to position herself behind him and she disappeared from view, as if hidden behind one of the pyramids of Giza. Raoul looked out. A Volkswagen jeep passed by. Four men, armed and observant, occupied it. The front seat passenger stared at Raoul as if he was a pubic hair on a soufflé, but the vehicle did not halt and Raoul began to breathe again. He looked to his right.

George stood outside in his long red coat, manfully sporting an open umbrella. Raoul thought he was too far away for him to attract his attention; so, kissing Natalie on the cheek, he left her waiting and strolled towards the concierge.

'Raoul? What are you doing out on a night like this? With such a small umbrella too, here, let me…'

Raoul placed his index against his lips. George shut up.

Close up now the chef said, 'I need you to keep watch for me.'

'Watch?'

'Yes. The Special Police came for Natalie.'

The little concierge looked up with wide eyes and an expression on his face as if Raoul had handed him a viper.

'Natalie?'

'Shh. Keep your voice down. I need to get her into the hotel. You go first and make sure there is no one about.'

'She escaped?'

'They didn't get her. I'm going to hide her. Many Germans around?'

'Most of the pigs are at the trough. Your food is too good for them, maybe a little arsenic would also be good. I will check the lobby.'

'No, not the lobby, George. The end archway, going to the courtyard. I'll try to get her down to the kitchen through the back door. Go and check. I don't want to be seen either.'

George shook his head. Raoul noticed he was sweating and fiddling with his umbrella.

'Go on.'

'Yes Raoul. I will check for you. What do I do if Schiller or one of his men is there?'

'Just come back and tell me and I'll think of something else.'

Together the two men walked back towards where Natalie

stood waiting beyond the corner of the hotel. There was more light now as the clouds began to dissipate. Raoul saw her slight frame step from her hiding place and approach them and George turned into the archway smiling at Natalie as he did so.

Raoul and Natalie stood holding hands in the darkness of the arched stone roof, hidden from anyone's view from the street. She looked up at him and he realised how scared she was. There was an unnatural crease on her forehead and her hand shook, trembling in his. He realised then he was not frightened himself. He felt he knew what to do whatever happened, and he would see this through. For love.

For Natalie.

He smiled to reassure her and George returned.

'It's clear. As far as I can tell, there is no one between us and the door. You have a key?'

'Would I go to the back door of the kitchen if I didn't, you silly man?'

'No. No, of course. Sorry…'

'George, thank you. You did a brave thing here tonight. If they catch me with Natalie anything could happen.'

'I'll wait here. If anyone comes, I'll whistle. Like this'

George pursed his lips, but no sound came. 'I can't get them wet enough.'

'George, forget it. Now go.'

George retreated back into the street under his umbrella while Raoul and Natalie flitted, as far as a man of his bulk could flit, across the stone courtyard, crossing to a stairwell which led down to a green-painted, iron door. Descending, Raoul drew out his bunch of keys. He fumbled for a moment before finding the correct one and opened the door. Natalie, crouching on the stairs above him looked down. He gestured her to follow and they entered the doorway, shutting the door behind with a bang. A short corridor led to more steps, and below them they could see an open wooden door with bright light shining through, creating a yellow arc across the stone floor. He was breathing with slow, deep breaths and he felt under control. It was as if now the tension had eased he could assume his normal persona and become the Head Chef once more. He could not escape the feeling that someone might be there. Perhaps Schiller had positioned men in the kitchen, though Raoul was inclined to dismiss the thought. All the same, he guided Natalie behind him and peered around the corner of the doorway. The lights, bright and bold, illuminated the kitchen and whatever the next moments might bring Raoul felt he remained in charge. He was the Executive Head Chef. He was the man who led the kitchen troops in this fight against the evil Hun. Whether there were Germans there or not, he would deal with the situation. He advanced, fists clenched.

Damp as they both were, no one gave them a second glance. They stood, still hand in hand, dripping water onto the bare, tiled floor and looked around.

Marek approached. He held a kitchen knife in his hand, which he dropped onto one of the benches. Wiping his hands on his apron, he said, 'I thought you went home hours ago.'

'Come, we need to talk.'

'Natalie? I thought you had gone too. What's going on?'

She reached out and squeezed his arm. A tear trickled down her cheek.

'Marek,' Raoul said. 'They are after Natalie.'

He wanted to say, '*and she loves me.*'

It was on the tip of his tongue, but he knew it would sound foolish. He understood how ridiculous this mixture of romance and danger would appear to anyone with an ounce of common sense.

Marek looked up at Raoul and frowned. He rubbed the black stubble on his chin, then lifted his chef's hat and wiped away a wisp of hair. Replacing it he said, 'I'm not surprised. Schiller was here about an hour ago, asking for her. He had a list of names.

'So you understand?'

'Yes.'

'But do you?'

'Yes, of course I understand.'

'You realise we can't just hide them all here?' Marek glanced at Natalie who looked at him with a wan smile. He shifted his weight to the other leg wiping his hands on his apron again and went on, 'There is only the wine cellar and the cool-storage, but then what? What if they search?'

Raoul said, 'Leave that to me. I know every little crawl space of the roof, every tiny passageway and I know we are never fully booked these days. Natalie will become like Gaston Leroux's Phantom of the Opera. There, but never visible.'

'Raoul. I'm not talking about Natalie. What about the others?' He looked down and a sheepish expression overcame his competent features. 'Look. I must tell you, the others are in the wine cellar.'

'The others?'

'Yes, Collette heard the Sauerkrauts talking at table. I hid all the people who had not registered. There are six of them.'

'Well that is no big problem in the wine cellar. It is easy to hide there.'

'You don't understand. Witold, the demi-sous has a wife and little boy. Mina has a husband and two children.'

'Where are they?'

'I put them all there. What could I do? Send them out into the night?'

'I don't understand. You heard about it this evening and they sent for their families?'

'No. It was yesterday.'

'You didn't tell me? You hid all these people here and never told me?'

'I'm sorry.'

'Sorry? No. Marek, my friend, you are a true hero.'

Raoul reached forward and embraced his head chef. He kissed him on both cheeks.

'Marek, Marek. We will manage the situation. Does Monsieur Robert know?'

'I… I didn't want to bother him. He is under a lot of pressure and…'

'They are all in the wine cellar?'

'Yes.'

'Lead on my friend. Life is becoming interesting. This is the sort of puzzle an Executive Head Chef is born to solve.'

He followed Marek to the steps leading down to the cellar door. As he and Natalie followed, he realised he did not care what happened to himself. All he cared about was Natalie. As long as he could keep her safe, he was happy. So what if there were a few others? He would think of a way. It was as if he had waited for this moment forever. The scorn and the teasing, the mental battles to reach his present position, all had prepared him for this point in time. He would hide them from Schiller and he would protect every one of them—especially Natalie—from the Germans, the Nazis and even Hitler himself. He felt he was at last becoming a man and he was gaining more self-respect than he had ever known before.

Chapter 9

ILE FLOTTANTE—A very light dessert made from egg whites and sugar cooked in a bain marie then unmoulded onto a custard cream and usually coated with caramel.
– Larousse Gastronomique

I

Marek, who had the second key to the wine cellar, opened the door. Raoul could feel with an air of trepidation how the three of them would be facing the silent blackness. Behind Marek, he still held Natalie's hand. It seemed perverse, but he was excited. There was impatience too. He wanted to kiss her, hold her in his arms and make love to her. Yes, even that. He was a virgin, but now at last, there was hope for him. As he went down the stairs he imagined he was approaching some wonderful vista where they could walk hand in hand and enjoy each other. She loved him and it was all he could ever have hoped for in a war-torn world that was changing from moment to moment and creating such misery for his people.

Marek flicked the light switch. They descended to the bare concrete floor. The smell of yeastiness came to Raoul as it always did when he entered here. He had never puzzled over it until now. That smell was one that characterised wine-producing chateaux where wine stood enclosed in barrels waiting to be bottled. To Raoul it was a smell representing patience and expectation. It did not belong in a cellar where the bottles stood for years, undisturbed and resting, ready for that cataclysmic moment when the nose and the fruit would be released. He had always accepted that smell as one for which there was no explicable reason and he had never before puzzled over it. He wondered why he did so tonight. This, the night in which he had found love and in which he now felt denied it by circumstance. And now, all he could think about was the aroma of his wine cellar.

Marek called out.

'It is safe.'

Silence.

'My friends, it is safe.'

He took a few steps forwards and Raoul, standing behind him, noticed movement behind the Bordeaux wines. Shadowy forms began to appear. There was Marie, the half-Senegalese who helped the junior demi-sous chefs. Here was Sol the pastry sous-chef. But look, who was this? It was a woman he did not recognise. She clutched a quietly mewling infant to her, agitating it in the vain hope it would quieten.

When they were all assembled, Raoul backed up onto the third step behind him.

'Please, dear friends, don't be alarmed. You are safe here for the time being, but we will need to make some arrangements for feeding you and find a place where you will be safe.'

He thought it was a good beginning. He was not a man for

speeches but realised something had to be said. These people would fear for the future. It was a future he was determined to ensure, though how he would do that puzzled him still. A thought came to him then. The far door at the end of the cellar had not been opened in years. As far as he knew it led to a tunnel, but when he took over as Executive Head Chef his predecessor had told him not to bother with it because it was damp and unhygienic.

Now out of necessity perhaps he should explore what was there in the hope it could become a bolt-hole for these unfortunate people. He stepped down and counted heads. There were twelve people excluding Natalie. She would make thirteen. Unlucky for some, but it was his father's birth-date and he always felt it was a lucky number for him. Raoul's large frame blotted out the light as he approached the barred and locked door beyond the Burgundies and the Rhônes.

Removing the heavy metal crosspiece, he leant it against the whitewashed brickwork, took a large iron key from his bunch and inserted it into the rusty lock. Nothing happened and he became worried in case he might break either the key or the lock. He felt Marek's hand on his shoulder.

'Here, my old man.'

Marek handed him a bottle with a spout, stoppered with a cork. Raoul poured some oil into the keyhole and turned to the assembled refugees.

'I don't know what is beyond this door but we may be able to use it if you have to hide. The oil will take a while to work.'

Sol stepped forward. He was a man of about Raoul's age but thin and small, with a hooked nose and a bald head. 'I can't stay here. I have a wife and two sons. I have to either get them or go to them to face whatever comes.'

'Sol, my friend, we will send someone to fetch them. Perhaps George will go as soon as he is off duty. He can bring your family here. A few more mouths to feed won't be a problem. Already we are wasting more food than an army can eat. Just tell me the address and I'll speak to George.'

Raoul could see Sol trusted him. He hoped he could be as good as his word. Spartaco, one of the sous chefs pushed forward. He was a serious fellow and Raoul never liked him because of his lack of humour, but tonight he felt none of those feelings were relevant any more.

'Spartaco, how can I help?' Raoul said.

'My wife, Milena. She is alone in our apartment. Maybe they have arrested her already…'

'I will send George or one of the porters to see. You have a pen?'

'Yes, here,' Spartaco, a tall thin man, scribbled on a piece of paper with a pencil.

Raoul took the scrap of paper and the pencil, then wrote down Sol's address too.

'Any more?' Raoul said, raising his voice in an effort to be heard. 'Anyone else have family who needs to come? We have plenty of room, but it must be tonight. The Germans will soon be watching to find out where all the staff have gone.'

'Raoul. Try the door,' Marek said.

Raoul did as Marek bade and still found the key stiff in the lock, but after several attempts it clicked and the door opened. He could see nothing in the bible-black that greeted his eyes.

'We need a torch of some kind,' he said.

Silence filled the cellar, but minutes later Marek came with a bunch of tapers. Once they were alight, the two of them advanced. The room greeting him surprised and relieved Raoul at the same time. A broad concrete floor spread ahead. It was dry but rough. A dank smell wafted towards him as he stepped in and he realised this was not a room but a huge passageway. Twenty yards on he could see two tunnel entrances. The left hand tunnel felt cold as he approached and the other seemed to be a dead end, for no air moved there. He pressed on with Marek at his shoulder.

What they found made them both gasp. This was no adjunctive cellar: it was a warren of underground tunnels. For Raoul it was like finding treasure. There was enough space for a hundred people as long as they could keep them warm and fed. In a big hotel the means to keep them warm was no problem. Feeding a multitude was nothing to him either. Was he not a great chef? Was it not his business to feed people?

He turned back with a smile of triumph on his broad face.

2

Schiller was smoking. The fumes in Monsieur Robert's office reminded Raoul of the little smoke-house on the banks of the Dordogne where his father used to smoke fish. He was sitting opposite the German and knew that behind him by the door stood two green-clad soldiers, each with a Mauser by his side. If Raoul needed reminding that things had become serious he needed only look over his shoulder. Schiller had his booted feet on the desk and was leaning back in the leather chair as if he owned the hotel.

Both men were silent. Raoul waited for the questions to start and Schiller seemed to want to prolong the moment. He watched as the German sucked at the cigarette and drew the smoke into his lungs. Schiller puckered his lips as if kissing someone and the smoke exited in a long plume of grey towards Raoul, who waved his hand to waft it away.

Schiller smiled and said, 'You seem uncomfortable.'

Raoul said nothing. Schiller was right. The chair was small and Raoul had needed to squeeze himself into it when Schiller had ordered him to sit.

'Six Jews. All working in this hotel. All disappear from the face of the earth in one second. Even their families disappear. Strange? Eh?'

Raoul shrugged. 'How am I supposed to know where they are?'

'I didn't say you did.'

'Well, I don't. I have no idea where my people are at any particular time. I'm the Executive Head Chef. I spend most of my time in my office.'

'Except when you cook.'

'Huh. I don't do much of that these days. My job is supervising and making sure the kitchens run smoothly.'

'But you cooked for General Müller.'

'That was exceptional. It was a favour.'

'You do favours for some generals and you won't co-operate with me?'

'But I'm here. I'm co-operating.'

Raoul shrugged and elevated his open hands.

Schiller took his feet from the blotter and leaned forward, frowning.

'Look, my fat friend, I know you know something.'

'I know you think you know that I know something, but your thinking about my thoughts is wrong.'

'This isn't funny.'

'No. It isn't. You are preventing me from doing my job. I know nothing about these Jews of yours. Can I perhaps have a list of their names and I'll ask the staff.'

'I can interrogate them myself. I have plenty of time. The Jewish workers do not. They will turn up eventually whatever happens.'

'Then why are you asking me?'

'This may become a matter for the SD. If they are communists and resistors my colleagues in the *Sicherheitsdienst* will want them found.'

'There have never been any communists in my kitchen. It is absurd.'

'How did you warn them?'

'Who?'

Schiller's face turned red. 'The Jews.'

'I didn't even know you were looking for them, though Marek the head chef said you came down while I was out, with a list of off-duty staff whom you wanted to speak to.'

'You were where?'

'I was taking some chicory to a friend's house.'

Schiller looked down at the desk and rifled through some printed pages.

'Yes. You were reported.'

'Then you know I wasn't here.'

'The Special Brigade officer you spoke to remembered you well. He said you had coffee.'

'It was chicory. I hope it choked him, he only took it because he thought he could impress someone by providing them with the real thing.'

'You don't understand the danger you are in. I have only to pick up the telephone and have you transferred to SD care. You won't find their accommodation as comfortable as Le Metro, I can assure you.'

Raoul said nothing. There was nothing to say, he knew that.

After a full minute of silence, Schiller said, 'You were visiting…' he glanced down at a sheet of paper on his desk, 'Natalie Dreyfus.'

Raoul remained silent.

'You deny it?'

'Of course not. She is an old friend. We grew up together in Bergerac.'

'She's Jewish.'

'If she is, she isn't a practising Jew. Known her for years.'

'She isn't registered.'

'No. As far as I know, she isn't Jewish any more. I think I saw her in church once or twice here in Paris,' Raoul lied.

'Any more? So you did know she is Jewish.'

'Well if she used to be that is.'

'You're lying.'

'I have no reason to mislead you, Hauptsturmführer. I am very concerned because I am missing even more staff now than only a few days ago. You think it is easy to run a big hotel kitchen?'

'All along you treat me as if I'm stupid. There are no stupid members of the SS. We are chosen because we have achieved our status. Did you know we trace every prospective member back four generations to ensure purity? We are tested intellectually and physically.'

'Very nice.'

'You think you can sit there and play games with me?'

'No. I just don't know what you're talking about half of the time. I'm just an Executive Head Chef. I have no politics and don't want to be involved in any either. Now, if you've finished with me?'

Raoul made to stand.

'Sit down.'

There was a calm and cold edge to Schiller's voice and Raoul began to realise he was facing another bully. It was like being at school. They always started with a pleasant face and ended by beating him. Until Pierre. Until someone somewhere stood up for him. Pierre was a long way away however. There was no one now to defend him or to look after Natalie. He wondered what he needed to do to get Schiller off his back.

'Hauptsturmführer Schiller. I promise you, I have no knowledge of any Jews. I gave no one a warning of any kind. Think about it. I was taking coffee to an old friend from Bergerac. When I got back here Marek said you were looking for some people but he wasn't sure of all the names. End of story. If I could find them, if I could get news of them, I would do so. Running the kitchens matters to me. I'm a proud man. I am French.'

Schiller scratched his groin. He shifted in the chair. 'We will talk again soon. Get out.'

Raoul stood up, pushing on the arms of the narrow chair

to do so. He smiled his most disarming smile.

'Hauptsturmführer, I'm sure we can work together on this one. I will make some enquiries and will report to you tomorrow. How does that sound?'

Schiller was silent. Raoul turned and walked past the two soldiers, snapping the door shut behind him. As he walked away down the green-carpeted corridor, he hummed the Marseillaise to himself. Schiller would never get her. Raoul would see to that. He would rather die than say a word of the pantomime that was going on three floors down.

Chapter 10

JUDRU—*A short, thick, dry sausage made from pure pork, a speciality of Chagny in Burgundy.*
– Larousse Gastronomique

I

Raoul's hand felt empty as he walked the street, entering the alleyway where Café Dimanche spread its green and dilapidated awning. If only Natalie's hand were in his. He realised he was not thinking sensibly but also knew he couldn't wait to see her again—alone this time.

To his right, the small cobbled square reached out to him, as if it needed his presence and his bulk to give it credence and substance. The green parasol over the single wrought iron table had seen better days and Raoul wondered whether he could offer advice on the running of the place, though he corrected himself almost at once.

Arrogance. That's what it is. Arrogance. I'm the Executive Head Chef of a big hotel and I walk the streets looking down on other places. No. I won't give in to that. It is like those filthy Sauerkrauts, looking down on what they don't understand.

He sat.

A memory came to him of how he and his parents dined by the Dordogne. He could not now remember the name of the place, but it was one of those cafés beneath the Chateau Beynac, by the river, where music played and autumn leaves drifted across the river-front. It was a time when he had felt at ease with the world. He was due to depart for Lyon the following week. His parents had taken him out to celebrate and the family had cycled to Beynac, to dine and look at the boats as they passed by on the Dordogne.

Raoul could recall how the waiter produced olives and bread as the Verney family perused the menu. In his mind's eye he could, even now, see the expression on his father's face as the langoustines arrived. Raoul had known as soon as he pulled off the front legs of the shellfish they were overcooked. He had grimaced.

Catching the look on Raoul's face, his father smiled at him and said, 'You know, Raoul, when we cook, it is like an author of a book who sees everyone else's writing as flawed because it is not written in the way he would have done it. Yet, there are many ways to dress a salmon, many ways to roast a chicken, and who is to say which is the best? It is a subjective matter of taste. As long as the food matches the ambience and the place, then who cares? You know and I know we would serve these little shellfish in a different way, but if the customers enjoy them like this who can say it is incorrect? Not me, not today. Look around. The sun is shining, bidding farewell to the summer heat. The river flows by as if it notices nothing. Can we really complain about a tiny softness when we chew these shellfish? No. The flavour is wonderful because I am here; I am with the people I love and I am drinking a beautiful wine from Alsace.'

The plump old fellow had raised his glass and clinked it against Raoul's. The three of them smiled, and as the phonograph played an American jazz tune in the background they celebrated being together. It was no one's birthday, no anniversary. They celebrated the warmth and love of family.

The feeling remained with Raoul, and even when he heard friends criticise him for the feast he cooked at his father's funeral, he knew he had done it for his father and he knew the old man would have revelled in the singing and dancing. Raoul's father was not a man to mourn and he had disapproved of grief. Often, he would say in Raoul's hearing how he thought it was a selfish way to carry on.

'You feel sad because you miss her,' he had said at Raoul's mother's funeral. 'It is selfish. You think only of yourself. Think more to celebrate her life. The joy she brought to our lives and the happiness she wrought. I miss her, but I won't mourn her. I think only of God's kindness in giving me that time with her and giving me a son of whom I am proud.'

Raoul wiped a tear from the corner of his eye as he sat in the street, on the hard metal chair at the black iron table. He wished they were still there, perhaps sitting opposite him, smiling and drinking wine, but he was a realist. He understood that however much one wishes, the past is gone and only the present matters for the future is unseen. Now, in Raoul's present the Germans were here like black crows in the summer sky, a gathering storm cloud on the horizon; his future had become unclear.

He took out his handkerchief and wiped his brow. He was

not sweating, but it had become a habit and he always felt better when he did it. It was the ritual of the Executive Head Chef and no one at the Metro made fun of him for it. Minutes passed but nobody came, so he stood up and opened the dark wood glazed door. A tiny bell rang as he pulled the door open and he reflected that a man of his size deserved a louder noise to announce his arrival.

In the window were two tables, ahead, several more, and to his left a battered counter barring the way to the kitchens, communication with the room only through a hatch. The hatch was closed. He leaned on the bar. To the side of the hatch were shelves with bottles. He always thought you could tell the personality of the owner from the quality of the drinks on their shelves. This establishment sported a full bottle of Pernod, an almost empty bottle of Scotch whiskey and four bottles of eau-de-vie. Several cases of wine stood on their sides by the wall beneath the shelf and a picture painted in pastels, hung above. It was a scene of a river in sunshine, and it reminded Raoul of home.

Presently, a small woman scuttled out of a doorway to his right, next to a flight of stairs. She reminded him of a small beetle, a dark, shiny face, black hair and a smoothness to her cheeks as if she had been toiling over a hotplate.

'I'm sorry but I was busy in the kitchen. I have no one to help behind the bar, but it doesn't matter because since the Sauerkrauts came, I only have three regular customers. Everyone else has left town or been sent away. You want a drink?'

'Yes. Yes please,' Raoul said. 'Pernod would be fine. Pernod with a little water.'

The woman smiled. It was a wan and weary crack in her

smooth features. Raoul thought she must be older than he was, despite her shiny black hair, tied back in the nape of her neck.

'I make the cassoulet when it's quiet. It's hard to get meat now with the rationing so I'm learning to be stingy. No one minds; most of them have only a few coupons anyway.'

'Today's cassoulet?'

'Mutton. But if you prefer, we have mutton. Otherwise if you come back tomorrow, you could have mutton for a change.'

She said this without any expression of humour on either her face or in her eyes, though Raoul knew she meant it as a joke.

'I have eaten already, thank you.'

He poured a little water into the yellow liquor and watched as it spread in a milky opalescence through the glass. 'I was looking for someone.'

'Here?'

'Yes.'

'There's only me here. A customer?'

'Natalie Dreyfus who works with me, suggested I try here. I was looking for her friend, Marcel.'

The woman gave him a sideways glance; a flash of curiosity perhaps, or it could have been caution.

'I don't know these people. Please finish your drink, I have to close up.'

'I thought you were serving cassoulet?'

'It's for this evening. I have to go out.'

'Marcel. I need to see him.'

'I told you...'

'Please, can you perhaps give him a message?'

'But if I don't know him, how can I give a message?'

'Would you kindly tell this man, whom neither of us knows, that Raoul from the Metro has a message for him from Natalie and he will return tomorrow at the same time.'

'You are the famous chef?'

'I am the Executive Head Chef at the Metro.'

He said it with pride. He wondered whether if he was a poor chef working in some soup kitchen in Marseille he would have said who he was in the same way. He realised how proud he was of his position. Pride before a fall—he knew that one. It had followed him all his life, he reflected.

'Well Monsieur le Chef, if I see this man whom I don't know and you don't know either, I'll be sure to tell him.'

Raoul swallowed the liquorice fluid down and stood to leave.

'I will return tomorrow.'

'I hope no one is following you, that's all. It would not be difficult to do that.'

'Yes, I'm not an easy man to miss. I will make certain no one follows. The message?'

'Until we meet again,' the woman said. She began to wash Raoul's glass as he blotted out the light from the door. The bell rang its tiny chime as he left.

Walking away, he reflected how this friend of Natalie's might be in some kind of trouble and it could make meeting him dangerous. He had no other contacts who might help get the Kitchen Jews away. They could not stay in the hotel for an indefinite time and even they knew that. If he succeeded in finding some way to help them get out of Paris it would mean parting with Natalie too, but where would they go? Would she return to Bergerac, to Pierre? He did not think it would be any safer there, since Pierre was registered and Natalie was not. Any idiot could tell they were related just by looking at their noses and their colouring.

Perhaps she could stay. But what sort of life would that be for her? She would always be moving from room to room, cellar to cellar, and almost never seeing the light of day. No. he loved her and he would get her away.

But what if the war lasted for fifty years? He would be dead before he ever saw her again. Perhaps if she left, he could go too. They could be together, together and safe, but he knew it would mean deserting his people, his staff. He bit his lip as he walked. He had to decide where his loyalties lay—Natalie or the little people who depended on him to keep their lives together even in the face of the dreadful world Paris had now become.

2

Natalie lay on her side, her right leg draped over Raoul's huge thigh. Through the window he could hear the rain, pattering, pattering like the soft thrumming of nervous fingers on the pane of his mind. He looked down at her face as she looked up. He touched her cheek with his left hand and caressed the side of her head, smoothing the ruffled hair back above her ear. Raoul experienced a warm feeling, as if he was once again a child, held by his mother, comforted and reassured, but in moments it came to him there was no reassurance here, only danger. Danger for them both, as if the one thing that now occupied his thoughts and spread this feeling of joy was a snake that could turn and bite at any time.

He knew that occupying this double room at the top of the hotel was risky and that any moment now the bedside telephone could raise its incisive tones, but he needed this first time with Natalie; he craved her arms, her face, and her body. Deep inside he wondered whether if he had been a different shape he would have had many women, yet he also knew no other women mattered to him. Not now, not ever.

'Natalie,' he said, 'I love you. I have never loved another. I know it's true.'

Natalie sat up. Her eyes now level with his.

'I know that. I feel it too. Why have we wasted so much time? If only we had each had the courage and strength to say what we felt. In the beginning, when I was young, I thought you didn't like me. I thought you shunned me because of that.'

'No. I was only shy. I never imagined anyone could want a fat, fat man like me. It puzzles me now too.'

'Don't you understand?'

'Understand? No. I puzzle over how God can pick this time to make us come together.'

'It is not the person you are on the outside. It is the man you are way down inside. I don't care if you are Catholic, Jewish or... or...'

'You can overlook my appearance?'

'Your appearance is Raoul's exterior. I have loved the man you are for years, but never realised you felt the same. I would have had your children... so much wasted time.'

'I suppose we are both too old now for that.'

'I think so. It wasn't that I was waiting for you, it was just I never found anyone who measured up to the great Raoul.'

'Great? No. Puzzled maybe. I'm puzzled by life. I'm puzzled by the Germans. I don't really understand why they are here or why they would want to be.'

She touched his cheek; a gentle caress, soft as his.

She said, 'It is one reason I love you. It is not because you protect me and the others, it's because you do it for such simple reasons. It isn't political or religious with you.'

He said nothing but could not take his eyes from her.

She went on, 'You help people because you are kind. The rest does not matter. It is enough.'

Embarrassed now, he threw the sheets aside and sat on the edge of the bed.

'If we don't go now, we risk being found.'

Raoul leaned back into the bed and their lips met. Reluctance tugged at his heart but he got up. Dressing, he sat in the armchair by the window and watched as she rose. Her breasts drooped a little and her body was thin, thinner than he had realised, and it made him think he would like to feed her. Perhaps he could manage to rustle up a meal from the Germans' leavings. What had they had tonight? Lobster bisque? Chicken liver paté? He remembered that his pork had become a firm favourite with the German "guests" and he smiled to himself as she dressed. Pork was appropriate for his Aryan guests, even though there was an element of cannibalism involved. Pigs at a trough. It was the only simile he could conjure up.

'I hate the Germans, you know,' he said.

'Hatred is what they specialise in. Don't become like them. It is hatred, prejudice and greed that has caused this war. The more we practise what they preach, the more like them we become. Have you read the newspapers?'

'No. No time.'

'Le Figaro is filled with their propaganda. Even cartoon caricatures of how they see Jewish people. Ugly, smelly and greedy. It disgusts me.'

'But when you know a lie is a lie, what harm can it do? No one in France believes the rubbish they print.'

'You think not? Before I went into hiding, neighbours informed on neighbours and people settled old scores by accusing each other of being spies against the Germans. They even call themselves our allies.'

'Well, there's nothing we can do about it but keep them happy until France can rise up and throw them out. It will happen one day. French people do not lie down and allow a foreign army to rape them. A time will come…'

'I hope you are right. I hope our country can resist.'

'I met Marcel this morning.'

'You said.'

'I didn't tell you he is trying to find a way to get you all out. You trust him?'

'You waited until now to tell me?'

'I'm sorry. I had other things on my mind.'

'Hmm. Yes, that was obvious. What did he say?'

'I told you. He is looking for a way to transport everyone away, either to the coast or to Switzerland. He knows many people who want to fight the Germans here, but I think he may be dangerous, you know.'

'Marcel is vengeful. If he has contacts, that is good, but I would never entrust myself to him. If he was leading me to an escape route, he would only need to see a few Germans and he would stop and kill them whether it risked my life too or not. I just hoped his friends would be wiser and more sensible.'

'Will it be all right?'

'Of course. We are careful'

'You really think so?' he said.

'Naturally.'

'I love you. Now I have found that, I don't want to lose it.'

He reached his arms out and she settled on his knee. He touched her face with his hand and their lips touched—a soft gentle kiss.

'We will always be together. I won't let them harm you,' he said.

'I won't let them harm you either.'

Raoul smiled up at her. Why did life have to be so complicated? His had always been a life of bain-maries and braising pans. Now it was one of stealth and caution. Caution to give nothing away and still make life unfold as close to normal as possible.

His one conviction now was that it was worthwhile. Raoul had found love for the first time in his life and he was not going to give it up to anyone, not Schiller, nor even to Hitler himself.

Chapter 11

KIR—*A Burgundy mixture of dry white Aligoté wine and cassis
(the blackcurrant liqueur for which Burgundy is famous).*
– Larousse Gastronomique

I

The autumn rain falling thick and fast had continued now for days, and Raoul wondered at times whether it was symbolic. Since the Germans took charge he had noticed that most of the residents in Paris struggled to find any reason for the sun to shine. They could not know that the reason for sunshine in his world was Natalie. His secret love kept him warm and dry. It filled his mind with thoughts of spring, and freed his spirit.

Leaving his apartment, Monsieur Lebeuf who lived in the apartment below had looked up at him as he put up his umbrella.

'Filthy weather, Monsieur Verney.'

'A bit of rain—no trouble, surely?'

He smiled. The heavens could open up with a deluge for all he cared. He was thinking of Natalie.

'They are putting posters up everywhere, you know.'

Monsieur Lebeuf was a tall man who reminded Raoul of a rabbit. His long ears and his overbite gave the man a rabbit-like appearance, a vision Raoul found he was unable to dispel. Sometimes he saw his neighbour skinned, spit-roasted and served on a bed of spinach.

'Posters?' Raoul said.

'Yes. They are trying to force-feed us their Nazi dogma. They think we are all proletarians.'

Monsieur Lebeuf was a schoolteacher and used words like that, though Raoul never minded. He had no interest in politics and would be the first to admit he could not tell Pushkin from Lenin.

'What dogma?'

'Work, homeland and family. It replaces freedom, equality and brotherhood. You've not seen them?'

'No, I don't walk past any billboards on my way to work.'

'How's it going, feeding the Sauerkrauts? You should poison them all.'

Raoul descended the steps. Close up to the man he said, 'Be careful what you say. There are spies everywhere and people are reporting each other. Not me, naturally, just be careful what you say all the same.'

Lebeuf looked at Raoul. His face became serious and his eyes narrowed.

'I know, it just gets on top of me sometimes. If this war lasts for a long time, our country will be on its knees. I hate that. Hate it. I'm proud to be French.'

'We feel the same my friend, but to last the course we must tolerate their presence and do whatever small things any of us can do. I think a resistance will come and maybe we can even throw out these German pigs. In the meantime, I will keep my mouth shut and my hands where they can see them. You know, some see what I do as collaboration, as Pétain recommends, but it isn't so. I just have no way to fight them yet. One day…'

'You talk sense, my friend.'

To Raoul's surprise the man came up a step, and placing a hand on each of Raoul's shoulders leaned forward, kissing him once on each cheek.

'Vive la France,' he said, under his breath.

Extricating himself from the embrace, Raoul said, 'An unusual morning. In five years, we have hardly spoken.'

'We must all stick together, no?'

Raoul smiled but said nothing. He realised the droplets running down the man's cheeks were not rainwater but tears, though he was still uncertain whether this man was reliable. He seemed unstable.

He began his march to work. The people passing him in the streets looked grey and dull, without smiles, no jolly conversation, just dreary faces frowning as they passed him in the rain.

He shrugged it all off. He was in love and walking on air. He felt his life had changed for the better as well as for the worse. He walked on. By seven-thirty he was hurrying up the steps of the Metro. He was late and it annoyed him. There was no excuse for an Executive Head Chef arriving late on a day when anything could be happening in the hotel.

George greeted him as soon as he entered and folded his umbrella. Arriving at work it was as if he had a guilty secret—one that aroused him and made him secretive. He felt desperate to find a time and a place when he could make love to Natalie again. The thought brought a smile to his lips and tumescence to his nether regions. He could not match his thoughts to the gloomy Parisians he had passed as he walked to work, however much he understood and empathised. Life had now become exciting. It was an excitement he had never before experienced and whether there were Germans in the hotel or not, his adolescent ardour reigned supreme.

At the reception desk he noticed General Müller. The man was remonstrating with the receptionist, gesticulating and shifting from one foot to the other. Raoul approached.

'General Müller. How nice to see you back.'

Müller turned towards him.

'Raoul. Will you explain to this young lady that I need to have access to my suite immediately? I have been travelling all night and I want to rest. All she says is that the room won't be ready until midday. It isn't any good to me. I'm tired. You will please tell her.'

Raoul looked at the receptionist's face. It was a more serious glance than his face betrayed. He knew the position.

'Beatrice, is there no way to rush through the cleaning? Ask Philippe if he can speed things up a bit.'

'Yes, sir,' Beatrice said. She was a thin girl, early twenties with brown hair and green eyes that narrowed as she caught Raoul's. She picked up the telephone and spoke into it in calm unhurried French, then smiled at General Müller.

'Philippe assures me the room will be ready in two hours.'

'And what am I supposed to do until then? Sleep in the foyer?'

Raoul reached out a plump arm and placed it on the

general's shoulder.

'My dear General,' he said, 'in the next two hours you will forget your tiredness and enjoy a breakfast so good you will wish it won't come to an end. You will be reluctant to go to your suite. Please…'

Raoul indicated the dining room with an outstretched arm. Müller, reluctant at first, muttered under his breath and led the way. He turned to his secretary, who followed behind.

'Don't bother, Schultz. You don't need to come. Raoul will look after me.'

The man clicked his heels, bowed and saluted. Raoul and Müller entered the dining room. The rococo fireplace stood out ahead, above which hung an oval painting of a young woman in eighteenth century dress reclining on a chaise longue. The gilt frame that had reflected the early morning sunshine in the summertime now looked dull and dark. To the right were French windows leading out to the terrace with its black iron railings and white marble slabs where, when the weather was better, patrons could breakfast or dine outside, looking across the close-cropped lawns between the elms towards the Tuileries Gardens.

The rich fawn carpet of the dining room with its opulent patterns of squares dulled the sound of their footsteps as they entered. To their left was an ice bucket containing an opened bottle of Krug '32 and clean champagne glasses. Each table held a white tablecloth adorned by a small vase of red flowers, overlooked by the high ceiling with its glittering chandeliers. Three Wehrmacht officers sat sipping coffee at a table by the fireplace and another table hosted a man in a black suit, a long black leather coat draped on the back of his chair. The man looked up as if studying Raoul. His dark eyes stared and his balding head reflected the light descending on his tonsure-like pate. The face was one that Raoul would have equated with an aristocrat, thin, dark-skinned and serious. There was something he could not quite place about the fellow. As he turned to his guest, he decided it was the feeling the man looked like a bully, but Raoul shrugged it off and paid no more attention.

Müller sat down at the nearest table.

'Champagne?' Raoul said.

'I will go straight to sleep at the table. Been on the road since yesterday morning. I've only come for a few days' rest, then I return to Berlin.'

'But Krug goes well with the dish I will cook you.'

'Dish?'

'Something simple, satisfying and nutritious.'

'Oh, very well, Raoul. You know the way to a man's heart.'

'Oeufs en cocotte. A simple dish, but it must be cooked carefully.'

'Eggs? I don't want eggs.'

'You trust me?'

'With my wife, my wallet and even my stomach nowadays, but eggs? I don't know…'

'Then come with me into the kitchen. We can drink a little champagne and talk as I cook. You will witness what I do with the eggs and you will become a convert.'

Müller seemed exhausted and unsteady on his feet as he followed Raoul into the kitchen. A cloud of steam rose from a counter to the right and the tiled floor was crowded with milling chefs and sous chefs. Raoul bit his bottom lip. He had to make time for Natalie and the others to vacate, clean and air Müller's suite. They had been there for three days. He knew however, as certain as eggs are eggs, that if anyone could clean and prepare a room in a flash, it was the staff of the Metro.

2

'First we slice the Bayonne ham into wafer-slim pieces. It has to be Bayonne. The flavour is…'

Raoul raised his pinched index and thumb to his mouth and kissed the air in that familiar gesture of love for the dish he was about to prepare. Müller leaned against the counter and smiled. 'You have such passion. Even I, a Wehrmacht soldier, cannot deny you, you crazy, hedonistic, fat chef.'

Müller took a mouthful of the champagne and chewed it like a connoisseur, as Raoul added the sliced ham to the buttered, cast-iron frying pan.

Raoul said, 'It must be crisp. So crisp it splinters, but not burnt. More champagne?'

Müller held out his glass. Raoul noticed the hand shook. He ignored it and continued.

'Now, we take out our ham-crisps and place them on the cloth, to absorb the fat. I usually warm the ramekin and then brush it with butter, like this.'

'When I went to university in England, bacon and eggs was always a popular way to start the day. Is that what you are cooking?'

'Rosbifs don't know anything of Bayonne ham. It has a flavour all of its own. Bacon? Bacon? Ridiculous!'

99

'I did not mean to offend your sensibilities, Raoul.'

Raoul smiled and clinked his glass against the German's. It was unfathomable, but he liked this fellow. He almost wished there was no war and they could meet in peace and friendship.

'Now,' he said, 'we splinter the ham like this and lay the shards in the bottom of the ramekin. Here, smell—is it not a wonderful fragrance?'

Müller had no time to agree as Raoul went on, 'And now, the eggs. They must be fresh and large.'

He cracked two eggs into the ramekin with one hand, the intense yellow of the yolks glaring up at him to his complete satisfaction. Next, he walked to the massive refrigerator and removed a large steel jug. He poured an egg-cupful of thick golden cream into the ramekin and sprinkled a pinch of paprika over the mixture. He ground some black pepper over the top with a pinch of salt, and inserted his egg dish into the big oven behind him. He had used twenty minutes. It might have been long enough; he was not sure.

'So, we wait four minutes. Just time for more champagne. If you would sit in the dining room, I will bring your meal at once.'

Müller staggered towards the wide double swing-door with his fifth glass of champagne. Raoul smiled and glanced at his watch. He knew he needed to be cautious not to let Müller get out of his clutches for one and a half hours yet.

He removed the ramekin and sniffed at it. Smiling, he garnished it with a sprig of parsley and placed the dish on a tray, with toast, a breakfast cup and a pot of coffee. If he sat with Müller and poured more champagne he thought he could gossip his way to the end of the longest two hours of his life.

Chapter 12

LANGOUSTE—A crustacean also known as the spiny lobster, thorny lobster, rock lobster and crawfish.
– Larousse Gastronomique

I

The sky was clearing and for once no rain fell. As Raoul trudged along the wind took the falling elm leaves, sweeping them into his path as he progressed through the flat autumnal Tuileries gardens. A crow cawed from high up in one of the elms and he wondered whether it was a sign of something, though he was not a superstitious man by nature. He was honest with himself however and he recognised his nerves were on edge. Too many close escapes, too many potential problems in hiding his people.

The numbers of secreted staff and their families had begun to swell. Unexpectedly, uncles and aunts, brothers and sisters had appeared and he now had responsibility for twenty-seven individuals excluding Natalie. When rooms were empty, they occupied them. When there were no rooms they sheltered in the wine cellars or the distant tunnels. On one occasion, when

Schiller did his rounds, he had to hide Sol in the freezer for a few minutes, but soon realised it was impossible for anyone to last more than a very short time in there. The poor man staggered out, lips and fingers blue, with ice in his hairline and eyebrows.

These secret guests always used the service lift and the back stairs to access their hiding places. And always Schiller lurked here and there; the suspicious Hauptsturmführer waiting for Raoul to put one plump toe wrong, when all would end as it had begun. The beginnings had been, after all, only a second's faltering acceptance of risk which now had snowballed into a day-long game of hide and seek. It was true, Schiller might spot one or two of them as they worked in the kitchen or cleaned a bedroom, but Raoul always thought the German would have no way of knowing who was who. If there were no distinguishing marks who was to say who was Jewish or Catholic? In the face of Schiller's apparent increasing suspicion Raoul still felt comfortable about the people he and Monsieur Robert were hiding in the hotel. But despite his confidence, one of his biggest problems was that he knew they could not be denied daylight forever. No one can live underground for years, and as a man from rural France he understood that. The need to get them all away burned like a beacon inside him and Marcel Maujean seemed to hold the only key.

No. It was no good pretending he could protect them forever. Some of them at least, had to be decanted somewhere, and today he was hoping for a decantation opportunity.

The Café Dimanche with its sad canopy loomed ahead and Raoul hastened his waddling steps towards it. He had only met Marcel twice and he remained uncertain whether he trusted him entirely. Natalie seemed to have reservations and Raoul needed more than a simple promise before he would entrust his loved-one to a man hell-bent on revenge. True, it was revenge against the Nazis, but all the same, he wondered whether Marcel was not just a loose cannon and someone whose basic motives did not coincide with his own.

Raoul entered the little café. The tables, as ever, were empty. He leaned against the bar and pressed the bell, breathing hard since he had walked faster than was comfortable for so large a man. A faint ringing came and the beetle arrived.

She looked up at Raoul. 'He's upstairs. You go up?'

'Would you ask him to come down? I walked a long way.'

'From Bergerac perhaps?'

'No. From the Metro.'

'A child could run that distance in minutes. You should eat more sensibly. Exercise a little.'

'Please ask him to come and join me. A little Pernod would be welcome while I wait.'

She pushed the bottle towards him.

'Some water?' he said.

'Here,' she said and shoved a small earthenware jug across the counter.

'You don't like me, do you?'

The woman smiled. 'I like you well enough. I just think you are lazy.'

'Lazy?'

'We should be fighting and killing the Germans. What do you do? You feed them, and worse, you feed them fancy food such as only Frenchmen have a right to appreciate. Anyway, fat people are always lazy.'

'Lazy? I do my job. In the background, I hide people. It is like a smokescreen. I make friends with the bastards because it protects my people and I wait for France to awaken from its slumber. One day we will all rise up and throw off the choking collar they have put on us. One day, we will all fight. It is just that now, no one trusts anyone else and neighbours inform on each other as if all good French principles have been abandoned. No. I am not one of those. I am an artist. I make wonderful, beautiful food. It is French and anyone can appreciate it, even our enemies. The Sauerkrauts enjoy it, but one day, we will rise up and shove it down their throats. Don't you see the lovely picture? A German soldier, choking, with bulging eyes and a blue-black face, fear in his eyes as he asphyxiates on Chateau d'Yquem and caviar? Now go and get your son and let me talk to him.'

She looked at him, silent and immobile. He glared at her.

She said, 'For that little speech, you can have the Pernod on the house even though it's a poor substitute for absinthe. Maybe I was wrong about you.'

She reached under the counter and brought out a small bowl of olives which she slid towards him before going up the stairs to the right of the bar. It was as if she was remunerating him for his little soliloquy. It was as if olives had become currency and she was trading with him for patriotism. God knew the franc had sunk into despair since the Germans devalued it. Twenty francs to the deutschemark; it was unthinkable. He thought that perhaps he preferred olives in any case; they were worth more to him. At least an olive remained true to its nature which was more than any currency could

104

claim.

Raoul tapped his fingers on the counter. He was sweating and he knew why. He understood that trusting another was not like in the old days. There was no Pierre to help. Auguste was not here either, with his wisdom and sanity. It was a mad world where anything could happen. The Germans might find his people. They could arrest him, and worse still Natalie might be taken. No. He would never allow that. He would rather die saving her than let those filthy Sauerkrauts get her.

It all made him dependent on Marcel, but he was such a fiery man. Marcel was angry and wanted revenge, whether it was borne of wisdom or hatred or even a simple wish to help France, it did not matter; the man expressed no caution or care. Perhaps he had a death wish. If he had, he would do no more than endanger everyone although Raoul knew he had no other contacts who could help. There would be no use in enlisting the aid of people like Lebeuf. It would be a blind alley from which Natalie and the others would never escape.

Marcel descended the stairs, his black shoes clacking. Raoul looked up at the young Frenchman's face. The lines showed more age than his twenty years justified. The checked shirt-collar poked up under his V-necked jumper and he was smoking a cigarette, stuck at a wry angle in the corner of his mouth. Raoul wondered how Natalie could be in love with him instead of this slim athletic young man. Clean-shaven, a rounded face and with brown unkempt hair, Marcel had the air of a college student, not a potential saviour of hunted people. He acknowledged Raoul as he came down, stood next to him and reached for the bottle. He drank from it and smiled. Raoul still wondered whether he could trust him.

2

Raoul layered the creamed, sautéed champignons and the sliced celeriac into the gratin dish. He added the breadcrumbs in a thin layer and sprinkled it with grated cheese. He placed the dish into the hot oven and checked his watch. The sautéed potatoes would be ready in ten minutes. It was enough time. He placed the frying pan on the hot plate and added the butter. Waiting until the butter was clarified and browning he added the pork fillet, careful not to disturb the layer of cracked pepper and salt.

He was sweating now and wiped his forehead with his handkerchief. The minutes were ticking by and he worried in case he had left too much time for the celeriac to cook, though he had only parboiled it for five minutes.

Celeriac is a forgiving vegetable; it serves up just as well if it is a little underdone or even soft.

He was pleased with his choice of main course and felt sure the Maître would approve. Raoul even understood why he was being tested like this. Fernand Point was not a man to allow his sous chefs promotion without frequent testing and today he had a special guest, though Raoul did not know whom it might be. He could see from the faces at the table that the first course of smoked duck on a Salade Perigordine had been well received. He had sorted and chopped the walnuts to just the right dimensions and used the balsamic vinegar in the vinaigrette just as his father once recommended.

He pulled out the gratin after turning the pork. When he carried through his dishes, the Maître looked deep in conversation with the dark-haired man and neither paid much

106

attention as Raoul served the food. They drank their Morgon and Maître Point leaned back in his chair.

'Verney, this is palatable. You may go.'

Palatable was as close to praise as he had ever received as a compliment from his employer and a smile spread across his face as he pushed the double doors open and entered the kitchen. Today the restaurant was closed and only Raoul and another sous chef were present, apart from a washer-up and porter. The Maître had told him it was a special occasion and he felt honoured to be singled out in this way. He was one of six sous chefs and all of them vied with each other for the Maître's attention. It was with a feeling of satisfaction he began to create his dessert.

The meringues were soft and chewy; Raoul had spent most of the morning making them and discarded the first batch because there was an unsatisfactory crispness in their consistency. When he mixed the second batch, adding chopped hazelnuts, he wondered if the nuts absorbed too much moisture, but he persisted and when he tested several, he found both the flavour and texture to be perfect. Selecting a large round silver dish, he began placing the meringues in a wide layer. He next created a layer of whipped cream. Another layer of meringue, narrower than the last, more whipped cream. Moments later, he looked at the pyramid of cream and meringue. The final meringue was the one with the perfect shape. The peak at the apex was perfect.

He poured the melted Swiss chocolate, mixed with a little oil and water in a delicious scented torrent over the mountain. Next, he studded the creation with whole hazelnuts and finished with a dusting of powdered sugar, dense at the top and fainter lower down to simulate a mountain capped by ice. He placed the dish in the deep-freeze for the few minutes before it was needed, wiped his brow again and sat down on a small wooden stool.

Raoul thought back to the first time he had tasted this meringue Suisse. It had been his birthday. Fourteen? Sixteen? It evaded him, but the thing remaining in his mind was the flavour of hazelnuts, chocolate and cream combined with the sweet, chewy meringue. It had been so moreish he could not satisfy himself with it until his father's special creation had gone. Gone like snow melting on the Pyrenees Mountains that the dish was supposed to emulate.

Here in Lyon, he missed his father and his home but he knew he was learning so much from exposure to the great chef who seemed to have taken him under his wing, once he had left college. Raoul always understood how he had left the College qualified but ignorant, unschooled in the real way of creating a loveable meal, for Raoul was beginning to love the food he made. Some had suggested to him he sublimated his real feelings into his food and what he really sought was a woman. Always laughing it off, he had often sat wondering whether the other sous chefs were right and he was only substituting one love for another in a frustrating lack of confidence. He had no way of knowing, but he knew there was no love of anything comparable to his love and passion for the food he made.

Raoul smiled as he entered the restaurant bearing his sweet before him like one of the three kings, bearing frankincense or myrrh. His was a mountain of pleasure and he presented it with a flourish. They barely looked up. A glance was all he received and he began to feel he might have made a mistake. He served the dish. Neither of the diners said anything. He stood, waited, and watched as they spooned the heavenly mixture into their mouths.

Monsieur Point looked up. 'You can go Raoul.'

'It is satisfactory?'

'Yes, yes. Off you go.'

Crestfallen, Raoul turned to go. A voice called him back. It was the dark man with Maître Point.

'This meal,' the man said, 'is one of the most pleasant I have had in a long time. My compliments to the chef.'

Raoul felt a burden lift from his shoulders. He glanced at his Maitre. Point looked up. Their eyes met and he said, 'You are getting better Raoul. Maybe a little less sugar on the summit.'

'I'm sure the climbers of Mont Blanc would agree.'

Monsieur Point smiled. 'Away with you. We are talking.'

Raoul still wondered whether the meal had been a success. There was no way of knowing. Here in this excellent restaurant praise was always in short supply but Raoul believed in himself. There were many areas of his life where he lacked confidence, but food was not one of them. He would get feedback but its nature always remained a puzzle to him.

Chapter 13

MEUNIERE, A LA—A method of cooking that can be used for all types of fish (whole, filleted or steaks).
– Larousse Gastronomique

I

Marcel indicated one of the tables to his right, and taking the Pernod bottle swaggered across the room and sat down. He put his feet up on a chair. The glass he had grabbed from the counter thumped as he placed it on the ageing checked table-cloth. He sat with one elbow on the table and looked up at Raoul, smiling.

'Come, sit. The Fat Chef comes to question me again. Perhaps you work for the Gestapo or the SD. Your inquisition is never less stringent than theirs.'

'I don't ever know what to think of you. You use these names in public as if you have no fear of these people. Well, I'll tell you—fear is a useful commodity. It can keep you alive when all else is falling apart. What do you know? A boy, nothing more. I have many people now who depend on me. I have a real burden and I need to relieve it. You understand?'

'Sit down, you fat fuck,' Marcel smiled as if he had paid a compliment.

Raoul sat. He said nothing.

Moments passed. Marcel said, 'Well?'

Raoul poured water into his glass to dilute the spirit and said, 'Look. I need your help. Many people are hiding not far from here, they need to get away. There must be a way. Perhaps to England or maybe Switzerland; I believe Switzerland is still neutral?'

'What are you talking about? You know what you are saying? I have no idea how to do that.'

Marcel sat forward and lowered his voice. He frowned as he said, 'I have no contacts or even ideas to get these people away. It is madness. No. You took them in and you will have to put up with the smell. All I want is revenge for my father.'

'I loved my father too. If there is a monument to him, it is in me. These people whom you seem to dismiss so lightly, are men women and children who have escaped the German clutches. They can't stay hidden until the end of the war. It could last for fifty years for all we know. They have to get away.'

'Yes, but it isn't my problem. You took on the responsibility; you deal with it. If I tried to find a way, they would catch me and kill me. You want me to risk my life for them? With nothing to show for it afterwards? Huh. You're crazy.'

'Natalie.'

'What?' He paused. 'Natalie?'

'Yes.'

'Fuck off.'

'You don't care about her. She said you were her friend.'

'You would go to certain death for a friend, knowing it would be the same for them anyway? It would be meaningless.'

'She said you would help. She said you cared.'

'Look, my plump friend. I know a few people but there is no escape route unless we put it together. You hear me? We have to put it together and trust no one. People are informing on anyone they don't like. For grudges, for jealousy. You think it's so easy? You know someone. You confide in them and they disappear. Get back to your cooking pots. I can't help you.'

'And Natalie?'

'Maybe for just one, I can help. I could drive her myself. Maybe Spain, I don't know.'

'No. Not only Natalie. Ten or fifteen people.'

'I don't own a railway. It's impossible.'

'You can do this. You would become a hero.'

'I don't give a shit about being a hero. I care about getting these Nazi pigs out of France. We all need to help with that. It isn't about saving a few Jews. It's about fighting the invaders. I can't help you.'

Raoul reached forward and grabbed Marcel by the arm. He squeezed. It was like crushing a lemon. His fingers compressed and Marcel grabbed Raoul's hand.

'Let go.'

'You do as I say.'

'Fucking Hell. Let go.'

'I need your help.'

'All right. I'll think about it.'

'Marcel. It is a matter of common humanity,' Raoul said

without relaxing his grip. The lemon was almost dry. 'If we have here a chance to help some people we cannot turn it down. If you could see the looks in their eyes, you would not hesitate. For the love of God, have you no common feelings of humanity? We have to do something.'

'Bastard.'

'I'll let you go when you understand.'

'I understand.'

'Good,' Raoul said, relinquishing Marcel's arm.

Marcel relaxed as soon as Raoul's grip did.

'Do that again and I'll kill you.'

Raoul smiled. He said nothing. Only the sound of the Pernod glugging into their glasses broke the silence.

Presently, Raoul said, 'Spain, eh?'

'It's possible. We would need a truck and I will need to drive to the border first with an empty truck to find out where we can stop. I know of a man who might be able to find some farms where the truck can stay overnight. It's going to take time. You have money?'

'Money?'

'I need to buy the truck don't I? I don't have any money. Six months ago, I was a student. Now they have sent my father away. You think this café makes money?'

'I trust you. I'll get to the bank. If you cheat me, I'll know and I'll come looking for you.'

'Feeling tough? You don't look like a man who can handle himself in a fight.'

'I never had a reason to fight. I have now.'

'Then you know how I feel. I want to kill the lot of them.'

'Fighting to protect others is a fact of life. Fighting because

113

you are angry is the province of youth and it will get you killed as easily as I can make an omelette. You will have to be very careful. There is an SS officer, who watches the hotel so don't come there. I'll come to you. This place is on my way home; I can stop by without anyone thinking it's odd.'

Raoul stood up, a little unsteady from the Pernod. As he opened the café door, Marcel said, 'Against my better judgement, I like you. I'll do what I can.'

Turning back, Raoul smiled.

'We all need each other. The Germans think that by saying something it is a fact. They change our country and this "family, work and home" shit they smear on the posters is supposed to make us change, but we won't. We must all stand together to keep France French. I'm glad you will help me. Life is hard for our people. They are as scared as I am.'

He closed the door to the sound of the merry little bell and turned left, heading towards his apartment. He wondered whether Schiller would know if he went to the bank. He shrugged off the thought; as far as he knew, Schiller was not following him, at least not yet, but he might if Raoul weakened and betrayed himself. He decided he would have to become inscrutable, like a woodcarving, his face must not betray him.

He had meant what he said to Marcel. He hated the thought of physical violence but his fear for Natalie was driving him on. It was one of the few times in his life when he wanted to fight back. It was as if he could see Pierre's face as he questioned Raoul's self-esteem—his loyalty to himself. But his faithfulness to himself was not in question, it was an issue bigger than that for Raoul. It was love. He knew he would

114

fight and die for Natalie and for the love that was so new and so precious to him.

He felt like a priest who has preached celibacy all his life but finds he loves women more than God. In a sense it was true: he had given himself to his job and had never expected to find love, nor had he dared to imagine any woman would want him as Natalie did. His thoughts of her warmed him despite the autumn breeze and he unbuttoned his coat. He would get his people out, but now he could not see the way. Ever optimistic, he felt sure something would come up.

Yes. That was it. Something will come up.

2

Raoul's jacket bulged as he returned from the bank. Half his life savings. All in cash, all in francs, and now he could feel it stuffed into his breast pockets like so much chaff, ready to fly away on the autumn breeze. He patted the bulge from time to time as he approached the hotel, his feet kicking autumn leaves as they drifted past him. George was not there as he pushed open the glass double doors. Beatrice stood behind her desk as usual, and a group of armed soldiers stood outside his office. He hesitated, patting the lump of money in his jacket and deciding to go straight downstairs. He did not wish to risk them noticing anything, however small it might be. No sense in attracting anyone's attention today.

Raoul smiled a greeting to Beatrice as he made for the stairs. Another day over and he had plans to make. General Müller wanted a banquet and he had to see to the menu and

115

the ordering, but that was easy. There were forty people. He knew how much to order for one person, and so all he did was to order forty times that amount. Of course, he would order sixty times one person's food. He had his responsibilities and he did not neglect them. He pictured the faces looking at him from the darkness of the tunnel or the open door to an empty hotel room. His heart thumped and a feeling of pity came to him. He would make sure they had food. Good food and plenty of it too.

On this occasion it was difficult because Müller insisted they have pork and he knew his secret guests would not eat it. In the end he had persuaded the General to accept that there had to be two meats on the menu. The beef would never appear and no one would question him. It was all so easy to fool these Germans.

He opened the green wooden door at the foot of the stairs. Entering the kitchen, he stopped. A frozen tableau revealed itself. His danger dawned upon him. It was as if he watched a painting in a museum. He swallowed and stood still.

Natalie sat at the small guest table next to the pastry counter. Marek stood next to her. Schiller stood with his back to Raoul. Lying prostrate on the floor at Schiller's feet lay George. Dark blood flowed from his forehead. Raoul was rooted. He could not have moved at that moment if a German Panzer was heading for him.

His mind raced. No one spoke, but it seemed obvious what was going on. Natalie must have come up from the wine cellar for some reason and Schiller must have been in the kitchen. Raoul calmed. There had to be a way to solve this.

He cleared his throat. He approached. Schiller stepped

back and to the side. Raoul could see the dull, blue shine of gunmetal and he realised Schiller held a gun.

'What have you done?'

Schiller regarded him with a cold stare. He indicated with the gun barrel for Raoul to move to the table.

'Put up your hands,' Schiller said.

Raoul walked to George's side. The man was still breathing and began to stir.

'Get over there,' Schiller indicated with his pistol.

Raoul did as Schiller demanded. He backed up to his right, a few yards from the table. His eyes met Natalie's. There was a look of fear and utter hopelessness in those eyes and Raoul felt anger rising within him. His face flushed. He had never been affected like this before. All his life he had put up with bully-ing. Always before, they had aimed it at him, but now Natalie was the victim. It did not matter to Raoul whether it was a schoolboy punching or a German pistol-whipping a French-man. It was the same kind of abuse and it felt intolerable.

Schiller said, 'I knew it all the time. You are an enemy of the Reich, you fat bastard. Now you will pay. Don't imagine you will stay that fat in a German labour camp.' He smiled, but there was no humour there, only malice.

'Please Hauptsturmführer, I don't understand. Why do you point a gun at me? I have done nothing.'

'Nothing?' Schiller's voice rose a notch in its pitch. 'You have been hiding this woman here in the hotel. You are guilty of a serious crime. Nothing will save you now.'

'I've never seen this woman in my life. What happened to George?'

'He interfered. If you try to, you'll get the same. '

117

'Me? I have nothing in mind apart from maintaining friendship with our German allies.'

'You think I'm stupid?'

Schiller stepped towards Raoul. He raised his right hand, holding the Luger pistol. He struck Raoul across the cheek. It happened so fast, Raoul could not react. The big man staggered under the force of the blow. He stepped back until his backside gained the support of the counter behind him. His head swam.

'Get those hands up. You hear? I'll shoot you where you stand, you traitor. Higher.'

Raoul raised his hands higher. His right touched a wooden handle. Above him he realised a heavy cast-iron frying pan hung. He could even picture it in his mind's eye. It hung above the counter. Next to it was a heavy cook pot, the one he seared the joints with when he prepared pot-roast. He could smell the garlic.

Marek took a step forward. Schiller turned, still watching Raoul from the corner of his eye.

Marek said, 'There is no need for all this. I know where the others are.'

'Others?'

Natalie gasped. She began to stand. 'No. You can't…'

Natalie. She reached out towards Marek and grasped his sleeve. Schiller stepped forwards towards her and raised the pistol to strike her too. It was then something snapped in Raoul's mind. He sensed a momentary flush as if from embarrassment. He felt his head throb and the blood coursing through his neck. A feeling of rage such as he had never known before flowed in him. It overwhelmed him. It overcame any sense of caution.

Natalie.

Raoul gripped the frying pan. It was as if the handle flew to his hand. As if his hand was meant to grip it. His fat fingers closed. He experienced a feeling of power, solidity and strength. With one movement he stepped forward onto his left foot. The distance between him and Schiller closed in a second. He swung the heavy, cast iron frying pan. It could have been the weight of a feather, gossamer even. The heaviness meant nothing to him.

All that mattered was Natalie. She was a gleaming presence threading its way through his mind, his heart and his life. He felt like a man on the verge of fantastic success who sees his hopes and dreams threatened by a grotesque, evil creature from some underworld and finds he must act and act fast.

Schiller began to turn as if by instinct; he must have known what was coming. The knowledge could only have lasted a fraction of a second. Raoul drove the heavy utensil down, with all his strength and all his massive weight. It struck the German on the crown of his head. He crumpled like a crushed meringue. The Luger flew, clattering across the floor.

Raoul was breathing hard. He noticed sweat perambulating down his forehead. A drop of it hung from his nose-tip. He felt faint. What had he done?

He knelt over the stricken frame that once was Hauptsturmführer Schiller. A pool of dark crimson was spreading across the kitchen floor. He noticed Natalie's hand on his shoulder.

'Is he…'

'I think I killed him.'

'Yes,' Marek said, his voice almost a murmur.

'What do we do now?' Natalie said.

Raoul said, 'Do? What can we do? We must run. Or at least I have to run. If he's dead, he can't talk, can he?'

Marek said, 'What about the body? We can't just leave him here for the sous chefs to step over as they prepare the banquet for tomorrow.'

'I...I don't know. I've never killed anyone before. How the hell do I know what to do now?'

'Hide the body. Get rid of it,' Natalie said.

Raoul was close to panic. He still felt faint. With a grunt, he stood up. He turned to Natalie and hugged her. Something in that hug gave him strength. He began to become the Maître again. He was the Executive Head Chef. He knew how to organise. If he could cook and prepare for a banquet, he could dispose of the poor, late Hauptsturmführer Schiller.

'Here's what we do. Marek, you get one of the sacks we use on the meat. No. Two. We'll put him in the deep-freeze. Hang him there with the sides of pork until we can dispose of the body. Quickly now.'

Natalie looked up at Raoul. 'But how will you get rid of the body? We can't put him in the tunnel. He will smell and anyway the people are sheltering there.'

'I don't know. I can't think.'

'Raoul. What do we do?'

'We must clean up.'

George groaned. He began to raise himself onto his elbows. Natalie knelt at his side and helped him to stand. He touched his forehead and then examined the blood on his

120

hand. 'What happened?'

He looked down and seeing Schiller's body and the pool of blood, he jumped back as if attacked by a pack of wolves.

'I... I didn't kill him did I?'

Raoul stepped up to him and placed a hand on his shoulder. 'No, my friend, you didn't.'

Confused, George looked from face to face.

'I remember he found Natalie and I tried to stop him pulling out the gun. What happened then?'

'Never mind,' Raoul said. 'I hit him with the frying pan. He won't bother us again.'

George sat down on the chair so recently vacated by Natalie. He held his head in his hands and shook it. Raoul pictured him with a cigar in his hands, knees bent with his eyebrows twitching up and down. Groucho Marx; the similarity was striking. He was jerked back to reality as Marek returned bearing two oilskin sacks. He realised the horror of the situation had brewed denial in his mind. He had to focus.

Raoul looked down at the body. He had killed a man. True, it was for a reason. It had been to protect the hiding Jews, but that was not his real reason, however much he told himself it was. It was for Natalie. He had known he would have died for her at any time, he knew he was committed to her. He had not realised he was prepared to kill for her in real life.

His life had changed again.

Chapter 14

NEWBURG——A method of cooking lobster created by Mr Wenburg a former Head Chef of Delmonico's the famous New York restaurant.
– Larousse Gastronomique

I

'All night?' Philippe said.

'Yes, all night,' Raoul replied.

'But surely these are not your duties?'

'We are very short of staff, you know that,' Raoul said. 'There is this big dinner tonight and it has to be perfect. I had a lot of work to do preparing the entrée and the marrowbone.'

'Was it worth it for German soldiers? I hope they choke on it.'

'Anything to protect our people.'

'Goebbels himself is coming. I suppose that to insult these German pigs would be a disaster for the hotel and its staff, as you say. No, you are right, we must do our best.'

They were standing in the foyer. Philippe had intercepted

Raoul as he ascended the steps from the kitchen. The early dawn light flooded the hallway as they spoke, revealing the beige carpet and the red, patterned wallpaper. Apart from the two of them, the corridor resounded to a strange silence made eerie by a portrait of Hitler hung on the wall, the piercing eyes seeming to follow them. It gave Raoul the shivers every time he looked at it. .

Philippe, a man of middle years with an old-fashioned toothbrush moustache and greying hair, remonstrated with an extended index. Beatrice looked up from where she stood behind the reception desk and he dropped his hand and lowered his voice.

'You take too many risks. How many are we hiding now? Thirty? It's crazy. I can't tell who's who anymore.'

'Don't worry. After the banquet tonight, I hope to make some arrangements to get them away. As long as the hotel runs properly, they won't even notice our extra "guests". It is almost funny. The great propaganda expert of the Nazis snoring in a room occupied by Jewish refugees only the day before. Heh, heh.'

Raoul's stomach and chest wobbled as he laughed. It was like a tidal wave of blubber but he did not care. He was in love.

'But what if they find them?'

'They won't.'

'What about Schiller?'

'He won't be a problem. Believe me he will never inform on anyone again. Trust me on this. Yes, trust me, I know a doctor.'

Raoul smiled as he enunciated his little joke, but it was

wasted on Philippe, who frowned and looked down at the carpet.

'Goebbels. You know what food he likes?'

'All I know about him is he's a top dog in the Third Reich. Müller kept telling me he was a dangerous man to upset.'

'Müller? He's still here?'

'No. Left yesterday afternoon. Had to return to Berlin. Pity really, I was cultivating him.'

'Eh?'

'Well I hoped to use him to lean on Schiller, but if he's in Berlin, well...'

'I don't understand you any more. One minute you cook for these bastards and next minute you make friends with them. Don't you care what they are doing to our country?'

'Philippe, stop it.'

They stood on the front steps. An armoured troop carrier passed by, its exhaust emitting a dense smoggy cloud. Neither of them reacted. Raoul wondered whether they had now become used to the sight of German soldiers.

'What were you doing all night down there after everyone else had left? You, the Executive Head Chef? Surely you should have made Marek and the others do the food preparation?'

'It is personal. I had to make sure everything is perfect. It is how we have formed our reputation. Anyway, what else have I to do with my time? I can't go anywhere with Natalie and we have no privacy. I might as well do my job. I was a good chef before I became a manager, you know.'

'You think this Goebbels chap will shut us down? If I lose my job Maribel will be beside herself. After twenty years in this hotel…'

'Calm yourself Philippe. I have created such food that even the God's would enjoy it.'

'You have?'

'Naturally. First they will have Mehlsuppe, it's a German favourite. Next, they will have a mille feuille de cervelle du porc using a panna cotta I have created using pig brain. Then I will serve a fish course that Marek has worked on. It is not the most important, but he seemed keen so I let him interfere…'

'Kind of you.'

'Oh Stop it. Next, is a sorbet to clear the palate. The main course is a filet de porc and a separate small cutlet with a piece of shin bone, cracked to reveal the marrow and with a Marsala sauce—also fresh vegetables and a celeriac gratin. Then comes a bombe glacé, with cherries interspersed into the creamy ice cream, and we end with the cheeses and port wine, like the Rosbifs do. Finally, coffee and petit-fours. It will be a feast for a king. Admittedly a German King, but all the same…'

'The only change I would make, Raoul, is I would make the bombe glacé into a bombe explosif and deal with the lot of them the way God demands. How can you prepare such beautiful French food for these Sauerkraut pigs? If I didn't know you better I would think you were a traitor.'

'Ha ha,' Raoul said, slapping Philippe on the back. 'My father would say that I should let people call me anything but filet mignon, because…'

'You there.'

The voice made Raoul jump. It was not the volume but the preciseness in the tone which conjured seriousness and lacked humour. He turned to his right and faced the man he had seen in the restaurant on the morning when he was with General Müller. The man still wore his long black leather coat over a neat, dark suit and this time he held a black hat with a grey hat-band, grasped between the fingers of his right hand. He was of medium height and this time Raoul took in his face with greater concentration. The eyes were dark brown and they emanated a kind of hostile superiority which Raoul recalled from the dining room.

'Yes?' he said.

'When is breakfast served? I have an early appointment and do not wish to be late.'

Raoul looked at his watch. Six-thirty.

'Breakfast is served for hotel guests at seven o'clock, in the dining room. We finish at ten. You are a guest?'

'Yes. I am staying here for the time being. Hauptsturmführer Schiller asked me to come.'

The tone of voice was non-committal. There seemed now to be a warmth and friendliness in it, belied by the serious face and furrows on the man's brow. In the absence of a smile the man's demeanour remained a puzzle to Raoul who said, 'Can I direct you to the dining room?'

'I thought you said seven?'

'I am the head chef. If you wish, I can arrange for your breakfast to come early.'

'You are very kind, but that won't be necessary.'

Raoul noticed the man had an educated accent and he detected only the faintest trace of a German. He blinked; his eyes felt tired. Lack of sleep began to take its toll, but the man interested him. He was not like the other Germans in the hotel. He radiated an air of knowledge and culture as if he was a man of the world and someone upon whom one could rely.

The man approached. 'I am Sturmbannführer Von Schwerin. You are?'

'I am the Executive Head Chef.'

'Yes. Quite so. You have a name?'

'Raoul Verney.'

'Monsieur Verney, I remember now,' the man said, clicking his heels and bowing his head a little. 'I am enchanted to make your acquaintance. I saw you at breakfast with General Müller the other day.'

'Other day?'

'Oh, well. Perhaps a while back. Although I have military rank as a Major, I also have other, more important duties.'

'I see,' Raoul said, puzzled. 'Breakfast?'

'I can wait.' The man smiled, 'You are going somewhere?'

'Yes, I'm going home for a sleep. I have been working through the night to create a banquet for Reich Minister Goebbels tonight.'

'Ah. Just so. I won't delay you then. You return tonight?'

'Yes. You will be there?'

'Yes. I will not be dining. I will be watching.' Von Schwerin smiled and raised his arms from his sides, hands open, in a disarming gesture. 'It is my job. Security you understand.'

'Yes. Of course. Is there anything I can do for you Sturmbannführer?'

'Call me Karl. There is no need for us to be too formal. After all, you are not under suspicion, nor are you in the military.'

Raoul flushed a little, 'No. Not military.'

'I bid you good day then.'

The German clicked his heels, and bowing once more walked past the two men.

Philippe said, 'What was that?'

'Security police. He spies on people, like the Gestapo in Germany. Don't you know anything?'

'He gives me the creeps.'

'Yes, I know what you mean. He seems friendly enough though,' Raoul said.

'No. It's like a shark who seems to smile before he bites you, but it's only him opening his mouth to eat you'

'I would be more than one mouthful. Either way, I'm off home to get some sleep before the banquet. I'll be back at three o'clock. Can you let Marek know when he comes in?'

Raoul descended the steps to the Rue Rivoli and turned right, leaving Philippe standing at the door watching his broad backside as he began his walk home.

He was tired and anxiety gripped him as he walked. Who was this new Sauerkraut? There had been a faint, indefinable feeling of threat from his steely gaze, his presence in the hotel, and his appearance just when Raoul had been working all night. What German officer would be wandering the hotel at six-thirty in the morning, enquiring about breakfast? It made no sense to Raoul's tired brain. He felt as if it was bursting after the previous night's activities. Visions of Schiller's body as he hacked and diced came into his mind and it revolted him. He could see the bleeding flesh on the slab. The dark, dead blood as it trickled on the counter, on the butcher's board.

Overcome for a moment, he stopped and vomited over the

Seine Bridge. He wiped his mouth with the back of his hand and realised he should not be seen doing that. It could arouse suspicion and he now had something new, something evil to hide. He analysed whether it was a thing to hide from the world or from himself. He had never been one to consider violence, and now he had killed a man. Yes, it was a German. Yes, it was an invading soldier and he would have taken Natalie away, but how could God forgive such an action? No. He felt he was Hell-bound and nothing could help him now. Raoul, the Executive Head Chef had become a killer and a butcher of men and there was no longer any hope for him in the afterlife. All he had was the present: his life now, today, this minute. He hoped that what remained of his life would be with Natalie and he knew he would fight for that. It was as if having killed once, any other deaths became minor; as if now committed, he could kill again and it would not matter. He was going to the fiery depths of Hell whatever happened. So, he might as well not look back; if he had to do it again to save the woman he loved, he would do so.

He could feel resignation setting in.

2

Raoul lay on his bed in his apartment. He looked up at a crack in the ceiling and traced it to the armoire which stood against the wall. The armoire was the only piece of furniture he had brought with him when he closed up his parents' house after they died. He thought about how he had sieved through their possessions, his father's clothes and his letters. The same feeling of despair filled him now. He wished Natalie were with him, lying next to him. He wanted to make love to her. He wanted her to take it all away.

Visions of Schiller's flesh kept recurring in his mind and he turned over, making the bedsprings creak. He closed his eyes and the visions still remained vivid, in colour, indelible. But how else to dispose of the body? Someone had to do it. It would have meant death to them all if anyone found out he had killed Schiller.

He turned back and thought of his father. There was comfort in those memories. He pictured him with his walking-stick as they strolled by the Dordogne the summer before the old man died.

'You know, Raoul, I'm very proud of you. You have achieved so much that I never dreamed of for myself. It makes an old man happy.' Raoul could almost hear his father's voice.

'Not so much,' Raoul remembered saying. 'You helped me become a chef. You paid for me to go to the College in Lyon. Without your help, I would still be here in Bergerac, maybe in the back kitchen of a café.'

'Don't minimise your achievements. Your mother always did that. There was a time when the chimney blocked and the stove became useless. She had many diners to feed. You know what she did?'

'What?'

'She lit an open fire in the yard and cooked everything on a skillet out there. Quite an achievement.'

'You were not there?'

'No, it was during the Great War. I think I was at the Somme then. I wrote many letters home. None of them arrived until I had returned, but writing them made me feel better all the same. Did I tell you how I blew up a machine-gun nest in that battle?'

'Yes, Papa, often.'

The plump old man leaned on his stick and smiled. 'Then you will have to be patient while I tell it again. It is the privilege of old age, that you youngsters must listen anyway. I was in a trench in the lee of a small hill…'

The old man's voice faded in Raoul's mind as if the scene were drifting away. Another view came to mind, this time of Schiller's liver. Raoul held it in both hands. The deep dark red of it seemed to fill his field of vision and then burst, splattering him in foul-smelling offal. He must have drifted off for he awoke with a jerk. He was sweating. He thought he needed a drink but knew he could not go to work smelling of alcohol. Life had to be maintained as if nothing had happened.

Business as usual. Cooking and eating and shitting and planning the menus. Oh my God.

Everything whirled around in his mind at once and he sat up; then he swung his legs out of bed and leant forward, head in hands, eyes closed. He felt so tired but dared not face the nightmares again. He looked at the alarm clock by his bedside. Twelve o'clock. Three hours to go.

Raoul wondered if he could face returning to the scene of his crime. He had decided it was criminal to kill a man with a frying pan like that. How could he have done it? But it was easy. It was as if in the heat of the moment nothing mattered but self-preservation and defence of the one he loved. Surely his love for Natalie was sufficient cause, sufficient justification, to excuse the killing. Maybe Schiller was evil.

131

Yes, that's it.

Schiller was evil, he arrested people and sent them away, he hated Jews and wasn't Jesus a Jew? Perhaps he should give confession. Perhaps absolution would help him. But no. He had not even been to church for almost a year. Last Christmas in fact. He was not a good enough Christian. If he had been, then maybe...

His ruminations continued until he thought they would drive him mad. He sought distraction from them. Crossing the room, he opened the sash window and looked out at the rain-soaked street below. Across the roadway, an old woman in a long black coat walked by, protecting herself from the rain with a black umbrella. She glanced over, perhaps drawn by the noise of him opening the window. Her tanned face was as wrinkled as the bark of an old forest pine. Her brown eyes gleamed up at him then turned red as if they glowed with some satanic fire, and she seemed to scowl. The expression was deeply accusing and he felt an icy prickle at the back of his neck. He drew back fast, bumping his head on the window. He rubbed the evolving bruise. It was as if she knew what he had done. He shook his head. No. He was imagining things now. He had to focus. It would be a long day and he needed to concentrate on what he had to do at work. His stomach rumbled, so he showered, dressed and walked out in his long blue raincoat, umbrella in hand. Lunch had become breakfast and he knew he was famished.

He could kill for a brioche and a cup of decent coffee.

Chapter 15

ORGANOLEPTIC—Describing the qualities that determine the palatability or otherwise of a food.
– Larousse Gastronomique

I

The moment Raoul stepped into the street his demons went. The cool wind on his cheeks and the smell of the damp Paris afternoon with its mixture of food cooking and wet stonework dispelled the thoughts pursuing him. His dark mood lifted and as he strode through the puddles in his galoshes he waved his closed umbrella. He could almost have been like Charlie Chaplin; he felt like singing that he was happy again for his thoughts had turned to Natalie. He could see her face, her smile, and he realised he had a chance to spend some time with her before he needed to work.

When he reached the Café Dimanche, Raoul sat inside because of the weather. Rain had descended for days and the Paris streets flowed with water. He did not care, he had his love as well as his smouldering hatred to keep him warm, but all the same he could see no point in sitting outside under the battered green awning in the damp. The bell rang its clear, merry tone when he entered, but it had begun to irritate. It was not the tone of the beast, it was that it always reminded him of the bell they rang when he went into school. It represented bullying and worse still a sense of failure; it all came back now every time he entered the café.

Marcel sat in the far corner wearing a hat and an open black coat, looking like an American gangster. Raoul crossed the wooden floorboards and sat on the creaking, unsteady chair opposite the young fellow.

'Good morning.'

Marcel said nothing. He looked at Raoul. In his hands he held a pack of cards and he split the pack, ruffled them into each other and tapped them on the table top to order them, then looked up and said, 'You play bridge?'

'Yes. My family loved the game. An art not a game, eh?'

'You know how to work a "squeeze"?'

'I never reached that stage. It was always a family game with uncles and aunts. When I was a small child, I used to bid five hearts if I had five red cards in my hand. They were very tolerant with me though. Of course, I play better now.'

'Raoul, my fat friend, we are going to work a squeeze on these German rats.'

'You see? My bridge is so immature I don't understand what you mean. Is your mother around? I'm starving.'

'Huh. I'll get her. She has croissants. No brioche.'

'Don't trouble her to come out. Croissants would be fine. Oh, and coffee.'

Minutes passed as Marcel disappeared into the kitchen. Raoul looked around. He was certain one could analyse

134

anyone's life from looking at their home, but this was no home, it was a place of work and he learned nothing from the portrait of Pétain, the bare floorboards and the sagging lathe and plaster ceiling. He began to wonder what kind of life this Marcel had experienced as he grew up. Had his mother always owned a restaurant? Had he been to school in Paris? He realised he knew nothing about the man. Marcel could have been a criminal low-life for all he knew. But he understood that Natalie had liked him and recommended him as a patriot and it was enough for Raoul to have handed over half of his life savings, including what he inherited after his father's death.

Raised voices from the kitchen interrupted Raoul's thoughts. He could hear Marcel's mother, the beetle, shouting a swearword, and a clatter as of plates falling onto a hard surface. He pictured her round, smooth, brown face and shiny black hair.

Marcel returned after a few more minutes carrying a tray. He held it before him with a look of irritation on his face.

'My mother does not like using the little real coffee we have in the place.'

'But it came from me to start with.'

'Yes but she's made some money from customers. Your coffee costs her part of her living. She doesn't like it.'

'Look Marcel, I came for breakfast, nothing else. If you want me to go, I will.'

Marcel paused. A look of seriousness overcame his gaunt features. His eyes looked tired. He placed a hand on Raoul's shoulder and said, 'No. Please stay. We need to talk. I have the truck.'

'You have?'

'Yes, I owe you six hundred francs. It was a bargain.'

'It's all right. Buy food and provisions for the travellers with the rest of the money. They have to get through. Do you dare tell me how you will get them out?'

'How do you mean"You"?'

'Well I can't do it. I have to work at the hotel. I would be no use as a resistance soldier.'

'You and I will have to make a dry run first, otherwise we won't know if it is safe, will we?'

Raoul shrugged. 'But I can't get away. I have my duties. Our country is overrun and the hotel is filled with Germans. You think I can take a holiday?'

'Delegate.'

'Delegate? I have twenty-seven people to hide. You think it's easy? I'm putting them into empty rooms, in the wine cellar, everywhere. One night they slept on the roof.'

'Raoul. It will be dangerous if we go with a truck full of Jews the first time. With an empty truck, people will remember us as legitimate. Familiar faces will be more likely to succeed. Trust me on this; I have sought advice from others who know. We leave tonight.'

'You don't understand. Tonight I have to be there for a banquet. How long will it take?'

'Two days, maybe three to get there, and the same back.'

'Go where?'

'Spain, but my run is only to a farm anywhere in Aquitaine, maybe Bordeaux. Someone else will drive them to Pamplona. It's in the Basque country and they don't sympathise with the fascists. From there they can maybe get a boat

136

to England, if the submarines don't get them on the way.'

'You are sure it can be done?'

'If it is safe, many others can go the same way. We have to find out.'

'You pass close to Bergerac—my home.'

'So?'

'I have friends there; you could rest there overnight.'

'I have been given a list of farmers in the Dordogne who will be helpful. On the way, we can decide which of them you know, if any.'

'You have the list here? I can look now if you wish.'

'You think I'm crazy? I can't keep that sort of thing here. Even if I did, anyone could be spying on us.'

'Look I can't go. I have to be at the Metro. There have been developments,' Raoul said, pulling a piece of crusty croissant off and putting it into his mouth. He chewed fast, nervous now for an obvious reason. The image of Schiller's liver entered his mind though it did not put him off his croissant.

Marcel said nothing for a full minute, studying the fat chef. Presently, he said, 'All right. I'll take the truck to Bergerac. First real trip I can take ten or fifteen only. Today is Tuesday, arrive Wednesday, hand over the truck Thursday. Allow another two days then another day for me to be back. I'll go tonight for the dry run. '

'So soon?'

'Yes. Second trip a week or so later as soon as I have confirmation that the first shipment has arrived. Make sure your people are ready.'

'They will be ready.'

Raoul picked up his bowl of café-au-lait and sipped it. 'Good coffee,' he said.

Marcel regarded Raoul for a few moments, then he smiled for once and said, 'You don't seem the sort to be a hero,'

'Hero? No. I'm a patriot but there is more to this than that. Could you turn out people who depend on you, knowing they will be deported and some of them shot? Impossible. Anyway, there is Natalie.'

There was the crux of the matter. It was all about his love for her. He knew it.

Maybe Marcel guessed. 'And Natalie. She comes too?'

'Yes. Not the first trip.'

'Why?'

'I need to know it is safe. It will be safe won't it?'

'I understand. Second trip. Finish your coffee and make sure no one is following you. We have to be very careful.'

Raoul slurped the remains of his coffee and finished his fourth croissant.

'Naturally, I will be careful. Au revoir, my friend.'

Raoul stood up. He was still hungry. Perhaps he could eat when he got back to the Metro.

He looked left and right as he went. Nothing. He knew if someone followed him they would stay out of sight anyway, and he did not have the skills required to fox them. No more rain fell as he made his way to work. He was early but if Natalie was available, he would find her. The thought warmed him as he walked, and although he took a long meandering route he was walking up the hotel steps twenty minutes later.

2

George was not there on duty in the foyer; he had taken a day's sick-leave. Raoul could understand that, after the blow to his head. Patrice, George's second- in-command opened the door for Raoul. He was a young man, maybe early twenties Raoul thought. His freckled face and fair hair made him look German to Raoul 's eyes. He remembered when the lad had joined the hotel staff two years before. At the interview he had impressed everyone with his knowledge of hotels and the theory of their management. For a junior concierge, he had shown unusual perspicacity. Raoul thought he would go far and although he had offered him training, Patrice refused to learn any culinary skills. He wanted management and experience in it. The young fellow was a climber.

After Patrice had finished telling him about George, Raoul asked "What time are we expecting Herr Goebbels?"

'Five o'clock according to Monsieur Robert. He was most particular that you and Philippe should be there to greet him.'

'Perhaps I should arrange some refreshment for him.'

'A bomb perhaps?'

'What?'

'Sorry. I meant a machine-gun.'

'Patrice. What has got into you?'

'Nothing.'

'What?'

Patrice looked down. After a few moments he said, 'Alphonse.'

'Alphonse what? They shot him. I've had to make a lot of the pastry myself. Poor bastard.'

'He was a... friend.'

'Yes. I felt it too. When I first arrived, he was very kind to me.'

'I want to kill all these bastards. I hate them.'

'Don't show it. We will win in the end. France will rise up and we will have our revenge—another Treaty of Versailles. However long this war lasts they cannot win—they are evil.'

Raoul was tempted to tell Patrice about the unfortunate Schiller's fate, but knew knowledge was a dangerous thing in these days.

'What will you do? Poison them all?'

'No. We have to have finesse. Only we French use finesse in everything we do. Wait and see.

Patrice turned away. He walked over to the concierge's desk and sat down behind it. He reached under the counter. Raoul followed and peered over the edge of the raised, polished surface scratched here and there with long use. To his horror, he saw a gun in Patrice's hand.

'What are you doing with that?'

'When Goebbels comes, I will send him to Hell.'

Sweat ran down Raoul's back although it was not warm in the foyer. He reached forward and grabbed the younger man's right arm. He squeezed and with a vice-like grip pulled the young concierge towards him across the desk. Patrice grimaced and struggled but it was as much use as a lobster wriggling in the chef's hand. Patrice dropped the gun and Raoul heard it clatter to the floor. He dragged the young fellow around the wooden obstruction which separated them and pushed him away. Stepping around the desk, he picked up the gun and put it into his trouser waistband at his back. Glancing

140

across the polished marble floor at the reception desk, he could see Beatrice frowning at him. Perhaps she was part of this lunatic plot too.

Patrice stood rubbing his arm and scowling. Raoul stepped forward and manoeuvring himself beside the young concierge, he put a pudgy arm around his shoulder and guided him towards the doors. Once outside where they could not be overheard, he said, 'It would have been foolish. I agree with you, but they would shut down the hotel, all the staff would be deported and the Jewish people we shelter would have been shot. A good price for one dead politician? No. I don't think so.'

Patrice said nothing. He stared at the Executive Head Chef. Tears formed in his eyes.

Patting the young man's shoulder, Raoul said, 'It's all right. We all hate them, but we must be patient, even you. Let us wait our time until all of France rises up and throws them out. That time will come. I know it. France will rise again, but it would be good if we live to see it. Even now there are people who are beginning to organise and to join together to resist. You could be very useful to those people because of where you work. You can only be useful if you are alive. We all loved Alphonse, but dying because he is not with us serves no purpose. I will inform the people I know that you are available for them and one day, they will contact you.'

Patrice still said nothing. He turned towards the roadway of the Rue de Rivoli and wiped his face with his sleeve. Although Raoul wanted to say more, he knew it was useless. It was a bad war and despite anything Pétain might have to say about it, the war was still being fought, even if it was only in the hearts of his countrymen. Raoul knew however, that the quiet in the French countryside was only the calm that comes before the storm, and the black German crows one day would all be hunted down and shot.

One day France would be free.

Chapter 16

PARISIEN—A lemon-flavoured sponge cake filled with frangipane and crystallised (candied) fruits.
– Larousse Gastronomique

I

Each time Raoul looked out of the swing doors of the kitchen into the dining room, he could see Von Schwerin staring back at him from his position by the entrance. He had known the man would be present but he had not counted on the fellow staring at him in this way every time he looked out. It was as if he knew about Schiller, though Von Schwerin made no move towards the kitchens.

The first course had gone down well. Raoul could tell because moments after the waitresses set down the steaming soup dishes before the uniformed guests, silence descended like a cloak all over the dining room—a sure sign they were enjoying their food. His second course was about to be served and he had no doubts it would be equally well received. He had slaved over the dish and he spent time chiding the sous-chefs to ensure the panna cotta was of the correct consistency—set but not too solid. He had supervised the sprinkling of the parsley and the pouring of the beurre noir into which they set the delicate pastry.

He knew it had to be tasty; they had to like it. It was as if in his hatred, he wanted them to consume each other. He wandered the kitchens with Marek at his side, glancing at the dishes, encouraging the waitresses and titivating here and there. Attention to detail was everything to him. He stood by the meat counter and for a fleeting moment thought about what he had done during the night. A wave of nausea swept over him, but he swallowed the water brash and continued his rounds.

He watched as the marrow bones were assembled and placed on the plates, waiting for the time when they would be released among the waiting Germans and their fat wives.

'Lucille,' he called, 'make sure those over there are served to the top table and no one else.'

It had been a hard night of preparation but there was a grim satisfaction in it too. These German soldiers were here to make France subservient and chastened and he understood it, but by keeping them impressed and satisfied he was dulling their ardour making them comfortable and replete and, he hoped, off their guard.

What he expected would happen afterwards was another matter. There was no one to attack them. No one existed out there apart from Marcel as far as he knew. And Marcel? All he seemed to be interested in was killing soldiers. The fellow had even told Raoul about one occasion when he had met a German officer on a Seine bridge and as the man leaned forward to light his cigarette from Marcel's lighter he had shot him three times. Twice in the chest and once in the face. Marcel said it was his hallmark.

It made Raoul realise that Marcel had killed many in revenge for his father's deportation. He knew also it achieved little. Whatever France needed, it was not a series of murders: it was a mass resistance, though he also knew he would never be the one to begin such an uprising. All he could do was shelter his people and do what was required to get them out of Paris and away from France.

By the time the waitresses had served the petit fours, and the coffee and Armagnac adorned the tables, Raoul heaved a sigh of relief. It was over, as far as he was concerned. Schiller was gone, the banquet had been devoured and life would continue in his beloved hotel. Only one thing disturbed his relief. Von Schwerin remained like a vulture standing by the doorway; a quiet sentinel staring at anyone who emerged from the kitchens, his eyes roving with suspicion.

Goebbels stood up to give his speech. Raoul tried to show interest as he peered through the double doors. Spoken in German, the eminent politician's words escaped him, though he heard references to peace and compliance with Nazi party edicts. To his horror, he heard his name mentioned. He stood still wondering whether they were going to subject him to some public inquisition. Perhaps they knew about Schiller and would denounce him in public. His German was not good enough to understand what Goebbels said. All eyes turned toward the kitchen doorway. Raoul stood mesmerised. He felt his stomach turn and a feeling of nausea swept him again but it was different from the feeling he had earlier. This was true terror. They knew. They would torture him and send him to his death somewhere. His heart beat in his chest and his mouth became arid as a dusty Algerian street in summer.

Goebbels, a tall thin man with frontal baldness and a lean hawk-like face, smiled towards him. Von Schwerin approached. All was lost and Raoul knew it was useless to run. He had never run since childhood; he had neither the physique nor the stamina for it. He waited.

Von Schwerin closed on him smiling. Philippe was right; it was the smile of a devouring shark.

'You are wanted at the top table,' he said.

''I… I don't…'

'Let me explain. Your German… The Reich Minister wants to congratulate you personally on the meal.'

'Congratulate me…?'

'Of course. No one is more appreciative of good food than Herr Goebbels. Come.'

Von Schwerin indicated with his outstretched arm and Raoul noted applause from the diners. One or two stood up, clapping. He crossed the dining room floor, his steps hesitant at first and then once it dawned upon him this was an honour, he strode with more confidence and vigour.

Approaching the table with its long white cloth where the "Great Man" sat, he wondered what was going to happen. Goebbels stood up and a thin serious woman at his side beamed at him as if she knew him. He swallowed and almost wished he could draw a gun as Patrice would have done. For them to single him out like this could only make him a target for Frenchmen everywhere.

Goebbels shook Raoul's hand. It was a weak sweaty grip and Raoul, eager to run away, tried to let go as soon as the grip loosened, but it was not to happen. The Reich's Minister began talking. He seemed to be extolling the greatness of the Chef, the beauty of the food and this time, everyone stood and clapped.

His cheeks radiating bright madder, Raoul bowed to the Germans and made to leave. As he crossed the floor, he found Von Schwerin had hold of his arm. The man was still smiling and seemed friendly.

He said, 'He honours you and the rest of the staff for the wonderful food.'

'Yes, just so.'

'He doesn't know what was in it of course.' Von Schwerin winked.

'Culinary secrets,' Raoul smiled.

'You chefs are so secretive about your cooking. Do you have secrets?'

'Secrets?'

'Yes. Do you hide things that perhaps I should know?'

Raoul pushed open the doors to the kitchens.

'I don't understand. What things?'

Von Schwerin followed him through.

'I don't care about the food. I just have some questions for you about Schiller.'

'Hauptsturmführer Schiller?'

'Yes. He has disappeared. We are all very worried about him.'

'I don't know anything about where he has gone. How would I? He would hardly explain his movements to a cook.'

'Cook?'

'He never called me anything else. I don't know anything

about him.'

'Perhaps we should talk. I am looking for him and need to talk to anyone who may have news. I'm sure you under-stand—a matter of security. We can't have our SS officers disappearing into thin air, can we?'

'No. Of course not. Perhaps he deserted?' Raoul suggested, his mouth no more moist than three minutes before. 'You realise it is pointless talking to me. I know nothing.'

'You may know things whose importance you do not ap-preciate. We can talk tomorrow. My compliments on a truly original and tasty meal. Why, it could almost have been German.'

Von Schwerin continued to smile. His eyes remained seri-ous and it was the eyes Raoul was watching. As the man turned and pushed through the swing doors Raoul felt faint. Reaching out to his side, he gripped a counter. He began to wonder if the SD officer knew the truth about Schiller. How could he? Almost no one knew and those that did would never speak of the dead man. Everyone would be shot if any hint of Schiller's fate were discovered.

Raoul remained clutching the counter when Marek slapped him on the back. He almost stumbled forward.

'Well, I should congratulate you on an excellent meal. I just wish it had been served to people who might appreciate it. These Germans know nothing of food or finesse. What did that one want? A recipe?'

'He wants to talk to me about Schiller.'

'Schiller?'

'Yes. They are missing him. Von Schwerin is investigating. He wants to talk to me tomorrow. You've said nothing to anyone?'

'Naturally. I still want to live.'

'Keep it that way. They can hardly torture me now that their Reich's Minister has congratulated me. If they only knew what they had eaten…'

'Eaten?'

'Forget it. My nerves are shot. I'm going to bed.'

'Alone?'

'Shut up. With all this security there is no way to be with Natalie, and you know it. Anyway, where are they tonight?'

'The cellars. All the rooms are fully booked until this fiasco is over. I'm taking leftovers down to them once the dining room is cleared.'

'No. Don't do that.'

'Why?'

'It's all pork. Take them only the fish, would you?'

'Do I look stupid? Of course I won't give them pork. The staff would maybe want some of the banquet remains.'

'No. Throw it. I mean that. No one is to share the food from the banquet with these German animals. You hear me?'

'Yes, all right. Calm down will you? What's bothering you?'

'Nothing. I just don't like the idea that anyone who is here will share the food from tonight with them. I made it for them and not for decent French people. Make sure of it, will you?'

'You sound like it was poisoned.'

Raoul pushed past his head chef. He glanced over his shoulder and said, 'Do as I say. As God is my witness it was a meal for pigs, not for the likes of us.'

Raoul wondered what would happen in the morning as he

made his way to his office where he planned to sleep on the couch. Von Schwerin might suspect. He knew the German could not possibly know the truth, but he had an uncomfortable feeling the man knew something. He puzzled over what it could be as he removed his white jacket and pulled off his shoes. Lying back on the chaise longue he speculated that if he kept his nerve he could fool the man. Von Schwerin knew nothing and Raoul would make sure it remained so.

2

A turgid black gloom surrounded the throng gathering in the wine cellar, but as the days were drawing in above ground and the weather on the Rue de Rivoli was icy at times, the temperature here was constant most of the year round. It was cool but not cold. A brazier stood against the left hand wall away from the wine racks and the refugees clustered around it, glancing now and again at Raoul who stood separated from them, ready to explain his plans. Natalie stood with him and he could feel the warmth of her body as she leaned towards him, holding his hand.

Looking up at his round face, she smiled and said, keeping her voice low, 'You're sure it will be safe?'

Raoul nodded his reassurance and said, 'No. But who is sure of anything in this war? All I can say is that Marcel has driven the route, he knows where to stop and he has papers. I don't know where he got them from, but he is more resourceful than I could have imagined such a young fellow to be.'

'Yes. He is nice.'

'Nice?'

'He cares. I know of no one else who would risk his life for us.'

'I would,' Raoul said, frowning.

'Yes. Apart from you and Marek.'

Raoul cleared his throat and raised his voice. 'My friends,' he said.

The assembled throng turned to face him.

'I will have to repeat the plan and I apologise for that. We have to get it right. You have chosen who is to go in the first run?'

Sol said, 'Yes. The children and their parents are first. Then the older people. The rest of us will remain.'

'Good. At five thirty the truck will come. You will all have to queue at the rear entrance to the kitchen. The truck will back through the archway and then you all get in. There is food and drink for the journey in the truck. Make sure you replace the packing cases once you are all on board.'

'Will there be enough room?' a woman said. Raoul thought she was the wife of one of the concierges.

'Yes, yes. Fifteen people can find space easily. It is a big truck but Marcel was not stopped when he tried out the route. If he is, you must all remain silent.'

'We have no weapons,' a young, thickset demi-sous chef called Aaron said from the back of the crowd.

'You won't need to fight anyone. It will be a short trip and then you arrive in Bergerac and the drivers swap over. Marcel will wait here and another driver will continue with the truck to the Spanish border.'

Aaron said, 'But if they search the truck?'

'The packing cases are heavy. There will be a double layer of whiskey between you and any searching soldiers. Marcel will not let them unload the truck anyway. You can rely on him to protect you.'

'I still want a gun. I won't let them take my wife.'

'If it works out against us, shooting soldiers will make your death certain, and your family's. If you obey them, there is always some chance to live.'

'All the same…'

'Aaron, listen to me. You can trust me and you can trust Marcel. He is a good man.'

There was an uncomfortable silence and no one seemed willing to break it until Raoul spoke, 'We should celebrate, my friends. Tonight is the last night for some of you and then it will only be days before the rest of you get out of here. No more hiding like little mice in the Metro Hotel. There is a case of champagne here, by the brazier, and you can help yourselves but don't drink too much. You will be leaving early.'

Sol approached. 'Raoul, will you be there?'

'Of course I will be there. You think I will send you all away and not bid you farewell?'

He leaned forward and took Sol in his arms, kissed both his cheeks and smiled as the refugees began opening the champagne. Three corks popped and within minutes Raoul found himself with flute in hand, clinking glasses with his people as they toasted their venture. He could still feel Natalie's small body next to him, soft, warm and exciting. After two glasses, he turned to her.

'We can take a risk?'

She stood on tiptoes and said in a low voice into his ear as he leaned forward, 'I would love to, but tonight isn't the night. There is too much at stake and I can't have you killing any more Germans for me, can I?'

Raoul flushed.

'Be patient. My love for you is always there, my dear Raoul.'

He squeezed her hand in the gloomy light but felt unable to do more to express the emotions rising within him.

'Where did you hide the body, anyway?'

'I don't want to talk about it,' Raoul said. A sudden vision of a descending cleaver and the crimson spray as it struck a leg bone thrust itself into his mind. He shuddered and turned away.

'I'm sorry,' she said. 'I didn't mean to…'

'No. It's all right. I just don't like to think about that poor man, even if he was German. It haunts me.'

'Raoul, how can you say that? He would have had you shot. All of us shot. There was no choice, was there?'

She reached up and touched his cheek. He smiled back at her, but it was a strange, wan smile and in his heart, there was no humour—only a chill.

Chapter 17

QUADRILLER—*A French culinary term meaning to mark the surface of grilled food (usually meat or fish) with a criss-cross pattern of lines.*
– Larousse Gastronomique

I

At five-thirty in the morning rain pelted the canvas roof of the truck as Marcel backed it into the service entrance of the hotel. He had driven the vehicle into the side street and with much revving and double-declutching finally found a good position halfway into the street with the rear of the vehicle projecting into the service area. Raul stood behind, and once he was satisfied he crossed the small courtyard and opened the green-painted metal doors leading to the lower echelons of his empire. He could think of no other description for the place in which he worked. He was in charge of the kitchens and now he was in control of the escapees. He ushered them into the pre-dawn light, in the rain, across glistening flagstones towards the truck.

Marcel was unloading crates to create a gap in the wall of

cases, just enough for the refugees to crawl through, and Raoul counted heads as they climbed in. Fifteen. Half of their number, but he knew they would be crowded, he knew it would be a trip to Hell. His only hope was they would get away, and he trusted Marcel to do that as long as it was possible for him to contain his temper and his urge to kill Germans.

As the truck pulled out Raoul stood alone in the courtyard. The memory of what he had done haunted him. He had killed a man then chopped his body into tiny pieces and disposed of it. The method of that disposal still horrified him. A human body fed to pigs in the pig-swill. Even when he excused himself on the grounds of self-defence the act itself made him shudder. One fraction of a second, one tiny moment in time, and it had become too late to change his mind. But what, when it came down to it, were the alternatives? He could never stand by and have Schiller arrest them. He knew he had acted to save lives, to protect Natalie. His Natalie, the woman he loved.

He missed her. Expediency and caution placed boundaries on their time together. This whole week the hotel was full and no rooms stood vacant and inviting, ready for the fleeting trysts they wanted to snatch. In many ways, looking forward to those meetings and the chance of making love were the lynchpin of his existence. Had it not been for this thought he would have left the Metro long ago but he knew he could not desert his friends and their families for his own self-preservation. No. He would stay and he would suffer the consequences whatever happened.

The night had been long and sleepless and he sighed as he climbed the service stairs to the ground floor. Now he had to face this Von Schwerin fellow and he wondered how his tired brain would cope with the questioning. He did not even know whether they would take him away or interview him here in his beloved hotel. He had called it "his" hotel though he knew that a conglomerate of business people owned it. Commandeered meant just that. It was supervised by the Reich but funded by Frenchmen. He could bet they never saw any profit.

Raoul closed the office door behind him. No sound came from the lock as he pushed it to. He extracted Patrice's pistol from where he had stashed it in the belt of his voluminous trousers. He placed it on the desk and sidled around it to sit in his chair as if the gun might fire its bullets by itself. He felt respect for the force of its power. He had witnessed the violence of a firearm when using a shotgun, though he knew nothing of handguns, not even how to clean one. Would he have to clean it? Should he learn to take it apart?

He had no gun-oil and no pull-throughs though he knew he was able to get some. Maybe Marcel could teach him when he returned. He sat down, still staring at the weapon. Would he have the courage to fire it if he had to? Raoul was afraid of the thing in any case. He picked it up with the same care as he would an almond pastry cup, and weighed it in his plump hand. Examining the safety catch, he wondered whether it was on or off when it was up. He decided it made no difference because he could not envisage himself ever using the thing, but he resolved to ask Patrice to teach him, on the assumption the boy knew what to do. Raoul did not.

He glanced at his wristwatch. Six o'clock. Von Schwerin had not confirmed an appointment and he thought he would have time for a coffee and a shower. When the German had said he had questions, Raoul knew it did not mean the kind of abuse Schiller seemed so prone to hand out. He doubted whether Von Schwerin would dirty his hands by hitting anyone. The "Von" in his name meant he was an aristocrat. There was a smooth feel to the man as if he dealt with matters such as questioning prisoners in a more subtle way than the bully-boy tactics he had heard the SS used. It made the fellow doubly dangerous. Raoul realised he could not deal with the man as if he were stupid. There would be nothing to mock this time and he knew it.

How would he hide the truth? He wondered if trying to do so would make him transparent to Von Schwerin. There would be no way to the man's heart, even through food or wine. Perhaps he was worrying too much; perhaps the man would ask a few questions and move on. There was nothing to connect him to Schiller or Schiller's death after all. The body disappeared like the food he cooked for the banquet. There was no looking back, no repentance, of this he was sure. Whether Père Bernard, his local priest at home would have called it mortal sin or not, it was a past event and nothing any inquisitor could do would change that. No, he would keep silent, whatever inducements they offered and whatever pressure he felt might be applied.

2

The five brioches sat upon the desk, with steaming black coffee and a little apricot conserve, filched from some German officer's secret supply. Lucille brought Raoul's breakfast up from the kitchen and as he sat at his desk he looked up at her freckled face. There were lines there he had not seen before and although she smiled, he knew there was no humour portrayed in her expression.

'Thank you Lucille,' he said, smiling.

'Monsieur Verney, can I speak to you for a moment?'

'Yes, of course. We have known each other for four years, you hardly need to ask.'

'We are all in danger.'

'Danger?' Raoul frowned.

'Yes, that German Von Something is asking questions of all the staff.'

'What questions? Anyway, he'll learn nothing from anyone who knows what we do. As long as we are all quiet, he will find nothing out that can threaten us. We are all together in this.'

'No. Not about Jews. He's asking about Schiller and also about you. He asked Beatrice yesterday whether you and Schiller were together the night before the banquet.'

'She said?'

'Nothing. She said she didn't see Schiller all day.'

'She shouldn't lie. Von Schwerin will know about it if she does. He only has to ask someone else if the man was here or not.'

'Should I tell her?'

'Yes. Tell her to stick to the truth. It's always the best option.'

'Is Natalie alright? I hope she is, I always liked her.'

'Yes. Thank you. I'll pass on your well wishes.' He looked up at her from the desk. 'Lucille?'

'Yes?'

'Don't worry about this Schiller. Even if there was something to admit, I would implicate no one. Don't be scared.'

'You are a good man, Monsieur Verney. The others are right about you.'

Lucille closed the door behind her as she left and Raoul opened the desk drawer. He fingered the rough butt of the revolver. He still wondered whether he would have the courage to fire it if the situation ever arose. Von Schwerin seemed to know something if he was questioning everyone about Raoul's interactions with Schiller. There was no proof of anything, he decided in the end. There was not even a body. Without a body how could anyone prove a murder?

He mulled over the idea. Natalie and Marek had seen him kill Schiller and he knew he could trust them though he had heard how the SD, the German security Police, extracted confessions under torture. He was not afraid of pain but he was also realistic enough to know that few people could stand up to days of torture. If they tortured Natalie or Marek, would they not tell? But they had no access to Natalie and Von Schwerin was not homing in upon Marek either, as far as he was aware. No. Von Schwerin was after him and Raoul knew he would have to be on his guard and give nothing away.

He finished his breakfast and stood up, shutting the drawer. Crossing to the door, he emerged like a fighter in the ring, guard up and ready for a tussle with the SD officer. There had been no sign of Von Schwerin and he had received no word of where or when the interview would take place. He felt like a man awaiting a doctor's appointment at which he would be told some bad news, but the doctor's receptionist was refusing to tell him what time to attend.

Raoul leaned on the reception desk and waited for Beatrice to finish her telephone call. She turned round to face him, smiling.

'And how can I help the Executive Head Chef of Le Metro, today?'

'Any messages?'

'No sir. No messages.'

'Von Schwerin was going to question me, that's all. He said today.'

'No, I've heard nothing.'

'You've seen him today?'

'Yes. He went out about ten minutes ago. Got into a big black car and the driver pulled away in a hurry. If he contacts us, where will I find you?'

'Me? I've got some menus to write and then some ordering, after which I shall go home for the afternoon. Back early evening, if they want to know where I am.'

'Very good sir.'

He retraced his steps and sat down in his office chair. He rubbed his chin and realised he had not shaved or washed. He sniffed his armpits. Wrinkling his nose, he decided the sooner he got home the better. He also hoped his worries about Von Schwerin did not show, but wandering about the hotel unshaven and smelling of sweat was no way to demonstrate a clear conscience.

He pulled the pad of paper towards him and examined the rough notes he had made, planning the following day's menus. For him, it was easy work. His experience was as extensive as his paunch and the work flowed from his mind with the same ease as creating a lemon soufflé.

Finished with the menus he took them to the office on the first floor and left them to be typed, and then attended to the ordering. They had just under a hundred guests, all of them German and almost all soldiers. Some were in transit, some taking a holiday in Paris. He hoped they would be knifed in the streets but such things were rare and the judgements by the military courts always severe. Last week they shot a man for punching a soldier who was molesting his wife. Raoul had read it in the papers.

Work finished, although he would rather have spent the afternoon with Natalie, but he knew the less he exposed her, the better. He resisted temptation and left the hotel. He crossed the Tuileries Gardens still wondering why Von Schwerin had not sent for him. It occurred to him he had no real evidence. The man might question him at SD headquarters, or perhaps they would use his office. He shuddered at the thought of being questioned by a man as unfathomable as this SD Major. There was a subtle expression of intelligence behind those brown eyes, and he would need to watch what he said.

Raoul glanced over his shoulder. He could see a small boy, perhaps ten or twelve cycling around behind him. He rode in circles. He glanced towards Raoul from time to time but paid him no other attention, just circled.

Raoul walked on, buttoning his coat against the cold breeze as he crossed the Seine Bridge. He placed a hand on his wide-brimmed hat to prevent it flying off and turned around once more. The boy on the bicycle was still circling, but no closer or further away than before. Raoul shrugged. Why would a child follow him? It was silly. The SD would no more use a child to follow him than he would use a ladle to serve a fried egg.

Reaching the corner of his apartment block he saw Monsieur Lebeuf opening the front door.

'Monsieur Lebeuf! Monsieur Lebeuf!'

The man turned and descended the stairs.

'Monsieur Verney. You come home early.'

'Yes, but back to work later.'

'You're lucky.'

'Lucky? How so?'

'At least you have a job.'

'Something has happened?'

'No. Nothing has happened, just that they sacked me. After twenty years as a teacher, they sacked me for speaking my mind.'

Lebeuf gripped the railing with pallid knuckles. A gust of icy wind took his coat, blowing it open and he struggled to keep it wrapped around his thin waist.

'Your mind?' Raoul said.

'Yes. One of the children reported something I said to his father and he complained. Seems he is in the Special Police.'

'I'm very sorry. What will you do now?'

'Now? There is nothing I can do now. Maybe I'll go home to Brittany. My cousin has a farm there. If he hasn't become a

Nazi too, I can stay with him.'

'Look. I wonder if you could do me a favour?'

'A favour? Of course, anything. Heaven knows I have time.'

'I think I'm being followed. A boy on a bicycle. He's been fifty yards from me all the way from the hotel. Whenever I stop he circles, and when I walk he follows.'

'I can help? How?'

'I'm going down the road and turning back. If he follows me like before you could perhaps ask him why, as he passes?'

In the event, the boy disappeared and neither of the two men were any the wiser. When they parted, Raoul asked Lebeuf to keep an eye out, but suspected it would not result in anything useful. He began to wonder if he was becoming paranoid, but decided to keep his weather eye out. The boy had him rattled.

Chapter 18

RIPAILLE—An informal French term for a hearty feast, where the food is abundant and the wines flows freely.
— Larousse Gastronomique

I

Jolted by the stopping service elevator, Raoul reached out a hand to steady himself. He checked his watch. One-thirty a.m. He wiped a little moisture from his forehead with his handkerchief as the doors opened and he stepped into the corridor. No sound of his footfall emerged as he walked along the soft-carpeted floor. Room five-o-six. He stopped, double-checked the number then inserted the master- key.

Pressing the gilt handle he entered the room which was submerged in darkness. A faint smell of perfume came to his nostrils and he shut the door behind him with a click, then locked it. The short corridor-entrance to the hotel room showed itself only by a dim light from the window of the room beyond, where the curtains remained open to the black-out enveloping Paris. A figure stirred in the double bed and the movement made him jump. With his heart in his mouth,

164

he approached. If it was the wrong room, anything could happen.

'Natalie?' he said. 'Natalie, is it you?'

The figure sat up in the bed. 'Of course it's me. Who did you think?'

Raoul sighed with relief. 'I used the master-key. It could have been a German General if I had got it wrong.'

'Then maybe you need to accept my orders at once.'

'Orders?'

'Yes. Remove those troublesome clothes immediately, or I will have you court-martialed.'

Raoul sniggered, putting his hand to his mouth for no more reason than to hide his breath. He began to undress.

Natalie put on the bedside-light. She was naked. The coverlet, as it fell away, revealed her breasts, her ruffled hair hanging in curly locks about her shoulders. Raoul could feel the tumescence of his arousal already, then he stopped. In his underpants and with his shoes still on, her beauty struck him. He took in her face, her body. A feeling of unworthiness came over him. Who was he to be so privileged as to get into bed with this beautiful, wonderful woman: the object of his affection for so long and the pinnacle of womanliness in his mind? He knew he did not deserve her and he also understood that he had wasted time. He had wasted most of his adult life alone when, had he only suspected, he could have been with Natalie. Had she not said as much? She had told him she always worshipped him. It seemed incredible that she saw him as big and not fat. She showed no revulsion at his wobbling paunch, his thick thighs and his enormous girth. He sometimes wondered whether she was only being kind and his physical presence in reality revolted her, but he saw no signs of that, only affection.

It was wartime; Paris, France's capital, besmirched with invading German soldiers and everyone felt depressed. But not Raoul. He had, in the midst of all the sadness and grief, found a haven and some solace. He had a beautiful woman who loved him enough to share the danger, share the love and he knew she meant it. He would die a thousand deaths and kill a thousand Schillers for this woman.

When he looked back to his youth, he realised he had hardly spent any time with Natalie because he had shrugged off the possibility she could ever want his company. It was as if, like Pierre, they had grown up in parallel without him ever understanding there was another person there, in Bergerac, who thought about him as much as he thought about her. Hopes and dreams that never came true except in fairy tales had suddenly risen and shone out enveloping them both in something for which he had never dared to hope.

'Are you going to stand there all night in your underpants?' she said, a smile on her lips.

'I'm sorry. I was admiring the view.'

'Stop talking. We don't have much time.'

'Time enough.'

'For what you want.'

'And you.'

'Yes,' she said her voice quiet now.

Natalie drew the sheets down and lay naked and welcoming. Tugging off his second shoe, Raoul fell onto the bed. She reached out a hand and touched the hair on his chest as he struggled to free himself from his underwear. He knew he must have looked ridiculous to any normal person, on his back, dragging the white cotton from his body, but he knew there was no ridicule in her caress. He knew she loved him.

Undressed now, he shifted to lie beside her and he caressed her breasts with a large hand. She reached for him and their lips met.

If Hell was at least a little like this, then the killing of Schiller was a godsend and Raoul did not care where it led, as long as he could be with Natalie.

2

He awakened when the dawn light flooded the room. No sunshine disturbed him, only a gentle brightness through the open curtains. Raoul's mind surfaced as if he emerged from a dream, though he had no recall of any mental images. He stretched his left hand out beside him and realised she had gone. Disappeared like a wraith in the night; hiding some-where in the hotel, in some place undefined and secret where even he had no knowledge today. The thought comforted him. Although he would have wished to be the one who secreted her, veiling her presence from the German occupiers, he felt relief that Natalie had the perspicacity and common sense to be away by dawn, to disappear like a nymph in the secret forests of his hotel.

Raoul sat up. He rubbed his bristly chin and cautioned himself not to think of Le Metro as his. He knew the score and understood there was no permanency here now the Germans had come. They could arrest him; they would shoot him if anyone discovered what had become of Schiller—for all he knew, it was now a secret all over the hotel. Even worse, they might discover what had happened to the body of the unfortunate German. Fed to pigs; consigned to oblivion forever. He wondered whether the man had a family, whether Schiller might have had dependants who, now he was gone, would be destitute. He rolled over onto his side and sat up, thick legs dangling over the side of the double bed like forest pines about to drop into a river. He examined the brown and gold patterned carpet. The pile was thick and opulent. He wriggled his toes in it. The feeling was an indulgence but also an appreciation of the environment in which he worked.

The thought of Schiller having small children or a beautiful wife who needed him, impinged again. Raoul shrugged. Schiller's family was not his responsibility. This was war, cruel, vicious war and no quarter would be given if they caught him out. No. Schiller was not his business. The man was gone, dead and forgotten and he knew it had to be so, whatever layers of blood clothed his own hands. The guilt came then. Stabs of conscience. He had killed someone; he Raoul, the one who always fled. In one world, he might have felt pride to have acted at last against a bully, but now, here, in this quiet bedroom, the fact of this murder brought nothing but a feeling of dread.

He began to dress. He missed Natalie's presence, and wished their time together could somehow become normal. He longed to awaken next to her in a quiet place—a place where birds sang and there was no hurry to rise. He wished they could walk together hand in hand by the Dordogne, and visit his favourite haunts by the river where he had grown up oblivious then of her affection for him.

Then a thought struck him. Had not Von Schwerin said he wanted to question him?

Nothing had happened. There had been no message, no summons. Perhaps the German had been called away. Yes, that was it. He was too busy to interview Raoul, the plump chef. He had said he wanted to talk about Schiller. Schiller's disappearance and maybe the suspicion of his murder. Yet nothing had transpired and Raoul began to feel as if it left him hanging, ensnared by some kind of noose. The interview, if it were to come, threatened him and he shuddered as he left the room. There was of course no need to tidy after himself; one of the girls would do that as soon as he informed Philippe which room they had occupied that night.

He walked down the stairs from the sixth floor. He thought the exercise would do him good. With each step, he recalled Natalie's hands upon him. He remembered how he had kissed her and the taste of her when he had lain between her opened thighs. The evidence of his arousal became obvious and he tried to distract himself by thinking of Von Schwerin. Why had no interview taken place? It was unlike the work of any kind of German military department as far as he could see. It smacked of a lack of efficiency which Raoul could not imagine the German War machine could promulgate. Yet nothing had happened. He began to feel reassured. The man clearly attached no great importance to the interview; he must surely suspect nothing?

That was the way he would present himself to Von Schwerin when the time came. He knew nothing; there was no need to question him. No one could link him to the man's death.

Schiller was a simple fact of the past. He had no form in the present. Raoul knew he had to forget, but he also knew he was not like Marcel. Marcel, with his guns and his hatred. The crime was one of self-protection and part of the war, though he recognised he was no soldier. He began to wonder whether the fact that he was not in the military, meant that he was guilty in the eyes of the Church and he was Hell-bound for it. He checked his watch as he descended the last few stairs and realised it was early.

All these thoughts disappeared in an instant. Standing at the desk was his adversary.

Von Schwerin.

The Major stood, one elbow upon Beatrice's counter, his other hand waving in the air with a nonchalant movement. He smiled and seemed to be chatting to the receptionist. Raoul stopped at the foot of the stairs. He stared at the man.

Von Schwerin continued to smile. His voice carried. He spoke French like a Frenchman and Raoul caught snippets of the conversation.

'A pretty girl like you working all these hours.'

Beatrice said nothing. There was a look on her face of sleepy boredom. Her brown eyes blinked as if her night shift was getting the better of her. Raoul wondered what time her relief would show. She drummed her fingers on the desk.

'Room four-o-three? Here.'

She passed a key to the German.

Von Schwerin took the key, weighted down with a heavy brass room number. He continued to smile.

'You are free in the evenings, sometimes?'

'No,' she said.

170

'There must be some evening when you could be free to dine?'

'No. I have a little baby at home. There is only my mother and I cannot go out at night.'

'Lunch maybe?'

'I'm sorry, I cannot.'

The look on Beatrice's face became troubled. Raoul realised she felt under pressure. He stepped forward.

'Sturmbannführer, you seem to be a very early riser.'

Von Schwerin turned towards Raoul. He expressed no surprise, as if the Executive Head Chef appearing at six in the morning was commonplace. The sickly smile remained on the German's face.

'Ah. The Head Chef. Early for us both.'

'Yes,' said Raoul. 'I slept in the hotel last night. Sometimes I use an empty room if I finish too late in the evening. You wanted to talk to me, you said.'

'Talk?'

'Yes. You said something about Schiller.'

'Yes. Schiller. No hurry. Perhaps later this afternoon. I am busy until then.'

'I finish work early today.'

'You do?'

'Yes. One o'clock. I will go home and rest. Last night was a late evening, entertaining your fellow soldiers.'

Von Schwerin crossed the hallway. He reached up and clasped Raoul's arm with his outstretched hand. 'My dear fellow. I would not want to overtax you with questions when you are tired after a late night. Please, there is plenty of time for such things. The Rosbifs are not invading today after all,

171

are they?'

Raoul wondered if the smile plastered onto Von Schwerin's face could be removed without a chisel. He said, 'Invading?'

'Only a figure of speech. They never will, you know. France is now part of a bigger country. We are all the same. Friends, allies. I will let you know when I need to speak to you.'

Raoul said nothing.

Von Schwerin began to make his way to the stairs. He paused for a moment as if pondering something, and turned.

'Who supplies you with meat?'

'Various people. Since Schiller took over the hotel, we have had supplies from many places, some of them in Germany.'

'No. I meant pork.'

'Pork?'

'Yes, on the night of the banquet, they had pork. I just wondered who could supply such a lot of meat.'

'We had some frozen and I sourced a supply from a farm outside town.'

'The name?'

'I don't recall, but I can find out for you. The name will be on your desk later this morning. You have a desk?'

'Desk? No, I am a simply a guest here. Deliver it to my room later. Now I need some breakfast.'

This was not a man like Müller. He held no desire to cook anything for Von Schwerin; of that he was sure.

'If you go through, I will ask the staff to make an early breakfast for you. I'm afraid I have duties.'

'Thank you. I will maybe use room service. It has been

very interesting to meet you again.'

As Von Schwerin made his way up the stairs. Raoul wondered what the man was investigating. Perhaps he suspected the truth after all. There was no body, so no evidence of Schiller's death existed. He shrugged and went to his office. Shutting the door, relief flooded over him briefly, but he still felt there was something creepy about Von Schwerin. Raoul had a distinct feeling the SD officer knew more than he betrayed, a chilly feeling that descended upon him. It would not be as easy as he had thought to fool the fellow. He sat down at his desk and opened the drawer. He stared at the gun. Visions of pulling the trigger came to him

Von Schwerin's face entered his mind. He knew he had killed once already. Could he do it again? Would he need to?

Chapter 19

SAVARIN—A large, ring-shaped gateaux made of baba dough without raisins.
– Larousse Gastronomique

I

The boy on his bicycle followed behind as Raoul made his way home. He wished he possessed the speed to catch the fellow. Every time he stopped he could see this child on a bicycle behind him, circling in his grey raincoat with that damned cap upon his head. The situation became tiresome. After a few hundred yards he turned and reversed his path until the boy became the quarry but the lad remained firmly ahead and Raoul knew he would never catch this little imp. In the end, after crossing the bridge, he gave up. Cat and mouse. It was stupid and a waste of energy.

Breathing hard, he reached the corner of his home street and noticed a figure in a raincoat with a wide-brimmed hat. He recognised Marcel at once. Panic struck him. The boy behind and Marcel in front. If the boy saw him speak or even gesture to Marcel the game could be up.

With his hand in front of him, he tried to gesture to his partner in crime to walk past. Within hearing, he walked past and said, 'It isn't safe. Walk on.'

Marcel seemed not to hear. He passed Raoul without even a sideways glance. Relief flooded the fat man. He felt like a man who having seen a ghost makes the sign of the cross and denies its presence. Marcel. What was he playing at? In broad daylight, approaching him like that?

The remaining refugees were due to leave tomorrow. Was the trip cancelled? Was there some urgent reason for Marcel to speak to him? He knew he had to evade his pursuer, but how? A thought came to him. There was a bookshop nearby. A bicycle would not be welcome in a bookshop. It was worth the try and he took a deep breath and turned into the shop.

Raoul picked up a book at random from a shelf. Trying to look as if he was reading, he glanced sideways to the back of the shop. Beyond the small ash counter, laden with books and a small till, stood the proprietor—an old fellow with long grey hair in straggles about his ears. The man's eyes remained fixed on Raoul's bulky frame as if he thought Raoul might steal the merchandise. Taking the book, Raoul approached the counter.

'How much?' he said handing the book over to the shop-keeper.

'One deutsche mark or twenty francs. Ridiculous I know, but even I have to make a living.'

The man yawned. Perhaps he had just eaten, Raoul reflected. He said, 'Yes. They are ruining us.'

'You have made a good choice.'

'What?'

'The book. It's very good. "The Castle" is easier to read,

but this one, his last, is deeper in meaning.'

'Err… yes.' Raoul realised he had not the faintest idea what the man was talking about. He smiled though he noticed he was sweating. 'Is there a back way out of here?' he said.

'Back way? The book is legal here in France even though it was written by a Jew. There is no need to worry.'

'No. Not that. My wife is having me followed. You see that boy outside? Behind me everywhere I go.'

'He's your son?'

'No, just a boy my wife sends to track me. I have a good reason to want privacy. You know—an affair of the heart.' Raoul winked and raised his open hands from his sides.

Their eyes met. The old man smiled and said, 'For such a thing I will be pleased to let you out the back way. Just between us men, eh? The courtyard opens into the alleyway behind. If you turn right…'

'Don't worry. I'll find my way. You are a gentleman.'

As Raoul lumbered along the cobbled street, relief came over him. He wiped his brow with his handkerchief despite the cold breeze on his face. He drew the collar of his navy blue wool coat up and pulled down the brim of his hat to keep out the cold and made his way to the Café Dimanche. Once there he waited, looking around to make sure no one had followed him, and then he entered accompanied by the tinkle of the bell.

Inside, he felt warmer and began removing his coat as he stood by the counter. He placed the book on the brown wooden top and removed his hat. There was one bar stool but when he tested it with his hand, it was rickety and he doubted it would take his weight, so he continued to stand there though no one came.

The counter-bell was not there and impatient, Raoul rapped on the counter with his knuckles. Minutes passed and he began to wonder whether they had abandoned the café. He was just beginning to put his coat on again when he heard a footfall on the pine staircase towards the back of the café. Raoul looked up and saw Marcel. He wore a grey suit and carried a coat and hat in his left hand. In his right, he bore a pistol.

'Marcel. I couldn't…'

'No. I understood. This place is too dangerous for us both now if they are following you. Is this about Schiller?'

'Schiller? What do you know about Schiller?'

'He's disappeared, hasn't he?'

Raoul said nothing.

'Save it. I don't much care anyway. I got back last night with the truck. It was an easy journey and no one stopped me. I left them and the truck in Bergerac and then picked it up empty three days later. We can repeat the journey Thursday. I'll come same time. Your refugees are ready?'

'Yes. We will be ready. You think they made it?'

'Yes. The other driver told me they got into Spain and he has contacts there who will help get them away. I don't know precisely how he will do that, but I trust him. He was a friend of my father's.'

'What will you do once we have finished? There may be many more who will need to get out of Paris. Jews and others.'

'This is my last trip. I don't like taking risks for just a fa-vour. I may go and set up a group of partisans somewhere south of here.'

Marcel sat down on the barstool next to Raoul. He waved him to an adjacent seat, but Raoul remained standing, his left elbow firm and stable on the counter.

'You are giving up?'

'No. I want to fight. Dying with a wagon full of Jews isn't going to make the Sauerkrauts go away is it? We have to kill them.'

'You are a strange man Marcel. So young but so angry.'

'Angry? Is that what you think? Does cooking make you stupid? No I'm not angry, I'm fucking angry. I just want revenge for my father, for my country. Is that so wrong? You hide Jews. You send them away but none of this will help our country end this war. The only way is to kill those bastards. We have to unite and make sure they all die at every opportunity.'

Marcel got up and walked around the end of the bar. He reached under it and produced a half-bottle of Calvados and then placed two small tumblers on the counter. Pouring two measures, he looked up at Raoul.

Raoul said, 'And reprisals? You think killing one German is enough? When that happens they kill ten in return. Don't you care? Our country is awash with Germans. They own our land. They take what they want and all you do is sacrifice our people on the altar of your vengeance. Don't you see?'

'I'll tell you what I see. I see a country overrun with filthy pigs who piss on our people. They might as well be dead as suffer what these German monsters are doing to them. Yes, ten may die for every Sauerkraut I kill but they're better off. They don't have to put up with these Nazis any longer. Why don't people see? We are all in a war. It won't end unless we all work together and take the same risks.'

'There is a little madness in you, I think. Anyway, what about the remaining Jews in the hotel?'

Marcel was breathing hard. He sat down again at the counter and sipped his drink. He waved a hand across the counter.

'Don't worry. I'll risk my life once more, then we're finished. One more truckload and that's it. You hear?'

'I hear, but I don't understand. There will be more.'

'Then they will have to find their own way to wherever they want to go. I can't do it for them. Why can't you see? We have no infrastructure. There is no organised revolt. All we have is a route to vengeance and it has to be visited upon every one of these Sauerkraut bastards.'

'I don't understand people like you. This is not a military situation. Killing Germans just because you have the chance is meaningless.'

'And Schiller?'

'Shut up about that. It has nothing to do with what we are talking about.'

A vision flashed across Raoul's mind of dark red liver. He shuddered and stared wide-eyed at Marcel. 'Look, my friend. I love Natalie. I don't want anything to happen to her. She will be on the next convoy and I want you to promise me you will keep her safe.'

'Naturally. She is a friend of mine too. I owe her much. After they took my father…'

'You believe in true love?'

'You're an idiot.'

'No. You believe in true love? I do.'

'I look at you and wonder sometimes if your cooking and

your wine have rotted your brains. Natalie is my friend. She offered me comfort when even my mother turned away. I owe her. She's a good woman. She is also the only reason I would do this ridiculous journey like ferrying a box of frogs through a crocodile infested river.'

'Frogs?'

'Oh, shut up. Whatever.'

Raoul smiled and stood up; he made to leave.

Marcel said, 'Why did you come?'

'I wanted to make sure the pickup would be when you promised, that's all.'

'I'll be there.'

'Then that is all.'

'Look Raoul,' Marcel said. 'I appreciate what you are about. I just don't share your views. To do this we need to remain friends. You understand?'

Turning, Raoul proffered his plump hand. 'Yes. I understand.'

The two men shook hands and Raoul made for the alley in which the café stood. As he left, he turned left onto the cobbled street. He turned right at the end of the road and walked with determination back towards the Tuileries Gardens. He knew he trusted Marcel but he felt a strong dislike of any man who could kill others with such distain. It was true he had killed Schiller but he resolved that event in many ways by feeling it was in self-defence. Defence of Natalie too.

He made his mind up to find her when he returned to the hotel, and make love to her. It seemed the only way to allay the misgiving rising in his heart.

2

Snow began to fall as Raoul rounded the corner into the Tuileries Gardens and snowflakes tickled the back of his neck as he entered the Hotel Metro. Glancing over his shoulder he discovered the boy on his bicycle again. It was as if the lad was something sticky on the sole of his shoe. He would not shift and Raoul wondered how he could do anything with such a pursuer. To hurt the child was alien to him. He shrugged his shoulders and continued. He thought to himself that if the boy made life difficult, then he would have to limit his activities by disabling the bicycle perhaps. What had he left to do in any case? It was a simple matter of decanting the remaining Jews and continuing with hotel life.

But there was Natalie. The moment the truck reversed into the hotel courtyard, he knew his life would be in tatters again. Left alone without her, life would hold little meaning for him. He was almost tempted to go with her and start a new life somewhere else; anywhere else for that matter—he no longer cared as long as they could be together.

When he entered the hotel, his confidence shrank. Beatrice looked up from the ledger in front of her and frowned at him as he began to shrug off his coat. It was a warning. The voice behind him made him start. He had not seen Von Schwerin as he came in: the man must have been leaning against the wall at the side of the door.

'Monsieur le Chef. I wondered whether you might show up.'

'Sturmbannführer. How nice to see you. I trust my people are looking after you?'

'People? You have people?'

'I'm sorry?'

'Forget it. Only a stupid joke. I need to talk to you. Can we go to your office?' Von Schwerin smiled though his eyes, as ever, were cod-cold.

Uncomfortable now, Raoul held his arm out, gesturing the way to his office. Puzzlement filled him. He had expected Von Schwerin's men to take him away for questioning, yet now the man seemed so civilised. Neither hint of threat nor any coercion came from the German. Raoul felt like a man covered in tarantulas. They tickled as they crawled over him but he knew how any wrong move would produce a bite.

He held the door open for the SD officer. Von Schwerin sat down at the desk opposite Raoul without invitation. In silence he drew a brown-stained, yellow meerschaum pipe and a tobacco pouch from his green tunic. Extracting a little of the dark ochre aromatic leaf he began to roll it between his palms. He took the pipe from his mouth and began to pack it. The two men continued to sit in silence. Raoul thought the ritual was symbolic. It smacked of obsession, but more than that it seemed it as if Von Schwerin was demonstrating his power. The German lit a match and blew smoke across the desk. This was not a man for Raoul to trifle with and the chef knew it at once. This time he did not try to intimidate with protestations over the aromas of smoke. He felt as if he had seen all the poor copies of Nazis but this was the real thing. There was something cloying and contrived too about this man's bearing. He could find no other description for what he felt. There was a subtle air of intimidation in the room now, unstated and subliminal, although nothing had transpired between them to make Raoul feel uncomfortable. There was nothing tangible here to make him sweat.

Presently, Raoul said, 'How can I help you?'

'Help me?' Von Schwerin said, blowing out a plume of grey smoke.

'Yes.'

'I suppose you could conjure up the unfortunate Schiller here and now or at least indicate where he might be.'

'Conjure? I don't understand. I haven't seen him for over two weeks, since before the banquet in Dr Goebbels' honour.'

'How long before?'

'I don't recall.'

'Well I'm surprised. He was here in the hotel the night before the banquet. I heard you stayed up all night too. Would you really have missed him?'

'I was in the kitchen preparing food. It was such an important occasion; I decided to prepare the food myself. It was very tiring, you know.'

'No doubt. I want you to cast your mind back to the evening. You didn't see Schiller at all?'

'No.'

'But maybe it slips your mind? You are certain?'

'Naturally.'

'Isn't that strange? Members of your own staff seem to contradict you.'

'They do?'

'Yes. The receptionist says she saw Schiller near the head of the stairs leading to the kitchen that night.'

'Which receptionist?'

'Doesn't matter. A receptionist.'

'So what? She could have been mistaken.'

'The concierge states that he saw you descending those stairs at approximately eight o'clock, shortly after Schiller went there. It suggests you were both in the kitchen at the same time.'

'It doesn't mean we met. The kitchens are large and if I was at one counter, he might easily be shielded from view by another counter. Anyway, I went first to the wine cellar.'

'Who else was present at the time?'

'I'm not trying to be uncooperative, but I just don't recall. I can't recall every time I go to the wine cellar, can I?'

'You know, before the war I was a policeman in Berlin.'

Raoul said nothing.

'Yes. I learned a lot about crime. Of course, there is little application for those skills here and now. It is mainly a matter of state security and ensuring that no Jews, blacks or communists are free to cause disruption. Not very interesting for an intellectual man I must admit. You understand?'

'Not really. What do you think happened to Hauptsturmführer Schiller?'

'I think someone killed him and disposed of his body.'

'No?'

'Yes. You understand the expression "gut feeling"? I have such a feeling. But don't worry. I will find whoever it was and I will ensure he or she is punished. Not personal you understand—just my job.'

'I don't know anything.'

'I didn't say you did.'

Von Schwerin put down the pipe. He exhaled audibly and said, 'Schiller interviewed you several times.'

'Yes. We were on good terms in the end. He was a worried man you know. He seemed desperate to impress his seniors. He seemed very depressed to me.'

Raoul shifted in his chair. He tried to cross his legs but the movement was awkward and he abandoned it. Von Schwerin picked up his pipe again and lit another match.

'Now you are a psychiatrist, not a chef, eh? You suggest what?'

'Nothing. But perhaps he ran away. If things were not going well for him... Of course I don't know if that was the case...'

'Perhaps so. The SS expects a great deal from its people but they are well vetted and few of them crack under pressure. But you know? What pressure could a man be under in occupied Paris? Germany has won the war. You are our allies now in the fight to establish the Third Reich.'

'Perhaps he was so depressed at the prospect, he killed himself. He was always very upset when we talked.'

Von Schwerin did not rise to the bait. He pulled his pipe from the corner of his mouth and smiled.

'No. I don't think he would have done that. I knew him. He was a strict SS soldier. He had backbone, you know. No. I think there is more to this than meets the eye.'

Raoul said nothing. He sat back in his chair and stared at the SD Major. A vision of Schiller's skull impinged. The smoke hung in the air. Neither of them looked away.

'I can't help you.'

'No. maybe not. I will leave you with one thought. If the man is dead and his body has been disposed of somewhere, I will find it. I am very good at that sort of thing.'

Von Schwerin stood up. He tamped the tobacco with his left index finger without flinching and shoved the lighted pipe into his pocket. He made for the door. Turning he said, 'By the way, the boy on the bicycle, he works for me. I would consider it rude if you approached him. He is only doing his duty.'

Raoul looked up at Von Schwerin. 'Boy? What boy? How do you mean rude?'

The German smiled. 'Of course. Your French humour. He is there for your protection, nothing more. He makes certain you are safe on your walks to cafés and on the journey home.'

'I don't need any protection.'

'Perhaps not, but there are many unsavoury people abroad in the Paris streets you know.'

'They don't bother me.'

'Maybe not, but all the same, if something bad can happen to an SS officer, it could happen to a chef, could it not?'

'I don't understand. Are you threatening me?'

'Of course not. I am here to protect you and the whole of Paris from undesirable elements. Until later. We may need to talk again.'

The door shut behind Von Schwerin and Raoul sat back into his chair and sighed. He began to puzzle over the conversation. If the man knew anything then why did he give it all away? No. He was fishing; trying to trick him, trying to make him slip up but Raoul knew he would not make that mistake. He even doubted that anyone in the hotel had said anything to Von Schwerin because hardly anyone knew the truth and the ones who did would not betray him. He stared at the blotter in front of him, drummed his fingers on it and then drew out his handkerchief. Wiping his brow, he reached under the desk and pulled out the bottom drawer. Leaning forwards, his hand grasped the bottle and the tumbler inside.

Raoul set the bottle of Pernod down and poured a measure into the glass. He had no water but he did not care. He needed a drink. One day to go before the tension would let up. One day more and Von Schwerin would have nothing on him. He would be just an Executive Head Chef trying to make life tick over as it always had in the Hotel Metro, the finest hotel in Paris.

Chapter 20

TENDE-DE-TRANCHE—A French cut of beef taken from the top of the thigh.
– *Larousse Gastronomique*

I

Raoul looked ahead at the empty courtyard. The snow lay like a layer of fresh, new goose-down across to where the truck waited. There was a yeasty smell of baking bread mixed with exhaust fumes in the air, even though it was early, and he wanted to smile at the odour though his heart dragged the corners of his mouth downwards instead of up. He clutched Natalie's hand as they crossed in the footprints of the others heading towards the truck. They had said their farewells; a whole night of them in fact, as if repeating their voiced love over and over again would make time stand still and let them bask in the fervour of the moment. It was a moment that passed too fast and was over before either of them could express their deepest feelings.

Raoul felt like a man who had once held the Holy Grail and now, in the throes of circumstance, had to pass it on to another who would never deal with it in the same reverend way that he knew he could.

Yet deep inside, he knew it was right. She could not stay and he felt somehow that he had to. The trouble was, he still couldn't shrug off the feeling that the others in the hotel relied on him, as a protector perhaps, but more likely as a leader. He needed this feeling that they would look up to him and he made his sacrifice today for them. He would part from the only woman in his life he had ever truly loved. What made it worse was that it was a voluntary decision and he questioned whether that meant he cared less for Natalie than his perceived duty. The conflict in his mind would not go away. He wondered too whether he would not be better to flee. Von Schwerin was after him and he could make a life with Natalie somewhere else perhaps. He shrugged away the thoughts as he shrugged off the snowflakes and squeezed her hand. The feeling of her cold, bony fingers erased all his negative thoughts and he felt warmth spread over him despite the bitter cold of the courtyard.

They stood at the tailgate of the truck and Natalie looked up at him. The brightness of the snow reflected on her face showing the little crow's feet either side of her eyes as she smiled up at him. Raoul felt there was a radiance to that look. It gave him strength.

'You have to go,' he said.

'Yes.'

Silence, then someone in the truck coughed.

'Come with me,' she said, still squeezing his hand.

'No.'

'We can make a new life in Spain.'

189

'We can't.'

Raoul shifted from one foot to the other; his galoshes made a sucking sound in the icy snow. He reached forward and touched her cheek. A tear appeared in the corner of his eye as he did so. Everything seemed cold and damp now. His heart was breaking.

'Then I'll stay,' she said.

'You can't stay here. Who knows how long this occupation could last? I could never forgive myself if they caught you.'

'Now I've found you, you think I would let you go? Come, get in with me. No one would ever know what happened to you. Trust me.'

Marcel approached from around the corner of the truck. 'We have to go now.'

He wore a long, grey raincoat and his black cap sat a little askew. His round face looked strained and his forehead was creased.

'One moment please,' Raoul said, holding up a hand. He turned to Natalie. 'You have to go. Something of me will always be with you whatever happens. Don't ever forget I love you. Now go.'

Even if she had slapped him in the face, the consternation of the next few moments could not have knocked him back any more. Natalie smiled at Marcel and said, *'Adieu, cher ami.'*

She released Raoul's hand and walked towards the steps leading down to the kitchen. Raoul stood watching, tempted to pursue her and sweep her up in his arms then jettison her into the truck, but he knew it was hopeless. His heart forbade him and so he turned to Marcel. A faint smile adorned his lips and he said, 'You'd better go. She won't listen to either of us you know. Women!'

'Get her back. She can't stay here forever. This is my last trip. I can get her away. Get her back.'

'You don't understand. It's my job, not yours. When she needs to go, it is my duty to take her. I love her, you know.'

'You're both fucking idiots. You know that? Fucking imbeciles. I'm going. We may not meet again Raoul, but I wish you good luck.'

'Look after them, they are my friends. My people.'

'What? Are you a fucking Jew like me now? Of course I'll look after them. They're my people not yours. Go cook some fucking Sauerkraut.'

Marcel turned around and stomped to the truck's open door. As if in an afterthought, he turned to Raoul, who still stood looking at him.

Marcel smiled. 'You know, I hate myself for it, but I admire you.'

Before Raoul could reply, Marcel mounted the cab and slammed the door. Raoul stood watching the departing truck and a feeling of hopelessness took him. He had now to continue to protect Natalie, to persevere in a hopeless game of hide-and-seek. But he knew equally well that Natalie had taken a burden off his sagging shoulders. It had been her choice to stay. He had not been instrumental in this and he understood that. He realised his feeling was selfish, but he could now be with her. He could make love to her and it would feed his soul. As long as he had Natalie life was, after all, worth living.

2

Raoul climbed the kitchen stairs, entering the hallway to the right of the long polished hardwood reception desk. He half-expected Von Schwerin to be there in the foyer. Two days had passed since the conversation in his office and nothing else had happened. Now, as he crossed the thick pile of the carpet, he stopped short.

A man stood with his elbows on the high desk with his face in his hands and a small bag on the floor next to his booted feet. There was something in the scene making Raoul puzzle; something undefined. Recognition came to him as the man drew his hands down, placing them flat on the counter. Müller had gone and now he returned.

It was the General's clothing which drew his eyes. Müller wore a scruffy brown suit and beside him on the counter rested a battered, brown felt fedora. He looked to Raoul like a man who had slept rough. His military trench coat lay crumpled and untidy next to the hat as if it too had become dishevelled like its owner. Raoul realised he had never seen the man out of military garb before and wondered why it was so.

He approached and placed a hand on Müller's shoulder. The fellow seemed distressed and when he looked up there was a gaunt, worried look in his face.

'General, how nice to see you again. You are staying for a while? Perhaps on holiday?'

'No.'

'But no uniform? I thought uniform was a rule in the army.'

'In the army yes, but if one isn't, then…'

'I don't understand.'

'No. I suppose you wouldn't. It will do you no favours to be seen talking to me. I just want a room for tonight, but I'm leaving early in the morning.'

Dark semi-circles underscored his eyes and there was a redness too as if tears had been and gone. The face was a troubled one and Raoul became curious to know what could upset a general of the occupying army enough to bring him to this point.

'Come, we can talk in the wine cellar, it seems to be the place we communicate best. I will open something special.'

He led Müller back the way he had come, then down to the wine cellar where the two men emerged in silence into the frigid subterranean gloom. Raoul switched on the lighting and fetched two tasting glasses from the armoire by the steps.

'What is happening?' he said, drawing the cork of a shoul-dered bottle.

'All is lost, I'm afraid. I've been relieved of duty, sacked from the SS and have to report to the Gestapo headquarters in Berlin when they send for me.'

'But why? You have done something wrong?'

'Ha. Wrong? No. I tried to do something right—moral. Now all is lost.'

Müller took the glass from Raoul's plump fingers and drained it. 'Damned fine that,' he said holding the glass out for more and wiping the back of the other hand across his lips with an air of hurried desperation. 'Damned fine.'

'Is there something I can do to help you? What will hap-pen?'

Müller grinned a humourless grin, 'They'll shoot me.'

'Shoot you?'

'If I'm lucky. At least this way my family will be safe.'

'I don't understand.'

'You won't have heard of the Solt group. We are a group of anti-Nazi idealists who meet from time to time and discuss the shortcomings of the political changes in our country. University professors, engineers, some senior staff in the Wehrmacht.'

'You've been betraying them then?'

'Yes. No… It's complicated.'

'What will happen?'

'I've been relieved of command and summoned. Usually, there is a phase of questioning, imprisonment and then they shoot the rebel. They've done it before many times. When the Party took over, many of the old school were assassinated or shot out of hand by the SS. They don't call it killing. They call it tidying up.'

'What are you going to do?'

'Do? Nothing. My goose is cooked. If I run away, my family will suffer. If I do as they tell me I will die but my family remains alive. You think there is a choice?'

'Can you not send for them? Can't you get them and then run away?'

Draining his third glass of wine Müller looked even more desperate. He remained silent, staring at the half-empty bottle between them. It loomed large as if it obstructed further conversation. Raoul shuddered, the cellar had become cold and unwelcoming. He said, 'If you can get them here, I can hide you all. It would be dangerous and difficult but it can be done.'

'Impossible. Where could you hide us? In the hotel? They would search and find us.'

'I am hiding the woman I love as we speak. She has been here since the autumn when the authorities wanted to arrest her and send her away. It can be done, though I don't know how long it would work for.'

'You are kind but I must fend for myself. We are all alone in this world. If it came to a choice between me or your woman, which would you choose? It is simple. You would give me up as soon as it became too dangerous, however good your intentions. No. I must find my own way to deal with my own misfortunes, though I admire you for your offer. You have been more kind to me than many so-called friends in Berlin. It seems my plight is contagious. No one speaks to me.'

Müller stared into his glass as if considering Raoul's offer. A minute passed. 'They will be watching my family, waiting for me to try to save them. They aren't stupid. No. All I can do is give them what they want. If they don't torture me, then I will be lucky. The Geheime Stats Polizei know precisely what to do.'

'Like the SD?'

'Same thing, same people, just a foreign branch.'

'Von Schwerin is one of them isn't he?'

'Yes.'

'He thinks I killed Schiller. He's after me.'

'Schiller?'

'I'm not giving anything up to him. He has no proof against me anyway.'

'You think he needs to prove his case?'

Müller finished off the wine and looked around as if impatient for more.

Raoul said, 'Surely he can't just arrest someone without any evidence, can he?'

'He can snuff you out like a candle and no one would be any the wiser. Stay away from him.'

Raoul opened another bottle. As he pulled the cork, he thought about Natalie and what she would do if he was taken away and shot.

'This one's a Burgundy. A Vogne Romanée. Forest fruits and raspberries.'

The description was mechanical, as if despite what they talked about, the wine was a separate issue like sailing a boat and talking about sautéed potatoes at the same time.

'For God's sake man, wake up. If they are after you, you need to get away, not hide me. At least they have no hold on you; you have no family.'

'But I have nowhere to run to. I don't have enough money to live somewhere else and anyway the staff here need me as much as any family.'

Raoul felt as if Müller's demeanour had become contagious. He was like a man who helps a stranger as a Good Samaritan, only to find he has caught plague from the object of his charity. He experienced a vague feeling that he wanted to wash his hands, but something kept him there. It may have been compassion; he was uncertain, but he felt as if Müller was speaking his last free words and there would never be another time or place for him to speak his mind again.

'Maybe you are right and it is time I went somewhere else, but it would have to be here in France. This is my country and my home.'

'Von Schwerin could find you anywhere in this country. Get out somewhere abroad while you still have enough leash. He'll draw it in sooner than you think.'

Müller stood up and grabbed the second bottle which was two-thirds full, and began walking to the steps. 'Mind if I finish this alone upstairs? I need time to think.'

'Of course I don't mind,' Raoul said, also glad to be alone for a few moments. He watched as the German trudged up to the kitchen. Müller kept his gaze down and did not turn. Words sat on the tip of Raoul's tongue but he didn't utter them. He knew Müller was suffering more now than if he was under arrest. It seemed to Raoul it was the uncertainty that hurt. A man like Müller could face death, he could face pain, but the precarious position of his family was something else. It made Raoul consider his own position. There was the same uncertainty there too, but he felt sure there would be a way out. Did he not have friends here in the Metro Hotel?

Chapter 21

UDE, LOUIS-EUSTACHE—French cook, a contemporary of Carême, who was one of the first to introduce the French culinary art to Britain.
— Larousse Gastonomique

I

Raoul awoke on Christmas Eve with a feeling of dread. He had slept little, still haunted by thoughts of Schiller and the red, dark blood dripping off the butcher's block as he hacked up the body. Several times in the last few weeks he imagined footsteps behind him but turning found nothing to account for the sound. He had not even seen Von Schwerin or his cyclist tail for two weeks. Common sense told him he was no longer pursued. Von Schwerin must have given up. Although he thought it was the logical conclusion, he often ruminated on whether he could relax or whether this was only a temporary lull. It left him with his conscience, nagging, constantly nagging.

His guilt harried and tore at him and at night the beast would not sleep; it haunted his dreams and wore away at his natural resilience until at times he thought or spoke of little else, even in bed with Natalie. She gave small comfort, and at times Raoul wondered if he really was being as foolish as she insisted he was becoming. She seemed to have no qualms about the murder. Whether it was self-defence or not, Raoul could not see what he had done as anything but a crime. The intrusion of his guilt had become stronger instead of attenuated by the passage of time as he has hoped it would.

It seemed to Raoul not that he had got away with the crime, but that the guillotine still hung suspended above his neck, waiting to fall and serve the laws of justice. He became irritable. The kitchen staff noticed the change in his demeanour most when they were under pressure because Raoul became a veritable ogre, glowering and shouting, whereas before, he would have smiled and made suggestions, often making a disaster seem like a routine. None of them wanted the good Doctor Jeckel back more than Marek, for it was he who bore the brunt of Raoul's new ill temper.

Long after Christmas had passed, they stood in the kitchen facing one another with Raoul remonstrating at the top of his voice and waving his arms in a wild, windmill fashion. Marek stood as still as a firing squad that takes aim and looked at Raoul with a glance to melt ice cream.

'You don't have to shout. You don't even need to raise your voice. I know the eggs are overdone. I have already put in fresh ones. What is happening with you? You're like someone else. Has the occupation changed you so much?'

'The occupation?' Raoul said, beginning to calm.

'Well, it's something. When they took over the hotel, you wanted business as usual. Every member of staff supported you. We kept calm and we continued. All the time since, you've done nothing but brow-beat, cajole and remonstrate. You think anyone here wants to stay now? Two sous chefs left last week and if you aren't careful, I'll be off too.'

'Where would you go? I wouldn't give you a reference.'

'Say it once more and you seal the bargain.'

Raoul hesitated then. Eight years working together and now this. It was like a rebellion. He felt like a man on a hillside of broken rocks: another step and he would cause a landslide. He wanted so much to have his old life back, to be in charge of his mind and his future. Now, it was as if guilt pursued him in every crevice of his thoughts and nothing could wash it away, not even Natalie.

It was Marek who brought him some control again, though he realised it was temporary. He valued his head chef; he also liked the man for his forthright manner and his honesty. For this reason, the outburst made more impression than it might.

Eight years. Eight years of my life and I've never recognised how much I value this man.

There was silence. The sous chefs and the chefs stopped in their tracks and watched. No pins dropped to break the quiet until, after fully two minutes, Raoul said, 'You're right. I'm sorry.'

He turned to the staff who remained motionless around him.

'I have been under a lot of strain. I apologise to you all for my harshness. I promise it will be better in future.'

Raoul felt moisture forming in his eyes and he turned quickly for a man of his bulk, almost knocking over a chef as

200

he did so, and made his way to the stairs. As he climbed he wiped away a tear with the back of his hand and strode to his office. Safe now behind his desk he opened the bottom drawer and extracted the bottle of Pernod, wishing as ever he had water, but too lazy or preoccupied to fetch any.

Schiller was gone but not gone. It was as if the man hung in the air and watched Raoul's every movement from behind, waiting to pounce, waiting to betray him. And Von Schwerin knew. Of this Raoul was certain; perhaps, like a genuine policeman, he really waited for evidence, or perhaps he only played with Raoul as a cat tortures its prey; he could not fathom what was going on. He understood that it was making him into a bully—the kind of person he had hated and despised all his life; one who abused his position making others suffer.

In his office, he swallowed the neat yellow liquid and shuddered as it rushed down his gullet. The numbing calm of the Pernod spread through him like cream added to a sauce. He was becoming someone he despised but he was aware he retained enough insight to turn it around. As he poured the second glass he knew he could do it if only the pictures in his mind would let up and give him some respite from the horrors tormenting him.

2

For three months, Raoul and Natalie continued their clandestine meetings, contrived sometimes at a moment's notice, at other times planned in detail, limited only by the fullness or

201

emptiness of the hotel. If either of them understood the risks, neither expressed their concern to each other. It was as if like ostriches they could make the world disappear, not by burying their heads, but lying in each other's arms hoping for the best. But the best for them was becoming elusive. The best would have been to be together day to day and creating a life together. War continued, and as it did their hopes of normality disappeared as surely as if they walked the streets openly.

Natalie for her part seemed to be languishing. Raoul often wondered how she managed without the wind in her hair or the sun on her skin, but she never demurred. Although he had questioned her about the restrictions on her life, she seldom replied except in monosyllables and as time passed he enquired less and less. It seemed to Raoul that even his relationship with Natalie was a cause of guilt. He knew she existed imprisoned by her love here in this environment through him and his actions. He had never admitted these thoughts in case she would be long gone, escaping to Spain or somewhere else that sheltered refugees from the Third Reich. The responsibility of that knowledge was a burden he dared not consider too closely so he distracted himself with work.

The General Staff planned a fish and goose soirée and he threw himself into the arrangements, from the ordering to drawing up the menus. He sourced the champagne from a small winery near Rheims where it seemed stocks still existed in good quantity. The Reich paid, happy to do so as the conversion rates rendered the franc at a miserable level compared to the deutsche mark. The result was, as the proprietor of the winery, remarked "robbery".

Raoul knew the party would be in full swing by midnight

and he had no concerns that he and Natalie might be disturbed, so they planned an evening together in the bridal suite, unoccupied as it was, despite the rest of the hotel being packed. Purloining a bottle of Dom Perignon, a *foi gras d'oie entière* and caviar, he felt sure that the night would be a memorable moment in his life. As it happened he was proved right.

Room 402 formed a pivotal part of his plan and he lay on the big double bed, staring out of the top floor window at the darkened city, waiting with enjoyable anticipation. The spring night held cold and sleet but he lay warm, comfortable and snug in his nakedness, propped up on two pillows waiting for the gentle knock with which he had become so familiar.

He checked his watch. Ten past midnight. He thought back to how, at Christmas, mass had been said in every church and every cathedral in the land and he, a murderer, had not dared make confession. But what could he have said? He had killed a man. A German. The act itself had been simple. A momentary descent of a hand, a simple blow to the head, a split second of pressure. In self-defence too. How could anyone condemn him for that? He struggled with his thoughts and came gradually to realise it was not the act of murder in self-defence that was taunting and cajoling him. It was his cold-blooded disposal of the remains. He wondered how he could have done it too. The cleaver in his hand descending on the skull and face of Schiller—a man—and someone he once had spoken to face to face. The gravity of it all drove his very soul to depression, to mourning over his own lost innocence, evaporated now amid furtive hiding and secretive liaisons.

By twelve-thirty he became restless. He opened the champagne and poured himself a glass. He stood naked looking out of the window. Paris was dark. The blackout across the city reminded him of finding his way in a fog once on his walk home. On that night he had been unable to see more than a few yards in front of himself and it had been as if he was alone, more completely alone than ever before in his life, without a friendly hand to guide him and without a companion to lead the way. He felt much the same now. Even his beloved Natalie gave him no guidance for his feelings of self-deprecation. By the time he had drunk three glasses, he became curious. The tardiness was uncharacteristic of Natalie. She had never been late before. He remained looking out of the window but disquiet began to absorb him and invade his thoughts.

Raoul lay down on the bed. He began to ruminate upon the killing and how he had no choice. A determined firmness began to form in his mind. He would not allow this thing to destroy his happiness with Natalie. Self-defence. That was the point. If he had not acted, Natalie would have been arrested and his world would have imploded, becoming meaningless.

Where was she? Had she forgotten the time? Did he need to start looking for her? Still she did not come and so he paced the floor. He decided if she did not come by one o'clock he would look for her. What could keep her?

The knock on the door, when it came, was not Natalie's. There was a firmness about it arousing a feeling of danger in Raoul. His spine tingled and he reached for his trousers as the banging continued. He could hear muffled words, but they sounded strange to him and he wondered what could be happening.

His trousers replaced, he approached the door and opened it a crack.

Two Heer soldiers stood outside. They held rifles and a figure loomed behind, though Raoul did not notice a face at first. Then all became clear as one of the soldiers pushed the door wide. The game was up.

Chapter 22

VEAU DE MER—The commercial name for porbeagle or tope.
– Larousse Gastonomique

I

Raoul sat on a bench in a tiny square room. The whitewashed walls glowed with a featureless reflection of the faint electric light shining above his head. In front of him was a plain wooden table and beyond it a hard-backed chair. In the corner stood a frame of some kind with a long, horizontal, metal bar across the top. Against the opposite wall he saw an enamel bath tub, three quarters full of yellowish water. A green-painted door on the right hand wall prevented exit, though a small barred hatch three quarters of the way up admitted noises from a corridor outside the cell.

The room was icy but Raoul did not feel cold. He thought he knew what was coming. It reminded him of sitting in the dust waiting for the bullies to kick him. He had no illusions but that he would be beaten. He also knew that if they had caught Natalie, there would be no information he could give his captors. He knew nothing about any conspirators and nothing about any political matters at all. That absence of knowledge gave a simple sense of relief. He had nothing to give them and as soon as they realised it they would shoot him and have done with the fat chef of the Hotel Metro. Marek would be promoted, life would go on in the hotel, and after his behaviour over the last few months he could not even blame his beloved staff for feeling well rid of him. He sighed and shrugged his shoulders with resignation. Without Natalie by his side, his life was a worthless thing to him anyway.

He sat like that for what he thought might have been thirty minutes then jumped when he heard a woman scream. It was a shriek of pain. A loud clang cut short the sound and he heard nothing else. There was a faint smell of damp earth from the bathtub as if it contained stale pond water and he wrinkled his nose in disgust.

The sound of a loud click drew him from his ponderings and he looked up from the bench. The sight of the man who entered shocked him and he felt heat ascend to his cheeks accompanied by a choking feeling of fury. On the verge of standing and rushing at the man who entered, Raoul half stood, before a green uniformed soldier pushed him back and slapped his face with the back of a very hard and bony hand.

He looked up and said, 'You. You betrayed me.'

Müller, in his green uniform, his black boots and general's cap, refused to meet Raoul's gaze. Looking at the wall behind the prisoner he said, 'I had no choice.'

'You bastard.'

'It was my family or you and your woman. For heaven's sake, I told you it might come to that. There was nothing else I could do. Besides, I owe you nothing. We drank some wine

207

together. You think that makes me a traitor? You think it makes you a member of the Party?'

Raoul said nothing. There was nothing to say. His anger seemed to hover in the space between them. What a fool he had been. He had told this monster everything for free. No pain, no torture; he had given Natalie to them of his own stupid accord. He wished again he were dead. No doubt they would hang or shoot him. His only regret now was he would never see her again. Natalie, everything. No love now for a fat fool who opens his mouth and puts his ladle into it.

'Look, it may not be as bad as you think. Von Schwerin has an offer to make and I urge you to listen. It will be much better for you if you co-operate.'

'I offered to help you and you gave us up. I suppose your re-instatement was part of the deal?'

'Yes. Von Schwerin is an influential man. I have been warned and my family is now safe. Surely you can understand there was no real dilemma. I will leave you to contemplate whether you will co-operate with Von Schwerin's offer or not. I would advise you to do so.'

Müller turned and made for the door. For the first time in his life, Raoul had murder in his heart. He was a big man. Never fast on his feet, his rage burned hot enough to spur him to action. Like a circus performer flung from a cannon, he launched himself at the departing German. Raoul's fat fingers grasped at the man's collar, pulling him back and to the floor. It was the last thing he was to recall for some hours. A bolt of lightning seemed to burst inside his head and all went black.

2

Raoul awoke slumped against the whitewash, his hands tied behind his back, seated on the narrow bench with his back against the cold brick of his cell. His vision refused to return in one go and his eyes focussed in aliquots. First the bench on which he sat came into view. He raised his head and looked up; his head swam. He felt dizzy. If he had been standing he knew he would have fallen. The room spun.

He squinted at the table and some clarity began to return. After minutes, he could make out a figure seated on the hard-backed chair opposite him. Raoul stirred, trying to right himself.

'Awake at last, Monsiuer Verney. I was getting worried.' The voice was Von Schwerin's.

'You attacked Müller. Unwise, but understandable. I have little respect for him myself you understand, but it has been a matter of expedience and efficiency.'

The man was fiddling with something in his tunic pocket. The meerschaum pipe appeared along with the worn leather tobacco pouch and a box of matches.

'Some people use a lighter. I prefer matches. They burn that bit hotter and there is no aftertaste of petrol. They are efficient. Purpose specific you might say. Like you. You have a purpose and now that you are in my care, you only have that purpose. But more of that later. I will give you time for your head to clear.'

Raoul watched and listened as if he stood outside his own body next to the table. He observed the two of them: the fat man on the bench and the German officer in his grey-green uniform smoking a pipe. He noted every movement as if fascinated, but with no strong feelings of any kind. A dull apathy occupied him and it surprised him. He only felt a mild revulsion and a feeling of resignation. In one sense he understood Von Schwerin. He was a man who believed in what he was doing and he had infinite patience in pursuing his aims. Von Schwerin had waited for the right information and the best opportunity to trap Raoul, and Müller's fall from power had presented itself as such an opportunity. He had waited and now all was complete. Why should he not take pleasure from smoking his stinking pipe?

'You know I've been watching you for months now. Since Schiller disappeared you have occupied a lot of my time. I've thought about you a lot and I've come to a conclusion. I know you killed him. I know you disposed of his body. I now know you've been hiding Jews in the hotel, under our very noses. Yes. You are a clever fellow; a very clever fellow indeed.'

There was nothing to say. Raoul listened and let his head clear.

'So. What to do now? On the one hand, we have your crimes against the State. Both crimes—murder and subversion carry a penalty of death. On the other hand, we have something I need from you. It may be possible for me to offer you an accommodation in exchange for a little service. You can hear me?'

'Yes. I hear you. You can't prove anything about Schiller.'

'I don't need to. In matters of state security I have the power to have you shot now or at any time.'

'I didn't do it.'

'You haven't been listening. I don't give a damn whether

you killed that stupid little man or not. The point is, I can have you shot if I suspect it. If that was of any importance you would already be dead and your nice Natalie Dreyfus would be on her way east.'

'Leave her alone. She's done nothing.'

'Of course she hasn't. I suppose in truth none of them have, but she will still suffer.'

'You bastard.'

'You don't understand. You think I care about you, your Jewish woman or even Schiller? Of course I don't. You have something much more important in your head and I'll come to that later. Now I'll leave you to think about what I've said. We have plenty of time, but poor Natalie? Well, I'm not so certain.'

'Where is she? What have you done to her?'

'She is safe. She will remain so for a limited time as long as you behave yourself. No more attacks on German soldiers.'

Von Schwerin stood up and Raoul watched as he departed. He was alone again until a guard came and loosened his wrists. Rubbing them, he looked up at the man's face. He was young, maybe thirty. There was no expression there for Raoul to read. To Raoul it was like looking at an empty frying pan. The man stepped back, all the time looking at Raoul as if he expected an attack. When the door slammed, he felt utterly alone, more so than at any time since they captured him. He wanted to die and nothing Von Schwerin could say would change that. He would give his life for Natalie if it was required but he had no idea what Von Schwerin wanted of him. He knew nothing. The entire conversation seemed incomprehensible when he looked back at it.

Raoul knew he had no contacts; he knew nothing. In the same vein, he understood that if Von Schwerin thought Raoul held information he would have begun squeezing him with torture or at least beatings. The man was not the kind of bully Raoul was used to. He seemed altogether different from the imagined torturers, with their beatings and blow-torches. Von Schwerin must be after something entirely different but what it could be was entirely beyond him.

Chapter 23

WUCHTELN—An Austrian dessert consisting of squares of yeast dough folded over a plum jam filling put in a warm place to rise, then baked and served hot, dusted with icing (confectioner's) sugar and accompanied by a compote of prunes.
– Larousse Gastronomique

I

It seemed to Raoul that Von Schwerin was playing with him. He languished, waiting in the cell for three days. During that time they fed him. He had chicken wings, potatoes and vegetables. As Raoul looked at each plate he felt an urge to complain. It was in his nature. The chicken was overdone, the vegetables were soggy too. He spooned the food into his mouth and thought of better feasts; some he had cooked and others he had tasted. The memories brought comfort but he knew the food he ate was another insult from the people who held him and he swallowed that as he swallowed the food. He did not even care much about his own physical well-being; all he cared about now was Natalie and whether there really might be some way out of the mire in which he waded.

On the third day Von Schwerin reappeared. He was smiling. His balding head appeared from behind the door as if he were someone who had popped in to visit a sick friend with a bunch of grapes—a cheery visitor. In one hand he held a bottle of wine and a corkscrew in the other two small wine glasses.

'Hello, my poor chef. They are treating you well?' he said. He smiled but Raoul saw the hard, cold look of the man's eyes and he remained impassive.

'I have a bottle of wine for us to share. Pecharmant—from your own part of France. A peace offering.'

'Peace? No peace between us until you are dead or you leave my home.'

'Now, now. Less of this resentful talk. I come with an offer. It is one you will enjoy hearing and you will need to consider it carefully before you reply. Your life and that of your little Jewish lover depend upon your response. I may sit down?'

Raoul remained silent. Von Schwerin pulled the cork.

'You don't understand me,' Von Schwerin continued. 'I am not like some of my contemporaries. I don't value pain as a way of obtaining what I want. Anyway it would be inappropriate in this case. You need have no fear of that kind of thing, since we are allies you and I—like our two countries. You just don't realise it, that's all.'

They stared at each other for a full minute.

Raoul said, 'What do you want? I have no information to give you.'

'Oh, but you do. Let us play a game. I will show you what I know and you can tell me what you wish to tell me. To begin with, I know you killed Schiller. Perhaps it was an accident. Perhaps it was not. His body has disappeared off the face of the earth, so it doesn't matter anymore—it is not a threat to state security. I know you have secreted Jews in the hotel. Natalie would not have been the only one. Am I correct?'

Again there was nothing for Raoul to say. He held no cards. Von Schwerin had them all, the full suit and all trumps.

'Since I don't need to prove any of my theories, your silence is in its own way helpful. You are like this wine, breathing before it performs its duty. You deny nothing so I think I am right.'

'You know nothing about me.'

'Well, I do know you love this Dreyfus woman. Don't misunderstand, I am all for love. I'm married, I have children. Romantic love is one of the most wonderful things in creation. I really do understand you.'

'If you understand me, then you know I will say nothing. There is nothing to say in any case.'

Raoul watched as the German poured two glasses of dark red wine from the bottle. Von Schwerin sniffed at the glass. He said, 'The problem with wines from Pecharmant is they have a lot of tannin and so require time to mature. Perhaps you too are like that. Perhaps you need time but it is a luxury I cannot spare you I'm afraid.'

Raoul picked up the glass. He sniffed too but out of habit, not to seek knowledge of the aroma. He recognised the wine from its nose. A '36 from somewhere near Saint George de Montclard—south-facing slopes. He knew his wine. He detected nothing to suggest it was drugged or poisoned, and anyway Von Schwerin was drinking too.

'Suppose I gave you access to this woman for a few short hours? Would you believe me then? I understand love, you see. It hurts me to think of two people who truly love one another parted and then shot. Look. Even if you refuse to help me, I will allow you both to be shot at the same time and even holding hands, if that helps you. You see. I am not a monster. I am a simple man who requires simplicity from others. The solution for you is truly simple.'

'What the hell do you want from me? I know nothing.'

Von Schwerin stood up and placing his flat hands on the table top, he leaned forwards until Raoul could smell a faint odour of cloves on his breath mixed with tobacco.

'I'll tell you. Natalie Dreyfus has or had a friend called Marcel. A young man, round face, brown bushy curly hair. She tells me nothing but I want this man. He used to be a textile worker like his father. Now he is a member of a seditious and violent gang who kill soldiers, wreck trains and attack military targets. I want him. He knows a lot of people we need to interrogate. You are the key—the catalyst.'

'Of course I know Marcel. He's only a boy. He couldn't do the things you say. I haven't seen him in months in any case and I have no idea where he has gone to. He didn't tell me and I didn't ask.'

'He helped you?'

'I didn't say that.'

'No, but you knew him and you have hidden Jews in the hotel, so forgive me but it is a natural assumption that you two are linked in some way.'

'You would let me see Natalie?'

'Let us not get the rewards before doing the work. I want to know exactly what your relationship is with this traitor, where he is and how he can be caught. Then you can see her.'

'I can't help you. It is true I hid some of my staff and Marcel drove them to Spain. I haven't seen him since. He said he would go south but he never told me where.'

'Spain? In one journey?'

'No they stopped in the Dordogne Valley somewhere. A farm I think.'

'Where is this farm? What is the name of the farmer?'

'I don't know. They never told me.'

'They?'

'Marcel. I never saw anyone else.'

Von Schwerin sat down and pulling a notebook out of a tunic pocket began writing something down. He craned his neck forwards and tilted his head looking up at Raoul; there was a smile on his lips and it broadened into a grin. 'Yes, I can see that what you have told me may be true. But to suggest the man is untraceable is unrealistic.'

He poured more wine. Raoul drank; the pleasure of the tannic wine in his mouth seemed incongruous. It forced from him a natural reluctance to like anything to do with this man. Müller, he could understand. He was a man facing death and possibly suffering for his family. This man however had no reasons other than ambition or his Nazi beliefs. He would have preferred to deal with Müller.

'I could go to the café where I used to meet him and maybe someone would know where he went.'

'Bravo. At last, a little common sense from you. You know, we may get to like each other in the end if we are not careful. I will have another bottle sent down to you later for this. A café you say? Where is it? What is it called?'

'I don't recall the name, but I can get there easily enough. I won't help you unless I see Natalie. Is she here?'

'And now you want to bargain? Some would say you are ridiculous: you have no counters and your cards are translucent.'

'Why is your French so good? Where did you learn it?' Raoul said, with a trace of annoyance.

'I speak fluent German, French, Russian and English. I studied languages though sadly not at a university. I had a particular kind of State-managed education you could say. I possessed the aptitude and the Reich provided the means. It is one of the things that separates us. Training. As a policeman I excelled, as a student of languages I became a master. Now, as an expert in protecting the interests of the Reich my superiors judge me to be the best. There is nothing a man like you can do to prevent me from my goal.'

Silence hung in the cell between them. It was as if the very air became thick as a béchamel sauce; as if the ingredients of their discussion had become turgid and opaque.

Presently, Raoul said, 'You will let me see her?'

'Who?

Raoul, now at the end of his tether, slammed a fist on the table. 'You promised.'

'No. I made no promises. You offer me very little and I give you much. Who did you see in this café which you cannot name and which you cannot identify on a map?'

'Look, I said I could find it. If you let me, I will go there. If you follow me even with that boy on the bicycle, I may achieve nothing. I will have to go alone. You have Natalie. What can I do?'

'You want me to give you your freedom. Let you go, like a dove released in the air to meet its mate? You think I'm stupid enough to comply with this? You have, as you said at the start, told me only scraps and you want the whole world in exchange. Think again.'

'Give me time with Natalie and then release me. I will fix a meeting with Marcel and let you know. You can take him then as long as you keep your word.'

'My word?'

'You said we would be together.'

'And what guarantee would you give that you would ever return? I am not so easily fooled. You think I can trust you? I don't.'

'You think I would leave her in your clutches?'

'I don't know. As a student of human nature, I am seldom wrong. There is something about you which makes me doubt you or maybe even your attachment to this woman. Perhaps I read it all wrong? Perhaps you don't love this woman and just want to save your own skin at the price of hers? Human nature is an absurd dancer whatever the music.'

'Look, let me go and I will give you Marcel for Natalie. What have you got to lose? Two dead bodies instead of a serious resistance fighter. Is it not worth the risk?'

Von Schwerin stood up. He walked to the door in silence.

'Well?' Raoul called after him.

Von Schwerin said nothing. The door clanged shut behind him and in the loneliness of the whitewashed cell, Raoul stared at the half empty bottle of wine and wondered whether he had whipped the cream too much. If it turner to butter he would never see Natalie again. If he had judged the stiffness of the peaks just right, he could change all this bad fortune to happiness. He remained puzzled by how he could achieve his aims—to rescue Natalie and still remain loyal to his beloved country. There was nothing more certain in his mind than that he could do this.

He had to.

Life was nothing without Natalie.

2

Faint dawn light coming through the bars of a tiny window above his head cut the darkness of the cell, casting striped shadows on the wall at his side. Already awake, Raoul reached up and let the light play on his plump fingers for a moment before he rose. He sat with his head in his hands then ran his fingers through his hair. He stood up to reach the bucket in the corner, but after two steps bumped into the table and swore a soft curse as he rubbed his shin.

They had not even expressed enough decency to remove their torture apparatus; the bath and the frame remained cluttering the tiny living space in which he had now spent almost a week. He had nothing to read, nothing to listen to and worst of all, nothing to do in a physical sense. He wished he could cook—to create something, to organise people and to be in charge of his life again. Raoul felt as useful as a skillet in the rain. Above all he wanted to see and speak to Natalie one more time before the end. He was certain that end would come soon. If Von Schwerin had accepted Raoul's suggestion to set him free the fellow would have done so long before, he was certain. No. The Germans had rejected the plan and Raoul waited only for the door to open and the feel of the cuffs on his wrists and the blindfold over his eyes.

He wondered at times what it would feel like to be shot and whether it was painful or if oblivion would come in an instant. He had put up with kicks and punches as a child, but shrugged them off. He knew however the pain of a bullet was deep inside and unless the firing squad was accurate his end might take time. He dreaded that. He guessed it would make him vulnerable to the bullies, a victim to their cruelty, if only briefly.

His thoughts returned to Natalie as if she were some guiding light. He knew however that she could do nothing to help him and it was now up to him to die bravely and without showing the Germans his fear. If Von Schwerin told the truth, at least they would die together and he would be able to look into her brown, soft eyes and find that love he had felt so honoured to accept.

Breakfast was a crust of hard, dry bread and a mug of bitter chicory. The brew bordered on undrinkable but he always finished it and thought of real Brazilian coffee as he did so. His mind fought back in that way; the filthy brew made him angry.

The guard always made him keep his distance as he placed the bread and chicory on the table. Today was no exception. No sooner had the guard backed towards the door than Von Schwerin pushed past him. He looked tired. Bags had formed under his eyes and his face looked grey compared to his normal tanned appearance. There were no smiles this time, simply a curt, 'Sit down.'

'You're going to shoot me?' Raoul noticed his hands shook so he placed them behind his back since he did not want any of his captors to see his fear.

'Sit, will you?'

Raoul sat. He looked up at the SD officer.

'You will find this Marcel Maujean and arrange for him to come back to Paris where we can take him. We will give you a convincing letter to take with you from a well-known partisan leader. After that, you and your woman will be free to go.'

'Just like that?'

'Just like that. I told you I am not inhuman. I will let you see her this afternoon before you go. How you find him is up to you but we will brief you on how to get word to us. You won't know how to use a radio transmitter I suppose?'

'No, of course not.'

'I presume you can use a telephone?'

Raoul refrained from answering.

'You will telephone and tell us the place and time of your arrival. We will arrange a suitable place, maybe on the train if you notify us before you leave. If you fail us, you can imagine what will happen to this Dreyfus woman?'

'You'll let me see her?'

'I gave you my word. My integrity is not in question, only yours.'

'There is nothing to stop you arresting me as well and then you have all three. Also, how do I convince Marcel to come with me? I am the last person he would expect to see in the forests around Bergerac. He won't believe I've run away to

222

become a partisan. He knows me.'

'He's in Bergerac?' Von Schwerin said reaching to his front pocket for his notebook.

'I don't know where he is. He could be in Senegal for all I know.'

Vons Schwerin looked disappointed and his hand fell to the table between them.

'You can tell him you escaped us at the hotel just in time and that you made contact with the group FTP-MOI. He knows them: they are all communists like him. The plan will work if you make your performance convincing. Remember the consequences of failure. I will send someone to brief you this evening and send you on your way.'

'It sounds too easy.'

'Often the simplest plan is the best. There is less to go wrong and less for you to remember.'

Von Schwerin turned and walked out. Raoul felt confused by the changes in the man. One minute he feigned friendliness, next minute he seemed unemotional and business-like.

Left alone now, he found he could hardly wait for the afternoon. To see Natalie even for a few minutes would restore his heart and soul. His only remaining worry was whether Von Schwerin could be trusted to keep his end of the bargain. He doubted that. Anyone in the SD had to be evil.

Chapter 24

XIMENIA—*A tropical shrub with edible, though rather sour fruit.*
— Larousse Gastronomique

I

By the time his disgusting meal of chicken wings and bread arrived Raoul could barely contain himself. Trying to talk to the guard proved unproductive. The answering grunt told him nothing and his mind alternated between belief and doubt, wondering whether Von Schwerin was playing some kind of game with him. He could hardly believe the man would keep his word and allow him to see Natalie, but try as he might he could think of nothing else.

He paced the floor despite the lack of space then sat at the table tapping his fingers on the brown scarred surface, next running his fingers through his hair. The room felt stuffy despite the chill in the air and he soon got up again and began pacing. Three steps and turn, three steps and turn. The constant repetition began to drive him crazy until the door opened again. Raoul turned towards it, his face lit up in a smile and his arms opened ready for her.

It was the guard. In silence and with pistol in hand, he indicated Raoul towards the bench. Raoul sat.

'No. Stand up and turn around.' The French was rudimentary.

Raoul did as the man told him and felt the guard draw his hands behind his back and clip on handcuffs. He heard the guard step back. A dim thought erupted that maybe they were taking him to be shot and the promises and the hopes were all part of an elaborate joke.

'Raus hier. La porte.'

Confused, Raoul stumbled to the cell door and exited into a narrow dark corridor. Pushed from behind, he made his way along to the stairs at the end and mounted them, all the time with the barrel of the guard's Luger prodding his back. Two floors up the guard halted him with a hand on his shoulder and directed him to a corridor in which wooden doors stood brown and forbidding in the half-light of the ceiling-mounted bulbs.

They stopped at a door labelled "Int. 201" and the guard removed the cuffs and gestured for Raoul to enter. Raoul placed a sweaty hand on the handle and opened the door. The room was awash with light from a large barred window, the linoleum floor reflecting the glare up into his eyes. There was a smell of disinfectant, and as his eyes adjusted after the gloom of the corridor he saw her. The door slammed shut behind him.

Natalie lay in silence on a bunk with her back to him. She might have been asleep, he did not know. He knew it was her, he could recognise her tiny, bony frame anywhere, anytime.

He heard the guard lock the door behind him and he approached.

In soft tones he said, 'Natalie, it's me. I'm here.'

She stirred, and as if movement caused her pain she shifted and turned with slow movements. On one elbow, looking up at him, she said, blinking through swollen eyes, 'Raoul?'

'Yes. It is me, my darling.'

Raoul knelt at her side and looked at her face. Yellow-blue bruises littered her face like leaves in an autumn park. Her lips, cracked and swollen, moved as she whispered, 'Raoul. Is it really you?'

He reached forward and with the back of his hand touched her cheek, barely daring to stroke it for fear of giving pain instead of solace. He placed his right arm under her chest and pulled her towards him with a slow and gentle movement, watching her face all the time, in case he caused her more pain.

Holding her to him he noticed how she winced with every movement and he felt his anger rising. It had been an unfamiliar feeling to him until only a few days ago. It brought to mind the betrayal by Müller, the entrapment by Von Schwerin, and now their beating of his one love; it was a torch igniting fires within him again. The fury had depth to it: hatred and a wish for vengeance for what they had done to her.

He touched her matted and unkempt hair and felt moisture accumulating in his eyes. He wanted to protect her but now he wanted vengeance too.

'What have they done to you?'

'Beatings. Questions. They said you were dead.'

'No. They just locked me up.'

'I told them nothing. They're going to shoot me. They said so.'

'No. I will get you out of here.'

The cracked lips parted in a smile.

'You were always so foolish. At least you are alive. As long as I know that, living is worthwhile. It will all end soon.'

'No. Von Schwerin wants me to work for him. He wants Marcel.'

She drew away, weak hands pushing and flailing against his chest and she looked up his face.

'This is a dream. It can't be real.'

'It's real. I don't know how much time we have, but I want you to know I love you and everything I do is for you.'

'Do?'

'Yes. They want me to bring Marcel to them. They promised to let us both go if I do it.'

'But you said no?'

'No. I said yes.'

An angry frown furrowed her forehead.

'You can't do that. It's treachery. Tell them nothing. Don't help them.'

'If I don't co-operate, they'll kill us both. If I bring Marcel, we can be together.'

'Raoul, you were always foolish in such things. They will kill us both anyway.'

'No. Von Schwerin gave me his word.'

She reached up and touched his lips with a forefinger.

'Hush. You don't know what you are saying. These people have no respect. They will kill us whatever you do. Don't bring Marcel to them.'

'I must. I have no other option. They will let me go to find him. Don't despair my love. I will return and bring you out of this shit-hole.'

She stared at the floor and shook her head. 'No. You will go if they let you out. Go far from here. If one of us lives, at least the memory of our love goes on. Don't fear for me. In a few days they will shoot me and then it won't matter for me. I would hate it if we dragged down Marcel with us. For France. For us. Tell them you've changed your mind and we can both die as patriots, not traitors.'

He pulled her to him. The feel of her angular body against his made him want to weep. Tears for all they had lost. Tears for his anger and his growing hatred. He had to do something, but what?

'Promise me,' she said.

'I love you. I will find a way. We will have a good life together. You'll see.'

A sound from the barred window made him look up. A pigeon had landed on the sill and began cooing. He wished he could fly away with Natalie, be free and unfettered by his hatred and by his remorse.

'Remember the time when Marek blew up the stove?'

'Yes,' she said.

'How we all laughed?'

'When you released the valve, he cried, I remember.'

'Huh, we had good times.'

'Gone now.'

'More will come, you'll see. Just stay alive for me and I will fight.'

'No. We have lost. We will both be shot and we will meet again somewhere, somehow. I feel that.'

'He knows I killed Schiller.'

She placed a finger on his lips again and leaned forward.

Whispering in his ear, she said, 'They will be listening.'

In equally soft tones, he said, 'I know. You must trust me.'

'I trust you.'

'I'm sorry for all this, so sorry. I brought it all upon you— the hotel and all. You should have gone with the others, but I let you stay.'

'Not your fault. Mine.'

'No. I should have…'

Once again she placed a finger on his plump lips. 'I am nearly forty years old. I made my decision and took my chance. It has come out against me. Who should I blame? You? No. I love you and I'm glad I stayed. We had a moment of love. It is enough in the desert of my life to find some small oasis with you. Remember what I said.'

'Said?'

She reached up and pulled him close. He noticed how she grimaced as she did so. She whispered in his ear, 'Save yourself. You cannot save me now. They will shoot me. I want you to go and never look back. Make a life in which I would have been happy and think of me. It's all I ask. I love you.'

'I will save you. Believe in it. I will get you out of here.'

His voice, whispered as it was, seemed to scream in his ears. What was he saying? Was he some kind of hero who would arrive with the cavalry like in some American cowboy film? Was he Errol Flynn?

He felt stupid then, embarrassed and afraid also that he

had said too much. He had no right to promise her anything. A fat chef captured for his stupid antics and bringing death and pain to the only woman he had ever loved, truly loved. He looked down at the broken face with the closed eyes, and he kissed the swollen and battered lips with more gentleness than anyone might have suspected for such a large man. Drawing back his face he smiled at her. It was an expression of his love, not his confidence, and he knew it. Deep inside he doubted whether there was anything that could bring them together now. Von Schwerin had won. Raoul had lost, and convinced of the truth of it, he frowned towards her.

'Don't be afraid,' she said. 'Dying is part of living. It is the only certainty we have, any of us. Life is meant for living and enjoying the freedom to love. We have had that in our way. It is enough'

'Trust me,' he said again.

'No,' she said. 'I had never lived until we were together. If I have to have that short life of a few months and nothing else at least I have lived. Does it matter whether it was months or years? There was no life before and if it ends, well, it ends. A short life compared to some people's, but with you I have lived enough to make time unimportant.'

'No, I will save you.'

She said nothing and they sat there for long minutes holding each other. To Raoul, it seemed as if she felt as hopeless as he felt angry. There had to be a way to save her and he needed to find that way. Holding her caused as much pain to him as it seemed to cause her, so he released her.

'Believe in me. I believe in you.'

'You were ever unrealistic,' she said.

He stood up and said in a loud voice, 'I have no option but do as they say. I will find Marcel and bring him to them. Von Schwerin gave me his word. It has to be enough.'

In his heart he trembled. He knew there was only one way to achieve success—at the cost of another's life. It sat ill with him but like making a complex menu, he knew there was a way round the complexities—a way to salvage the burned offering. Like scraping carbon from the burned toast he would make something of the cards he held. What was it Marcel had said? Play a squeeze. He had never understood what it meant but already a plan began to form in his mind.

2

Ejected into the street, Raoul wondered where he was. He walked east. He remembered how the SD headquarters were west of the Tuileries Gardens and he knew also he had to get home and spend some time thinking. He walked along, dragging one foot after the other thinking of Natalie and how the SD had made her suffer. Why had they beaten her? It made no sense. She knew nothing. She had no more information than he had. He wondered whether it was a simple ploy of Von Schwerin's to make him capitulate, but he could still make no sense of anyone wanting to beat a woman for nothing.

He reached into his pocket. The money they had given him burned in his hand. He wished he could throw it away, but he knew better. He thought about the man who had briefed him; he had been grey-haired, with a small moustache and side-swept hair. He had not worn uniform and Raoul wondered at the time whether to attach significance to that but decided, as the briefing went on, he did not care. He only half listened as the German recited what he was to do.

'How much time do I have?'

The German shrugged his shoulders. 'As long as it takes. Three weeks maybe.'

'Even if I find him, he could be a long way away. I have to make some contacts first.'

'Not our problem. All I can tell you is that she will be shot in three weeks unless we hear from you.'

'I can trust Von Schwerin?'

'Look you stupid, fat pile of shit, you have a job to do. Listen to what I have to say and memorise this number. There will be someone there every day between six in the evening and eight. You understand?'

'Yes. I understand.'

'Then it will go well, but you will need to hurry. We don't wait over-long. A firing squad can be organised in minutes. You hear?'

'Yes. I'm just a cook. Repeat the number. Can I write it down?'

'No.'

Raoul memorised the number but made up his mind to write it down as soon as an opportunity presented itself. He had no need to obey their rules. He understood what was at stake and would get the job done, whether they helped him or not.

3

He trudged along the street, his feelings glum and his mind on Natalie. Three weeks to bring home the bacon. He had no idea where to start looking or even how to make contact with anyone who might know Marcel's whereabouts. Even before they pulled him from Natalie's arms he had decided to go to the café and try to locate the beetle-woman. He thought she could help him or at least give him some news of the man he hunted. He took a right, and passing the bookshop glanced in through the grimy window. The old man behind the counter was still there, the same books sat disconsolate in the ebbing daylight with their faded covers curling, looking as attractive as an escargot someone has crushed underfoot. His stomach rumbled and he decided to go straight home. It was the first time he had returned to his apartment without any worries about being pursued or followed. There was no boy on his bicycle. No one was looking for Schiller's killer—they knew who had killed him, so there was no need to seek him.

Raoul reached the steps and began to climb. The light was on in the apartment below. A sudden desire to tell everything to someone came over him and although he did not know his downstairs neighbour well, there had always been something of the rebel about the fellow. It was as if he was casting around for allies in a place where there seemed little likelihood of finding them.

He knocked on Lebeuf's door. The faint sounds of a phonograph playing an overture of some kind came from the room, and a few moments passed before the rabbit-faced school teacher opened up. He was wearing a patterned dress-

233

ing gown and English slippers as if it was late, though Raoul felt it was only about eight o'clock. They had not returned his watch and he was not immune to the absurdity of telling him what time to telephone and stealing his watch at the same time.

'Monsieur Verney, how goes it? You've been away?'

'In a manner of speaking, yes; away. Can I come in?'

'Of course, come in, come in,' Lebeuf gestured with his left hand, his right still clutching the edge of the door. He backed away when he realised Raoul could not pass him and he smiled at his mistake.

'You are alone?' Raoul said.

'Yes, I live alone.'

'Me too, you know that, I suppose.'

The two men stood facing each other in the hallway. Both shifted from foot to foot in silence, the awkwardness of the moment seeming out of all proportion to the circumstance. Raoul shut the door behind him and followed his host into a geographically identical apartment to his own upstairs. Lebeuf said, 'You've never been inside, have you?'

Raoul looked around. In the corner stood an armoire, the door open displaying rows and rows of bottles lying on their sides. Above the mantel hung a portrait of an old woman, grey hair tied back and a blue shawl over her shoulders. Her eyes seemed to follow his every movement and it made him feel uncomfortable. A card table with four chairs stood in one corner, opposite the window, the green baize resplendent against the dull grey of the wallpaper. The rug underfoot was worn thin like its owner. A settee and a chaise longue stood in the middle of the room.

'Last time we met,' Raoul said, 'you said you were leaving.'

'That was then. I'm staying now.'

'They've reinstated you?'

'No.'

'So how do you live? You have another job?'

Lebeuf laughed. The hollow sound emerged from his thin throat like a clarion call. There was something wild about his eyes. Raoul reflected how the occupation could drive anyone crazy.

'Wine?' Lebeuf said, gesturing towards his armoire.

'If you can spare it, it would be most welcome. You are a generous man.'

'Not really. I came into some money, that's all. I can't tell you where, let us say I had some successful hunting a couple of weeks ago.'

'I had not thought you were the sort to hunt. We hunted with shotguns where I grew up in Bergerac. Mostly pigeons, but hare and pheasant too. Where did you go?'

'You ask a lot of questions Monsieur Verney. Let me open the wine.'

Lebeuf pulled a cork and poured a glass for Raoul. He took it with gratitude and sniffed it until his host had filled his own glass. When he had santé'd and clinked glasses with his neighbour, he tasted the wine. It was not a Bergerac but it was good wine, maybe from the Medoc, but very palatable all the same.

Raoul said, 'Lovely wine. You were saying?'

'I wasn't saying, but you were asking. You're not one of them are you?'

Lebeuf's eyes narrowed as suddenly as if Raoul had insulted him.

235

'One of whom?'

'You know what I mean.'

Lebeuf looked uneasy. He backed towards the armoire. Still facing Raoul, he fumbled behind him. With a flourish, he produced a German Parabellum. The gun shook in his hand but its barrel pointed square at Raoul's chest.

'Step back,' Lebeuf said.

'You are making a mistake. I am as French as you are. What has happened to you?'

'Happened? Nothing. I have discovered my true role in life.'

'Role…'

'Yes, I kill Germans. I take from them what they have taken from me. I make a good living from the dead. If you're one of them…'

Raoul smiled.

'You're not the only one.'

Lebeuf gestured with the barrel for Raoul to sit down. Looking up at the schoolteacher Raoul smiled again; he felt as if he moved in a dream-world. Their eyes met. His grin broadened and he began to laugh at the absurdity of it all. At a time when his life and Natalie's hung by a ravelling and time was ebbing away like the sand in an egg-timer, this man wanted to kill him for all the wrong reasons. It was ridiculous. He began to laugh. Lebeuf too began to smile and then laugh. An infection was spreading between them and soon neither of them could maintain a straight face. As soon as they looked at each other they laughed.

Lebeuf sat down on the edge of the chaise longue. He became serious at last. 'You're not one of them are you? They don't laugh. They only kill.'

'The Germans?'

'Yes, naturally.'

'How could you think I'm one of those—collaborators I mean...?'

'I think maybe I'm going a little strange in the head. I've no one to talk to since my wife, Matilde, died.' He gestured the table with an open hand. 'We played cards with friends. Even they have been exported somewhere to a work camp.'

'I think I understand. I too have much on my mind.'

Raoul stared at the floor. A picture came into his mind of Natalie, seated on the bunk in her cell, her left hand extended towards him as they took him away.

'I wanted to talk before. Now I don't. Can I have more wine?'

Raoul reached out a plump arm, his glass empty. Lebeuf filled it and said, 'What did you mean before—about killing Germans?'

'What did you mean about killing Germans?' Raoul said.

'Long story.'

'I have all night. I have a tale to tell as well.'

'When we last met, you know—on the steps, I told you what happened at the school, how they sacked me. I think I told you what I thought of it all.'

'Yes, you did, but you said you were leaving.'

'That was just what I intended. I went into the city and began drinking; my bags all packed and enough money for the ticket to Brittany. It was raining and I slipped as I came out of some bar or other. It was a noisy place—it doesn't matter which one. I reached out with my hand and grabbed a shoulder. It belonged to a German officer. He too was maybe a little drunk, but he punched me on the jaw. As I fell he kicked me in the stomach. He was breathing hard and when I looked up he began to clutch at his chest. His face went white; he was sweating and gasping his last. He fell to his knees. I stood up as soon as I had the strength. He lay at my feet then he stopped breathing altogether. If I wanted to curry favour with the German bastards I would have called for help, but it was late, it was a small street and there was no one nearby. It made me excited, don't you see?'

'But why? You didn't kill him.'

'No, but I dragged his body into a basement entrance. It was dark, hidden from view. He had a gun, a dagger and a lot of deutsche marks. He had almost five hundred. You know what that is in francs? I took it all, then I came home. I thought maybe I could live on the money for a while before going to Brittany.'

'A lot of money, I suppose, but not real riches. You have some left?'

'Yes, but that wasn't the end. I had a gun. I knew nothing about weapons, nothing about war, only teaching children to read and write. I was a useless person you see. After Matilde died there was nothing for me in life but my job. I threw myself into it to heal and to forget. No one ever trained me for revenge. I had bullets in the gun, but I didn't even know how many. I was not a professional. You understand? I had no idea what it was that God had planned for me. Now I know. I tried to practise with that Luger pistol. I was sure there would be at least six bullets. There are actually eight. I went to the Bois and when it was late and no one was about I fired a shot.

238

Just one. I was scared, but I hit the tree I was aiming for. I ran away holding the stupid gun in my hand. I heard shouts. Still I ran, but two soldiers came and they stood in front of me pointing rifles. I held up my hands, hardly realising how I still grasped the gun. They began laughing. They were young men, no older than my eldest son, Jules. I saw their guns wavering as they laughed and I knew they were not professionals. Don't you think that if you want to march into another man's country, abuse the people and cheat everyone, that you would owe it to yourself to be professional—serious. These German piglets were nothing of the sort. I shot the first one in the face and the second in the chest and it was easy. I am a Catholic and I know Hell exists. Maybe I will go there, but may God forgive me, it was easy. Three in the morning, Bois de Boulogne, two dead soldiers, and it was like marking an exam paper. I took their money too. No bullets, so I became worried; if I needed to do the same again I could run out of bullets. I wished I was a professional, like these young Germans had not been. Then I realised, to get more bullets for the Luger, I had to kill some officers. They had more money anyway and they carried the right ammunition.'

'You depress me.' Raoul said draining his fourth glass. The wine was growing on him.

'But why? I was having the time of my life. The bastards took my only life-anchor away and now I have a new career. It is a good one. I can at last make a difference. I progressed, you know.'

'You progressed from what you have told me? I don't believe it.'

'You disapprove?'

'No. I admire you but I could never do what you do. To take a life is a sin. I'm not religious but I know that Hell is there for any of us who takes another's life. It says so in The Bible.'

'Ha ha ha,' Lebeuf slapped his knee. 'We will have another bottle. This conversation tickles me. It is so long since I laughed, you know that? So long. This time a pinot noir. I think it is a Beaune but I don't know so much, just what I like.'

Lebeuf opened another bottle. Raoul finished what remained in his glass and smiled as the man poured a generous glass, disregarding the principle of only one-third. He began to wonder how he could make use of a slightly deranged school teacher who seemed to have an unerring knack of killing Germans.

'You want to hear the rest? It's short, don't worry.'

'But what happened? You are a teacher, not an assassin.'

'You know, Voltaire—you've heard of him?'

'A politician?' Raoul said, grasping for something to say.

'No, no, no. A writer—a great man. He wrote a book called Candide. It is about optimism. Despite everything bad that happens to the main character, and they are terrible things, he believes that everything happens for the best in this best of all possible worlds. Of course, Voltaire wrote it as a satire but there is truth in it. Every time I kill a German officer I think of Candide, I think of my country and I think how lucky I am to have no one who needs me—no one depending upon me. So I am free to move. I have been out to the countryside and practised. I can shoot the eye out of Pètain's face on posters at fifty paces, never a miss. I hadn't realised I could have talent. I always thought I was an average man who struggled with everything. Now I know. I am a natural born remover of Nazis. I don't care if I go to Hell. For once in my life, I am doing what I am gifted at and enjoying it.'

'How many?'

'What? Germans?'

'Yes.'

'Twenty-two and a half. That is, if you count the first one as a half. I only robbed him.'

'You have done that?'

'I told you. More wine?'

Raoul held out his glass.

'And you? What about you? You have a story you said? You kill these vermin too?'

It began to rain outside and Raoul could hear the pit-pit-patter on the windowsill. A vision of the frying pan descending on Schiller's cranium came into his head. He shuddered.

'I don't know what to say.'

It occurred to him that even if this was all false and Lebeuf was lying to entrap and betray him, it did not matter. Von Schwerin knew he had killed the man. There was no case to prove. All was known now. He shifted in his seat.

'Look, I too killed a man. He was threatening my woman and I killed him.'

'Good for you. He was German I hope?'

'Yes, yes. But I suffer. Now they are making me work for them.'

'You work for Germans?'

'No. Not exactly.'

Raoul explained Natalie's arrest and his own. He revealed his plan to trap Marcel. When he had finished, he looked Lebeuf in the eye. He said, 'Look, one day I may ask you for a service, an accommodation, and I wonder whether you might perhaps oblige me.'

'Bring on the entrée, my culinary friend. It will be a pleasure. You want me to kill this Von Schwerin fellow. Say no more. It is done. Tomorrow? The next day perhaps? It will be my pleasure to serve you and to serve my country. Do you think he carries a lot of money with him?'

'I don't even know your first name. I am Raoul.'

He stood up with as much formality as a consumed bottle of wine could allow and held out his hand. Lebeuf took it and looking straight at Raoul, said, 'I am Vincent. We could make a good team. I will kill the pigs and you can cook them.'

Neither of them laughed this time. The look in Vincent's eyes was more serious than Raoul would have expected from the wine and the demeanour earlier.

He took his leave after obtaining Vincent's telephone number. There might be a time when such a man would be useful, but now he needed to sleep. He still thought of Natalie and as he sat in his own apartment, the vision of her at their parting continued to recur.

Chapter 25

YASSA—A Senegalese dish consisting of pieces of grilled (broiled) mutton, chicken or fish (originally monkey) that have been marinated in lime juice and highly seasoned condiments.
– Larousse Gastronomique

I

At nine o'clock the next morning, Raoul was getting used to disappointment. Café Dimanche was resoundingly shut; even the dilapidated table and chairs were conspicuous by their absence outside. The sagging green awning still hung askew over the grey and red-painted fascia above the door. A little wintery rain began to fall as he wiped the window with his hand and stared into the gloom of the empty, unlit café. One of the tables lay on its side and a chair looked smashed though he could not get a clear view.

He tried the door; it was locked.

Raoul backed up into the lee of the wall opposite, sheltering from the rain, and waited. Twenty minutes later, nothing stirred and his hopes began to fade. The cobbles gleamed brown and grey in the morning light and there was an aroma of coffee, though he could not locate the source. A man in a black overcoat and a flat black cap cycled past him. Their eyes met, but there was no recognition, no contact and it occurred to Raoul he was wasting his time. No one here could help him, only the little black-beetle woman who had scuttled away and left her home untidy, perhaps wrecked.

He was getting wet beneath his umbrella as the wind swept the droplets of rain against his trousers and he regretted ever coming on this fruitless errand, but he had no other port of call, no one else to tax over the missing partisan. Suddenly, as he stood debating what to do, he saw her. In the distance her movements reaffirmed his impression that she was a beetle. Black and shiny in the rain the woman arrived. Her shoulders looked hunched in her black coat and black hat. She glanced at Raoul and looked away as if her ignoring him would make him disappear into thin air like a bubble on heated fudge.

'Madame,' he called.

His cry evoked no response and he repeated it louder until she turned, forced to do so by his increasing volume.

'You,' was all she said.

'I'm looking for Marcel. I need to find him. It's urgent.'

'Go away. I don't know where he is and I want to be left alone. Can't you leave a poor widow alone?'

Her brown eyes glared at him, but driven by desperation he refused to take her denial for an answer.

A man walked past beneath an open umbrella. He stared at Raoul but was gone in an instant. Raoul's heart was fluttering and he noticed he was breathing fast. An uncomfortable feeling of tightness around his chest- a crushing discomfort— came to Raoul then and it scared him.

He felt weak and his legs seemed to be made of rubber. He stepped forward and almost fell towards the old lady who reached out a hand to steady him, though what she thought she could do if he fell, Raoul could not imagine.

'Please, let me in,' he said supporting himself with an outstretched hand on the door frame.

Without further remonstrance the old lady opened the door and Raoul staggered in. He made for the only chair still standing. It occupied the centre of the bar and he sank into it, grateful to come off his legs. The room began to spin and he clutched at the bar to prevent himself from falling. He was fighting for breath and his head swam. He heard a clink of glass upon glass and then she was back, holding a brandy balloon in her right hand. She proffered it and Raoul drank, without a word. The Calvados burned as it found its way down his gullet and he felt an odd relief at that. With a closed fist he thumped his chest.

'Indigestion, I think. I am sorry to upset you.'

'Upset? I'm not as upset as I was when the Germans came and wrecked my café. They came, the bully boys, in their green uniforms. Searching they were, looking for Marcel. Want my boy and they do this to sniff him out, the pigs. You've seen the signs maybe? Instead of "Rauchen Verbotten" the little children rub out the letters so it reads "Race Verte". It's true they are a race apart. Evil, they are. And you?'

'What? I'm not evil'

'No, not what I mean. What are you doing here? You'll bring them back.'

The old woman, as if gripped by a sudden impulse scuttled to the door and leaning out looked up and down the street.

She locked and bolted the door and returned to Raoul, her paranoia obvious.

She said, 'It's not safe. He knows it isn't and he hasn't told me where he is in case they question me. Now, if you feel better, I'll let you out.'

Raoul looked up at her, he was sweating now. Drops of moisture ran down his forehead onto his cheeks and a droplet fell from the tip of his nose. Taking out his handkerchief, he wiped his face.

'It's very important I speak with Marcel. Very important. I have a vital message to deliver from Paul Brossolette. He needs this information. Is he still in Paris?'

'No, he went south somewhere, it's all I know.'

'Is there someone who would know? Please, it's important. Life or death.'

She looked at him as if in doubt.

'No. I told you, he doesn't tell me anything because it's too dangerous. Please go.'

Doubt also trickled through Raoul's mind, like a butterscotch sauce on a meringue. The woman was his only lead. All he could hope to do now was try to find someone who could find Marcel, but how?

He left the Cafe Dimanche with a heavy heart. The old woman locked and bolted the door behind him as if it could keep out the world, though Raoul knew that if the Germans or the Police Special Brigade or any of the SD came back it was a flimsy protection and would not delay them many seconds. Marcel had been right, whether he could trust his mother or not, it was safer for her not to know where he was.

He still felt unwell and sweated as he walked towards the

Hotel Metro. His chest felt as if a horse had kicked him on the breastbone. Perhaps someone at the Metro might know how he could contact resistance groups which he had read were distributing leaflets and causing trouble for the Germans.

On the way, he stopped and sat on a bench in the Tuileries Gardens. He watched the fountains spraying, and began to ruminate again. Disposing of Schiller's body. Natalie's face. Vincent Lebeuf with his deranged intentions to kill Von Schwerin. It all swirled in his head until he felt faint.

2

'Raoul. Raoul!'

The voice came to him as if from a long distance, far away across verdant meadows and yellow cornfields. He had a sensation of moving up, ever upwards into bright sunshine, almost like being pulled from a well or some tiny confined space. He opened his eyes.

Glaring light filled his fields of vision and the face he saw was not that of some archangel, it was Marek. Raoul looked around and found he lay in his office on the couch, that place of refuge where he had spent so many lonely nights, before Natalie. His thoughts always came back to her. Where was she? As if to taunt him, memory returned. Of course. She was imprisoned. The thought came to him how he was a most unlikely knight in shining armour. The horse might have collapsed under his weight. The image brought a faint smile to his lips and he said, 'I have the armour but no sword.'

'What? What are you saying, Raoul?'

'Where am I?' Raoul said, though he realised where he was and he began to wonder why he asked.

'Your office. They found you in the Gardens. Philippe found you on his break, got help, and we brought you here. You need a doctor, maybe hospital.'

'No. No time. I have things to do. I can't stay here.'

Raoul struggled to sit up, but his arms felt weak and would not support him, so he sank back onto the pillows behind his head.

'Relax yourself, my friend. You are not fit to go anywhere. Where have you been?'

'I'll tell you in a moment when I get my strength back. They questioned me.'

'Who? The Special Brigade?'

'I'll tell you. Bring me some wine. Anything, just wine, oh and a pêche flambé. I could kill for that,' he said.

'I'll bring you some broth. No fancy stuff. You aren't quite right yet. Lucille has called the doctor.'

Every moment that passed he felt better. The confusion cleared and he found the strength to sit up. Propped up with pillows, Marek in attendance, he felt quite well again.

'Marek, I can't stay here for long. I have a duty to perform.'

There was no one else in the room and he explained his predicament to Marek.

'You work for them?'

'No. I need to make a plan to get Natalie released and to save Marcel. I need to persuade him back to Paris and then try to find a way.'

'But you are collaborating.'

248

'Natalie. She needs me to do this.'

'Natalie. You think she would allow you to sacrifice a man who fights for France in exchange for her? You're crazy.'

Marek paced the floor. He said, 'You can't do this.'

'But I have to. I have a plan though.'

Marek sat down on the edge of the couch and Raoul explained what he intended.

'Now I know you're mad. It won't work. If the partisans don't shoot you, the SD will.'

'No. Listen. It will work if I can just find him. I have to find someone who has contacts in the FPT.'

'FTP you mean.'

'Well, whatever the Communists are called these days.'

Marek stood up from his narrow perch beside Raoul on the couch. He said, 'You could ask me, for example.'

'You?'

'Yes, I've been in contact with them a long time. I even wrote an article for *Le Franc Tireur* a few weeks ago. Under a pseudonym of course, but all the same, I'm connected.'

'You are? Under my nose too. I don't believe it Marek.'

'We only work together. You don't know me.'

'Have you… Have you done things…'

'What killed Germans? No. I distribute leaflets sometimes, but that's all they want from me; that and information about who is in the hotel. You think you are the only one who did anything for our county?'

'You're from Bohemia aren't you?'

'I haven't been there in twenty-five years, Raoul. You think France isn't my country? Of course I'm French. You make me mad sometimes.'

'Sorry. How do I get in touch with them?'

'You rest here. Leave it to me. If I can't find out where he is, at least I can get a message passed to him. You want I should tell him about Natalie?'

'Yes, tell him the truth. I have my plan and just need him to cooperate.'

Marek left then and Raoul was alone in his office. He considered drinking some Pernod, but thought better of it. He was worried now for his health. He smiled at the thought. Natalie in German hands, Marcel putting himself in danger all the time and he worried for his health. It was ridiculous.

Chapter 26

ZINGARA—A sauce or garnish containing paprika and tomato (zingara means 'gypsy' in Italian).
– Larousse Gastronomique

I

'He wants to meet you.'

Marek stood by Raoul's desk and shuffled from foot to foot. His demeanour seemed odd to Raoul, but he understood that. Who would trust a self-confessed collaborator?

'That's fine. I can't expect him to trust me after what I told you. You know Marek, what I said could be a clever ploy by Von Schwerin to entrap us all. He's very shrewd but I don't think even he would work that one out. Where can I meet Marcel?'

'I don't know. I only know that he will contact us when he wants to.'

'Time is short, you know. If anything happens to Natalie because Marcel is slow, I'll shoot him myself.'

'You would?'

'No. I just mean…'

'We are still serving food to these pigs, you know.'

'Yes. How about salmon laced with botulism?' Raoul smiled as he spoke.

'How do you do that? Even though you never had the guts to do it I would, given the chance.'

Raoul chuckled. He knew it was impossible. He could not avoid Marek's barb however. It could have saved a lot of bother if he had just poisoned them all in the first instance at Goebbels' banquet.

Raoul said, 'You serious?'

'No. I wouldn't hurt a fly. But you? Maybe after killing a German you might consider…?'

Their eyes met. A smile came again to Raoul's lips and they found themselves chuckling. He swung his legs off the couch. He rubbed them as if they needed the circulation to return and he looked up at Marek. Neither man spoke. Each of them realised Raoul took a risk. The doctor on the telephone thought Raoul had been the victim of a heart attack and he insisted upon ten days' rest. Raoul had swept his advice away with his hand and refused to see him. 'No. My ticker is as strong as an ox's heart. To lug my body around for forty years, it would have to be.'

He had not taken the advice seriously, but at Marek's insistence, stayed resting on the couch for the remainder of the week and waited for Marek to bring him news. It had been a long wait, peppered with dreams and visions of Schiller and Natalie. Natalie and Schiller and sometimes Von Schwerin would appear in one of his dreams, but the latter was always dressed in white, always with a heavy crucifix around his neck. At times Raoul had thought he was going mad but in the end

252

he put it down to not eating enough. He started each morning with a generous helping of eggs Benedict. Mid-morning he ate a snack of Danish pastries and coffee. At lunch he felt he had to be modest and ate only lightly of fish or sometimes a Weiner schnitzel with pommes Anna and roasted vegetables.

Marek showed his kindness in providing only the best wines. Raoul often started the day with champagne; at lunch he drank Bergerac rosé and finished with a good Armangnac.

Dinner was never a disappointment for Raoul; he could rely upon Marek to use his culinary skills to produce wonderful meals ranging from fillet mignon to porc Andaluz. In the evening, to keep up his strength, he ate foie gras with fresh brown toast and plenty of butter, washed down with beautiful Burgundies from Première Cru estates. The Metro had a wine list second to none and much of it hidden from prying German eyes. To Marek who often joined him, it must have been a rare treat, but to Raoul it was only what was expected in a good hotel, where he was the master of the wine and food.

2

It took two more days before Marek brought him news. He entered the office and Raoul could see at once his face was serious and strained. Raoul looked up from his double helping of eggs Benedict and smiled to try to put him at ease, but it made no difference to Marek.

'You have your meeting with Marcel,' he said.

'Excellent news,' Raoul said.

'No it's not. He wants you to travel to Bordeaux. He won't

meet you in Paris. Says it's too dangerous.'

'Me? Travel to Bordeaux? Doesn't he realise I've been ill? Can't he come here?'

'Raoul. You are always so unrealistic. If he came here, what would happen? The SD would be all over the place in no time; Marcel would be arrested and they would still have Natalie in custody. I think he has a plan and it may be better than yours. Who knows?'

Raoul said, 'All I want is Natalie. You know this. If I have to go to Bordeaux, I'll go. I'm fit and strong thanks to your good food, don't worry. I'll go.'

'Should I come with you?'

'No. Who would run the kitchens, if you go too? No. You stay here and I will go. Can you ask George to buy the tickets? I'll need two seats you know. My backside won't fit into one. Could you ask him to get there and occupy the seats for an hour or two before the train goes—just until I arrive? There will be no seats near the time of departure and I wouldn't like to stand all the way. Oh and can you fetch another bottle of Labégorce Zédé, and some of your chicken liver pate with a few brioche? I think I'm becoming a little peckish again.'

Marek left with a smile on his lips. He seemed to Raoul to know just how to hit the spot where his stomach was concerned. He lay back on his cushioned couch, looking around the empty office.

Ha. You'll beat them yet. That Von Schwerin won't beat you. But what if Marcel won't play along? I hope he co-operates. Surely he has to see it's the only way to get Natalie out of their hands? God, I wish she were here now.

She was wrong to tell you to leave without her. You could

never do that. How could you have been so blind to her love? All those years wasted and now all that stands between us is Marcel. He'll understand. He must. Natalie? Where are you?

Marcel is her friend. She said they were good friends. Would you risk your life for a friend? But he already has. He risked his life getting your people out to Spain. He's brave. You're not brave. Look at you. Great lump of pig fat.

But you can do this. Von Schwerin underestimates you. He thinks you're a peasant. He thinks he can squeeze and squeeze and you'll pop. He doesn't know what you went through in school. He doesn't know how you resigned yourself to pain. Until Pierre. Yes, until Pierre Dreyfus came along. Big, strong feisty Pierre. And now you owe her, like you owed him. They're both so strong and what are you?

Resilient. Yes, that's it. I'm resilient. I hope this chest thing will get better. Maybe you should have seen the doctor. Rubbish. Maybe some tablets would help the breathing. Ha! You don't need doctors. What do they know? Nothing. You were just needing to eat. It was losing weight in that damned prison. Made you weak. Where's Marek with that damned pate?

Raoul got up and rummaged in the desk drawer. His fingers found the handle of the gun after a few seconds. He picked it up and played with the safety catch. He could not work out whether the "s" meant it was safe or unsafe. Deciding it made no difference, he placed the gun under his pillow.

So now you're a man of action, Raoul Verney? A killer armed like an American cowboy? No. I would never use it. But if you had to? If they made you shoot someone?

No. But for Natalie? Maybe for Natalie. No. Shoot someone? It's out of the question.

But you could if you had to. Yes. I could if I had to but I

255

won't. Then die with it in your hand. Raoul Verney, you're a fool.

Then I'll die a fool but knowing I did not kill anyone. But you did, didn't you? You killed Schiller. Easier with a frying pan maybe but all the same...

Raoul felt uncomfortable with his thoughts and Marek's return brought relief from the unpleasant ruminations which seemed to pursue him on and on. The taste of the pâté took it all away. The Margaux brought back thoughts of cedar, tobacco box and cassis. He drank half the bottle before finishing the pate and the brioche.

At least if he got killed it would be on a full stomach.

Chapter 27

CHAMBRER—*A French term meaning to bring a wine to the temperature of the room in which it is to be drunk.*
– Larousse Gastronomique

I

Raoul found it hard now to understand how, as he grew up, he had always seen Bordeaux as the big city. Compared to Lyon or Paris, it was just another town. What had all the fuss been about? He sat on his two booked seats and recalled the German soldier as he had stood above him.

'I need this seat,' the man had exclaimed.

'No room,' Raoul explained.

'You are too fat. Move up.'

When Raoul showed his tickets, the fellow had scowled. He said, 'Your arse is so big you need two seats?'

'Naturally. What would you expect from one of the greatest chefs in all of France? If you wait without complaint in the corridor, I will let you come to the Metro Hotel and I will cook for you. Meanwhile, I think you will not be comfortable squeezed up to me anyway.'

The German seemed doubtful for a moment or two then retreated into the corridor, shutting the door of the compartment with a look of irritation on his face. France and Germany were still allies after all.

Raoul turned to the woman next to him. She wore a long grey overcoat over her skinny frame and a scarf that covered most of her head. Her eyes looked troubled. Raoul thought she was his own age.

'You have to stand up to these vermin. How can we be called French if we do not?'

She said, 'It's easy for you. You are somebody. I am nothing. They would send me away on a train to a work camp if I even sneezed at them. You must have a high position to be obeyed so easily.'

'No. I just don't like bullies and the way they carry on.'

An elderly man opposite leaned forward. He said, 'You know, you set a wonderful example, but you can't expect us to follow it. They shot ten people in Bordeaux only a week ago in reprisal for one German death. You think we can fight back? I don't think so.'

'We can fight back. It doesn't have to be military action. We can be uncooperative instead. Think about it. They control everything. They don't control our hearts. Not our minds. We have to fight to preserve what is France. We let go of that idea and we become German. All over the country our people are repressed by these German soldiers. Somewhere, sometime, our nation will face the bullies and fight back. You care? I care. We all need to stand up and decide which side we are on. It isn't Vichy France. It is France…'

Two fellow travellers of similar age to Raoul stood up.

258

They applauded him and he rose and took a bow. When he sat down no one said anything and quiet descended. He looked out of the window at the green countryside feeling pleased with himself. Perhaps his little speech fed the growing resentment for the Germans and their rape of his homeland. Wide fields, green and lush in the early spring stretched for miles before his eyes. Small farmhouses, meandering tracks and tall pines filled his eyes but in his head, he saw only Natalie. She was wasting away in that hell-hole and God alone knew what they subjected her to. He became anxious then. Only a few days left. What if Marcel refused? What if his plans went wrong?

The door of the compartment opened and a guard entered, his flat, black, peaked cap and dark blue uniform separating him from the military and to Raoul giving reassurance that not everyone in uniform was German or collaborationist scum. As he proffered his tickets, it came to him in an instant. Was he not a collaborationist too in his way? No. He was going along with Von Schwerin's plan to free Natalie. He was a kind of double agent. Comforted by the thought, he reached into his coat pocket and extracted his copy of Le Figaro. The headline today read "Xavier Mallat takes up appointment as director of the *Commissariat Général aux Questions Juives*" but since Raoul had no understanding of such things, he did not read further. He placed the newspaper on his knees and continued to stare out of the window.

Boredom set in. He was uncomfortable and his stomach began to rumble so he rose, making his way past the other occupants of the compartment, stumbling over feet, apologizing and smiling as he opened the door. As he left the compartment, one of the men who had applauded his little speech followed him.

When Raoul sat down in the dining car, the man sat down opposite him. He was a small man with a black beard trimmed short, beneath a sallow pock-marked face. The dark eyes looked up at Raoul from beneath a fedora with a black band and the man smiled. Removing his hat, he placed it with care on the seat next to him but kept his hand on it as if it might fly away at any moment.

'Have you booked this sitting?' Raoul said.

With a faint eastern-European accent the bearded man said, 'For a man on Reich business, you draw too much attention to yourself. There is good reason for you to be as inconspicuous as you can.'

The waiter arrived and rearranged the cutlery on the white damask tablecloth, turning the wine and the water glasses upright. He waited for Raoul to order. Frowning at the menu, Raoul found it hard to concentrate. Who was this fellow opposite? Was he a member of the Resistance or was he sent by Von Schwerin to watch him? Still confused, he waved the waiter away then called him back and ordered a bottle of rosé and a jug of water. The stranger ordered Vichy water.

Looking across the table, Raoul said, 'Who are you? And what's this about Reich business. I don't know what you're talking about.'

'Just what you heard. Don't draw attention to yourself. It's bad enough that your size makes you instantly visible and memorable. Have some sense.'

'But who are you?'

'You don't need to know who I am. You just need to follow the German's orders.'

The Vichy water arrived and the waiter opened Raoul's wine. He poured a little and Raoul tasted. He did not offer any to the stranger. He still could not understand on which side the man worked.

'Who's orders?' Raoul said.

'What?'

'Whose orders do you mean? You work for Von Schwerin?'

'Who?'

'The SD.'

'Are you stupid? SD? Of course not. Marcel sent me to keep an eye on you. He knew you would embarrass yourself. He seems to know you better than you do yourself.'

'How can I believe that? You could work for either side. I had no instruction about anyone "looking out" for me. You'd better leave me alone.'

'Calm yourself, my friend. I will keep my distance, but I will be there if you get into any trouble, you know—like a guardian angel.'

'I don't need a guardian angel thank you. You can lead me to Marcel?'

'No. He is how do you say? Ephemeral. Like a mist, he comes and goes as he wishes. He will contact you when he's ready. All you have to do is follow your instructions. You're sure you've got them right?'

'Yes. Of course. I'm not stupid.'

The waiter interrupted them and Raoul ordered his lunch. Consommé with bread followed by cassoulet with ham. He requested a double portion because he knew how stingy the chefs on these trains were with meat.

'You can find your way to the meeting place? At the…' the beard said as the waiter departed.

'Well everyone knows where Le Chapon Fin is. I've even cooked there for a while a long time ago.'

'Indeed,' the beard said. 'I cannot stay with you in case someone sees us together. If you catch sight of me later once we arrive, ignore me. It's safest. Le Chapon Fin, that's on Allée de Tourny, isn't it?'

'What? No. Rue Montesquieu just around the corner.'

'Yes, of course. You go straight there do you?'

Raoul's eyes narrowed. 'I thought you knew where and when?'

'No. I'm from the Paris end of things. I was just asked to make contact with you and follow to keep you out of any entanglements. You know—police and so on.'

Satisfied with the answer, Raoul tucked his napkin into the collar of his shirt as soon as the bowl of consommé arrived. He asked for more bread.

'They give such small portions on trains you know. I sometimes think the war is just an excuse for pilfering. This consommé is thin too. Tastes as if the chef has watered it down.'

The beard looked up at him. He licked his lips but said nothing. As Raoul slurped the last few spoonfuls, tipping his plate away from him, the man stood up.

'No doubt I will see you soon enough. I'll be at the rendezvous in, let's see…' The man looked at his watch.

Raoul looked at his own wristwatch, 'If we get in in two hours, it will be eight hours.'

The beard smiled a yellow smile and walked away down the corridor between the clean white tablecloths, swaying with

262

the train, his hat now atop his brown hair.

As Raoul began munching the cassoulet, a thought struck him.

Why would Marcel send anyone?

He picked a piece of ham out of a gap in his teeth with a toothpick and shook his head.

Makes no sense. Marcel knew; he understood where and when and anyway, how could he get into trouble checking into a hotel? Guardian angel indeed. Ridiculous.

2

Raoul alighted in the Gare Saint-Jean clutching his leather portmanteau and wondering whether a taxi would be available in the early evening or not. So few drivers had fuel and it meant those who did, charged exorbitant prices for only short journeys. But at least they were not Paris taxi drivers, who were as likely to spit at you as they were to take you to your destination. Jostled by the crowd of descending passengers, Raoul gripped his tickets and began walking towards the barrier where a lone ticket inspector stood clipping tickets and answering queries. He jumped when a hiss of steam released from an engine rose above the hubbub of the passengers thronging to exit the platform. In front of him, the crowd backed up since the inspector could only attend to one at a time and Raoul stood shifting from one foot to another, impatient to be away.

Ever sensitive to smells, he wrinkled his nose. It was an odour of perfumes and body smells, sweat and haute couture.

He wished he had used cologne on his handkerchief; at least it would mask the stench of humanity surrounding him. In one way he was sorry he had such sensitive olfactory skills, honed from youth by zealous parents encouraging him to understand food and wine. Steam floated like ghosts across the platform and he looked at his fellow passengers, wondering what it was separating him from them with such insistence.

He realised that he felt they milled around him without any great aim. They hurried, yes it was true, but there was no real urgency. Whatever they had to do, motivation had flown away for such people as these. If they worked hard, if they manufactured the very wherewithal of life, it was all wasted for a Frenchman nowadays. Everything was taken, stolen or bought for a pittance by the occupying Germans even though Pétain had promised they would not move south to the unoccupied territories.

Raoul glanced over his shoulder, searching the sea of faces for the man with the beard. He was not visible, so he shrugged and waited in the queue. When he emerged, he crossed to the bridge where he recalled the taxi stand stood and joined another queue.

The taxi ride took only twenty minutes and he alighted in the narrow cobbled street outside the Hotel Continental, opposite the theatre. He looked down the road towards the small square where no one moved. All was dark, though he remembered it as a place of light and music, open cafés and laughter. A black and white photograph came to mind, one his parents had kept in a wooden frame on the hallway table. It showed the three of them standing arms around each other in that square. They had eaten, what was it? Yes confit duck, yes that was it, his parents were a little merry from the wine and all of them had been smiling. In his mind he homed in on the laughter on his lips and he remembered feeling he had wanted that moment to last, last forever, though at the age of eighteen he had understood it could not.

Raoul stood outside the hotel. The place was not a grand affair but seemed homely and welcoming. He crossed the foyer and the old woman behind the desk looked up. She had a wrinkled face like a worn and abused parchment, and it cracked, splintering into a smile as she welcomed him and gave him his key. As he mounted the stairs to his left, she said, 'These are troubled times but we all must do what we can.'

Raoul turned and looked down at her from the first few stairs he had climbed. He said, 'This I know, but it is hard. You know the Metro in Paris?'

'Of course. It's an underground railway, isn't it?'

'No. The Hotel Metro.'

'Ah, yes. Of course I've heard of it.'

'I am the Executive Head Chef.'

'Hah,' she said, 'top of nothing.'

'Nothing?'

'Yes. The Germans are here and they take everything. They steal art from the Louvre. They steal our best wine and they take our best hotels. I heard about the Metro. Full of Germans and no French people. If you cook for them you betray us.'

'There was a time when I would have said you were wrong. I always thought that life would become normal again. I thought they might leave us alone.'

'You were wrong.'

'Yes, but it is never too late to change one's philosophy.'

'No?'

'Tomorrow, I will land a blow to the Germans who destroy our land, or at least begin a plan.'

'If you are one of our heroes then you had better shut up. Shut your mouth at all times. If you don't, someone will put a grenade in it.'

As Raoul turned and went up the stairs he realised she was right. Had he kept his mouth shut to Müller, he would not be in this predicament. He recognised it was a conundrum in which he felt so desperately inept and naïve. What the evening would bring, he could not analyse. All he could think about now was his Natalie and how he would convince Marcel to help him.

Chapter 28

DIOT- A small vegetable and pork sausage made in Savoy.
– Larousse Gastronomique

I

During the journey, Raoul had become used to the idea that he had a follower, a guardian angel. The man never gave him his name, but all the same he welcomed the feeling he was no longer alone and that Marcel was looking out for him. Opening the door of his room he entered, shut it behind him and leaned against it. He noted the bathroom to his right, the oatmeal carpet and the two casement windows on the far wall. An odd discomfort greeted him and he began to sweat. The feeling was akin to indigestion but somehow more powerful, more depressing somehow. He felt as if a tight band encircled his chest and his left arm tingled in a dull nagging parody of sensation.

He dropped his bag on the floor and stumbled towards the bed. Sitting on the edge, he rubbed his chest and lay back, his legs hanging off and his feet still on the floor. The sweating continued, but he felt better within a few minutes. Glancing at his new watch he sat up again. He had to compose himself. Only two hours to go before the meeting, though he could not help but wonder what the meaning of the discomfort in his chest could be.

Raoul had received instructions to be here. Why had Marcel not come to Paris, instead of dragging Raoul all the way to Bordeaux for a meeting to learn about a meeting which in itself was fictitious? He lay back again and closed his eyes. All he could see were visions of Natalie as he had seen her in that cell. Bruised and battered, hopeless and dispirited. That was no way to remember her and he knew it. He closed his eyes.

Rain pattered outside on the sill. The tall casement windows stood shut and secure. He must have slept for a while for when he looked at his watch again it was seven forty-five. It was time to go. He got up and walked to the window. Opening it, he looked out into the rain-bespattered street, breathing in the atmosphere of a damp city evening. Raoul detected the garlic-laced odour of cooking food; he smelt the harsh aromas of wet stone and the rank smell of gasoline.

The sandstone face of the theatre opposite shone light-brown and glistening in the rain across the alley. Looking left, he saw the square, looking right, the narrow street ended at another square. Towards the end of the narrow, rutted street, on the left, opposite the hotel was the restaurant.

The sight of the place brought back memories. In his training he had worked there for one week. Le Chapon Fin was the oldest restaurant in Bordeaux. Famous people, politicians and celebrities, had dined there and for Raoul it felt a privilege to construct and cook his tasting menu. He smiled as he recalled the lobster bisque, the sea bass in octopus ink and the fillet mignon. There were only messages of praise and no complaints.

Glancing at his watch once more he came back to reality, and entering the bathroom inspected his appearance. The dark rings below his eyes reflected only his lack of sleep he thought and the sweat on his brow suggested nothing to him. He had a job to do and he would do it.

Raoul closed the hotel room door behind him almost with relief. He was glad the moment was passing. To meet Marcel and unburden himself to the man seemed to be the most important thing in his focus now, whether Marcel was a youngster, almost a boy, or not. But he wondered whether he would expend effort in saving Natalie. He began to question whether they were actually friends; maybe he would not risk his life to save her. Raoul descended the stairs holding hard onto the bannister. The cold iron felt cooling and comfortable to his moist, sweating fingers.

In the foyer, the old woman had gone, replaced by a young man who smiled as if the world was clean and fresh, though Raoul knew it was not. It was a filthy place, infected with Germans and Nazi dogma. What had become of his country? They called it the free sector of France. They said France ruled here in the south, but he knew better. As soon as a military excuse cropped up, they would move in to control all of it, even Bergerac, his home.

Turning right out of the hotel, Raoul remembered his home and his parents. The thoughts had become more intrusive as the war progressed. He often wished he could speak to either of them for reassurance or comfort. An involuntary shrug raised his shoulders as he walked the few yards toward

Le Chapon Fin. The green awnings, tidy and clean, shaded the frontage from the streetlights and he began to look around, wondering what he should do once he stood outside. He had not long to wonder.

Shuffling from one foot to the other with his back to the entrance under the awning, he waited. The harsh metallic smell of the damp street came to his nostrils. Rain began to fall and he wished he had an umbrella, but he had not thought to bring one and his mind pictured the folded black canopy residing in the hall stand at his apartment. Raoul had mixed emotions then. On the one hand, he wanted to be home, sitting by the fire and drinking a glass of wine. Another part of him welcomed the chance to put things right and salvage the most important person in his world.

He had been standing for just two minutes when Marcel appeared opposite. A cool wind rose and it whipped the sloping rain to a shower as he watched. Marcel, dressed in a brown suit and an unbuttoned, heavy coat came around the corner to Raoul's left, walking from the eastern square with slow, determined steps. Raoul smiled and raised his hand to wave. To his consternation he saw Marcel's gun as soon as he came within ten yards. The gun pointed at him, blue, metallic and hard.

Fifteen yards away Raoul called, 'Marcel. There's no need for that.'

The young man stared past him and said nothing. Sweat began to filter its way through Raoul's shirt. He could feel it running down his back. Was Marcel going to shoot him? It made no sense. He watched, mesmerised, as his friend raised the pistol with both hands. Raoul swallowed. It happened fast, as if time concertinaed in Raoul's mind.

But what about Natalie? Had he come so far only to be shot by the very man he hoped would be his salvation? The situation seemed ridiculous. He had told Marek everything. Surely no one could mistake his intentions?

He jumped when he heard the shot as if it came from somewhere close to his ear. He could not tell whether he ducked or fell. The sound reverberated in his head and the alleyway rang to the report of the pistol as he fell to his knees.

2

Marcel's hand tugged at his shoulder. The hard brown fingers grasped him, the knuckles white. He could smell the cordite from the gun barrel smoking in Marcel's hand. The lad shook him.

'What are you doing, kneeling here? Get up. We have to go.'

Raoul said, 'What is happening?'

'For the love of God. Get up.'

Raoul glanced over his shoulder and what he saw froze him to the spot. A figure lay slumped against the theatre wall. The brown stone gleamed in the lamplight and the pool of blood beneath the body looked black in the faint rays. The bearded face and the sightless eyes thrust a picture of the man into his mind. The man from the train. The man who said he worked for the FTP. As he pulled himself up, he said, 'But he worked for you. He was one of your men.'

'You fucking idiot. He's with the SD. I know his face from

271

Paris. He's one of the men who arrested people from your own hotel.'

'He isn't. He said…'

'My God. You have a lot to learn. Get up. We have to get out of here.'

Marcel dragged Raoul along the alleyway leading away from the restaurant. In a stumbling run Raoul had no choice but to follow the man who clutched his lapel with such force. The alley turned left and then they followed it round to the right. They emerged into a wide boulevard and Marcel pulled Raoul to a halt.

'Walk now,' he said.

'You…You killed him'

'Wake up. Hasn't it sunk in? They've been watching you since you left their damned prison. They're after me. That's all.'

'You knew?'

'Yes. I knew. I was watching since you arrived at the Continental. Get in.'

A black Renault pulled up. Raoul drew back but Marcel, grabbing his lapel, pulled the fat chef towards the open door.

'Get in, they're with us. Why don't you know what's going on?'

Raoul scrambled into the car and his head jerked as the vehicle took off. Why didn't he know what was going on? Everything around him seemed confusing, and there it was again, that feeling of indigestion, central, crushing, in his chest.

Sitting in the front seat, Raoul twisted as best he could but he couldn't gain a view of Marcel who sat behind him. He desisted and looked out of the car window. The buildings sped past in the blackout. Closed shops, some with boarded-up windows, emblazoned with slogans in red or black paint, shouted at him as they sped by. He shoved his hand in his coat pocket and drew out his handkerchief. With fat fingers shaking and grasping, he wiped his forehead and settled back as the black Renault sped away. The butt of Patrice's gun poked hard in the small of his back as if it were a constant reminder of his uselessness.

You can't cook with it can you? It's no more use than you are. You always get it wrong. Where is the man who saved Jews in the hotel? Who was it who killed that Schiller? Who got rid of the body? Wake up. Wake up.

The car's headlights caught the shiny black cobbles as the vehicle sped along in the rain and he soon lost track of the streets. At first he wondered where they were headed, but as images of the alleyway and the image of the dead bearded man came to him, he saw nothing. Ten minutes passed and he resigned himself to the new situation. Both Marcel and the driver remained silent and Raoul decided this was not the time for conversation. He wanted answers but was afraid to open his mouth. He felt foolish.

He glanced at the driver. For the first time he realised it was a woman. Skinny and long-legged, wearing a beret on her blonde head, she drove like a tornado. She double-declutched and dragged the car around corners, ignoring other traffic, speeding past cars and cyclists alike until Raoul felt dizzy watching her. He wanted to introduce himself, know her name but she kept her eyes glued to the road.

The beard was SD. Why had he not realised? He wondered

273

whether he was becoming as stupid as Marcel seemed to think he was. The sudden thought that he had led the man to Marcel stabbed his mind and he bit his lip in remorse.

Stupid. Stupid. Like telling Muller about Natalie. You're endangering your friends with your stupid mouth. Stick to cooking and eating—it's all you're good at. You're not good for anything else. Stupid. Stupid.

Twenty minutes of helter-skelter driving and the woman slowed down and began to drive like a tourist. She joined traffic, queued behind the few cars in the streets and, Raoul hoped, became invisible. He looked out again to find he was heading north along the river. Crossing a bridge, they headed east towards his home. The rain continued to fall. Heavy, large drops of rain descended and he could see little of where they were going through the overburdened windscreen wipers. He thought about Natalie again. It was becoming a habit now. Constant ruminant imaginings of what she must be going through.

Marcel tapping his shoulder brought him back to reality. He could hear him leaning forward and saying, 'So far, so good. I just wish you hadn't exposed me to that assassin.'

'Assassin?'

'Yes, a Czech renegade they used to kill people.'

'But if they killed you, they would learn nothing, it makes no sense.'

He may have been acting on his own, who knows?'

'I'm sorry, I didn't know. I'm finding things confusing. I'm not used to…'

He felt Marcel's hand grip his shoulder. Marcel said, 'Don't worry my culinary friend. I had you followed too.'

'You had me...'

'Yes, Madeleine was with you all the way.'

'Madeleine?'

Marcel chuckled. 'Sorry, you deserve an introduction. Madeleine, this is Raoul. Raoul, this is Madeleine.'

Raoul glanced to his left. The woman smiled. He took in her hatchet silhouette, the long, thin generous nose, the tanned face and the wisp of blonde hair beneath the beret. She reached to her right and squeezed his forearm. She said, 'Don't worry, you're doing fine, Raoul. You were in no danger. I saw you both at the table on the train and realised he was fooling you. I'm surprised he didn't bring a wagon-load of soldiers, but I suppose he thought he could handle it himself. Hold on...'

She turned the wheel and Raoul felt the pull of the car leaning him towards her.

'You must think I'm stupid.'

'No. Not after what Marcel told me about you. But maybe you need to watch what you say to strangers eh? Like we tell small children.'

Madeleine grinned, her white teeth flashing in the light reflected from a pair of oncoming headlights. They were alone on the road now and the car was bumping along a rough lane, tall elms marching either side.

'I'm sorry.'

Marcel said from the back, 'What about Natalie?'

'They're holding her. I have to telephone them to tell them where you are once you go to Paris. I had no other way to save her.'

'It's not important. I know what we are going to do.'

275

'You do? I had a plan to…'

'I have people in Paris now. I will need you to do exactly what I say. I'll explain when we get to where we're going. Relax yourself, Raoul. You are not alone anymore. I want to get Natalie out too.'

'Natalie? But why?' Raoul shouted over his shoulder.

'She is a friend. She was kind to me when they took my father away. I owe her. Have you never cried on a woman's shoulder in your life? Natalie is a gentle soul and if I can help her now, I will.'

The car sped on in silence after that and Raoul began to realise he was no longer in a position to plan. He had a feeling akin to being a child led by the hand of an adult. Marcel was calling the shots. Marcel was the leader and he killed people. It was more than Raoul could do. Then a flash of memory came to him. He could see Schiller, lying on the kitchen floor, his head bloodied by Raoul's blow. No. He could kill too but only to defend Natalie and he knew it was the only thing that could condemn him to Hell. He could almost feel the Devil's spurs biting into his flanks, but he came to the conclusion he didn't care anymore. For his woman he would kill a hundred Schillers, Von Schwerins and bearded assassins, if only he could save his Natalie.

Chapter 29

BOCUSE, PAUL—A French Cook (born Collonges-au-Mont-d'Or, 1926). He comes from a long line of restaurateurs and cooks who have been established on the banks of the river Saône since 1765.
– Larousse Gastronomique

I

Raoul heard the ringtone as he pressed the black resin of the earpiece to his sweat-moistened ear. He could hear his own breathing into the mouthpiece as he waited. Leaning over the small table in front of him, he placed a flat hand on the polished wooden surface and waited.

'Yes?'

'I am Raoul Verney. I have a message for Von Schwerin.'

'The Sturmbannführer is not here. I can take a message.'

'No. I want to speak to him in person.'

'I will ask him if he can speak to you. You have news for us?'

'Tell him I will telephone again in five minutes. I'm in a dangerous place. I cannot wait here forever.'

Raoul relinquished the earpiece, hanging it on the hook at the side of the mouthpiece. He fiddled with the brown curled flex and looked at his watch. An oppressive silence surrounded him and he turned to sit on the chaise next to the telephone. Loosening his collar with moist tremulous fingers he looked around, then tapped his fingers on the table and waited. He was still sweating.

The farmhouse was old, hundreds of years old he guessed, though he was never a judge of such matters. Beneath his feet a round, faded Persian rug lay on the brown tiles flooring the hallway. To his right was a staircase and ahead a passageway ending in a heavy oak door separating the kitchen from where he sat. That was where Marcel and Madeleine waited. He glanced at his watch once more and stared at a portrait hanging on the wall to his left. It was of a young woman, perhaps twenty, seated at a table across from another girl of a similar age. They both wore lace bonnets and long eighteenth century dresses, one pale blue and the other a now faded red. They wore frills of lace at their wrists and their necklines, and one of the girls held up a ring in which a single gem sparkled. The smile on her face was one of triumph and pleasure. Raoul knew it was an engagement ring and the scene of the newly engaged girl showing off her ring to her admiring friend irritated him. He knew the chance of his being able to give a ring like that to Natalie one day now hung by a thread. He felt bitter that it was so, but he had a streak of pragmatism too, and it kept him sanguine.

What was it Marcel had said? 'Don't let them intimidate you. They want me much more than they want to kill you or Natalie. They want me alive, too.'

He looked at the wristwatch again and picked up the ear-piece. Tapping the crossbar on the mouthpiece he repeated the number to the operator. He waited.

'Yes?' a voice said at the other end.

'Sturmbannführer Von Schwerin?'

'Yes. Who is this?'

'Raoul. Raoul Verney. I have news for you.'

'Well?'

'Maujean knows everything. He said he knew what you planned from the start, as soon as he saw the letter you sent with me. Said it was a forgery.'

'It is a pity for your woman. You understand what this means. Truly, I am sorry.'

'No. Wait. Don't hang up, there's more.'

Raoul realised his voice had escalated in pitch. He thought he sounded like a strangled pig.

'Well?' Von Schwerin said.

'You don't understand Marcel. He is no coward. He said he would give himself up if you spare his life and let Natalie go. He said to tell you he has a great deal of information in his head. Information you might wish to pay for.'

'You must think me stupid. Why would this killer consider giving himself up? I suppose he loves this Dreyfus woman too? A little old for him isn't she?'

'He has a close friendship with her and he wants your word you will not have him shot.'

'Spare his life? You are mad. He's a killer. He will have to stand trial and face justice.'

'I can't tell him that. He would never come if he thought that was your intention. You have influence. You could pardon him if he makes a statement against the Resistance movement or the FTP—tells you things. Is he not more use as a political tool and informant than dead?'

Silence. It was as if Raoul could hear the man thinking. He knew Von Schwerin enough to know there was a chance he would go along with Marcel's plan. The man wanted advancement, he wanted political success. It had to be enough bait. It had to.

'How do I know you aren't trying to trick us?'

'You don't.'

Silence again. It dragged on and Raoul was poised to ask if anyone was there.

'Very well. Bring him here and I will let you and the woman go. If you fail to bring him here by tomorrow evening, I will have to make an example of her.'

'No. I can't do that.'

'Can't? You will do as I tell you. You realise how this Dreyfus woman will suffer if you do not? I won't be able to protect her from the others. Maybe you don't care for her enough? If you care for her, you will obey me.'

'Marcel won't come there. He said you have to meet him with Natalie and then exchange prisoners.'

'An exchange? I am supposed to trust you?'

'Can I trust you?'

'I am an aristocrat. I am a man of my word. You insult me.'

'I'm sorry. I did not mean to.'

Raoul heard himself apologise and he grinned. It was as Marcel had said. He was becoming intimidated by Von Schwerin.

280

'Where does he want to meet?'

'Pont Neuf, at six in the morning day after tomorrow. He wants you to be at the right bank with Natalie. No other soldiers to enter the bridge until the exchange is complete. We will approach from the left bank. If there are any troops on our side of the bridge, he will know, he said.'

'It sounds too good to be true. How can he give himself up? Doesn't he realise what will happen to him?'

'He says he doesn't care. He wants Natalie safe. It is friendship. Don't you have close friends?'

As he spoke, Raoul wondered whether he was pushing the German too far and too fast. He shuffled from one foot to the other in agitation, but managed to keep his voice clear and level.

'And I suppose I release your woman at the same time as Maujean crosses to me?'

'Yes. But you must keep your soldiers back until he is with you.'

'You mean?'

'I will need time to get away.'

'He will be unarmed?'

'He will not have a gun and he will keep his hands where you can see them.'

'If anything goes wrong my men will have orders to kill you all. How do you know I won't do that anyway? It would save a lot of trouble, would it not?'

'I didn't think you were that kind of man.'

'No. Not that kind of man at all. I keep my word. You had better keep yours. Pont Neuf at six.'

The telephone clicked and there was silence. Raoul sighed

in relief. He could almost feel her in his arms. But would the plan work? There were too many variables. Anything could happen and as his father had been so fond of saying, it usually did.

2

Above the drifting mist arising from the Seine, the dark shadow of the Tour Eiffel stood stark and bleak, rising against the black and deep-blue backdrop of the Paris dawn. Ten people stood in the street, Raoul among them. He looked at Madeleine wondering what she was bringing to this affair. On her shoulder a sniper's rifle hung from a webbing strap and her right hand clenched the strapping tight, her knuckles showing bleak and pallid in the burgeoning pre-dawn light. She wore her beret pulled to one side and her brown raincoat looked grey to Raoul in the emerging dawn.

'It's time,' Marcel said. 'Madeleine, you know where to go. Henri you're with me at the bridge and you Francois and Alois, as we arranged. The rest of you, you all know where to be. If you aren't there, it will be unpleasant. Compris?'

Henri, a tall man with a limp, about Raoul's age, grinned.

'If we don't know where to place ourselves by now, we never will.'

Marcel said, 'We have no margin for error. It must be as precise as if we had rehearsed it many times.'

'Relax Marcel. We all know what to do. We're professionals.'

'No,' Marcel replied. 'We are amateurs; very good amateurs but amateurs nonetheless. Remember that. Think fast and do as we planned and nothing will go wrong. Make a mistake…'

'I still don't understand what you will do once I have her,' Raoul said.

'Never mind me, Raoul. Think only of what I told you to do. You can do that can't you?'

'Yes,'

'You'll need to move fast though. Von Schwerin will have a lot of men at his end of the bridge and maybe others ready to come at us from behind. Madeleine will cover our arses though. You can trust her.'

'In this fog?'

'If it hampers her, think of how the Germans will feel.'

Raoul checked his watch. Five-thirty. He did not relish the walk. He felt breathless and his "indigestion" had returned. He rubbed his chest.

'You alright?' Marcel enquired.

'Yes, yes… just indigestion. I'm fine.'

The group split up and Raoul watched as each of them seemed to go in different directions with unhurried purposeful steps, disappearing into the mist. Five of them made for the riverbank where the path ran parallel to the Seine. The grey waters seethed as the rain fell in earnest. He began to worry he was the only one here who was anxious. He felt like the youngest child in a school party visiting a historic site—unknowing and lacking in understanding, stumbling after the teacher hoping not to be left behind.

A hand grabbed his shoulder and he turned to see Henri grinning at him. Raoul said, 'What?'

'Relax, my friend. When it happens, it will be so fast you won't even recall it later. Action is always like that. Only a fool would not be scared. Brave is when you do the job anyway. Cowards can't suspend their imagination and that's what makes them back away. Think only of the job and making it a success. Don't forget to be on the right hand side of the bridge.'

'Easy for you to say, you've done this before.'

'Believe me, I'm as scared as you are. I have no desire to die.'

'Will you two shut your mouths? This isn't a picnic. Here, Raoul follow me. Don't forget what I told you. As soon as I'm within arm's length, you hear?'

'Yes. I understand. It's just…'

'You'll be fine. After the Metro Hotel, I refuse to believe you are not as good as any of us.'

The heavy spring rain let up and it began to drizzle on the men as they made their way towards the bridge. Perhaps because they were so early, Marcel stopped them twenty yards from the roadway where the bridge began. All three looked across the bridge. There seemed to be no movement, though even Raoul knew the Germans would be there. A fishy smell rose in his nostrils as if he were near the sea and he wondered where it came from, though the proximity to the river should have made it obvious. He felt dizzy now and a faint edge of confusion set in. He thought about how his mother had once told him that seagulls brought luck and he looked up hoping to see them. There were no birds; no one stirred in the gradual progressive lightening of the day.

'Marcel?'

'What?'

'Why so early in the day? It will be almost impossible for Madeleine to shoot in this light, surely?'

'She is the best shot I have ever seen. She has eyes like a night-owl. If she can't see to shoot you, nor can they. It's all about having an edge. Like coming at your enemy with the sunlight behind you. It gives you an edge. Let's hope the mist doesn't thicken.'

Raoul shivered. 'We have fifteen minutes to wait.'

Marcel produced a blue pack of unfiltered cigarettes. 'Gitanes?'

'No. You know I don't.'

He grunted, and extracting a cigarette tapped the end of it on the packet to get rid of the loose tobacco. He put the Gitane to his lips and cupping the matches, lit the end; he held the cigarette so no light showed to any observer across the bridge. The aromatic smoke stuck in Raoul's nostrils like the fumes from a bonfire, and he sneezed. They stood there waiting as if they were waiting for a tram: as if they were travellers and their early arrival did nothing more than ensure they would be on time to board.

To Raoul it was as if he waited for a firing squad to load their guns. His heart fluttered.

Chapter 29

CHEVAL, Á—Describing small pieces of grilled (broiled) beef
(steak, hamburger or entrecôte) with one or two fried eggs on top.
— **Larousse Gastronomique**

I

With his first footfall onto the Pont Neuf, Raoul peered across
the bridge. It was now light enough for him to see the opposite side with sufficient clarity to make out the dim shapes of
an armoured vehicle and two black cars parked across the road
blocking it. He felt a gentle hand in the small of his back and
heard Marcel speaking in a quiet voice.

'Off you go. Keep right.'

The depth of the silence struck Raoul as he began to walk.
He felt like a man embarking on a cruise liner, but no one was
there to check his ticket or point him in the right direction.
The upslope made him slow down but he continued to walk.
He felt dizzy, though he knew he would not fail her. He was
here. He was real. He would win, whatever his stomach
decided to do. Raoul belched and felt the pain in his chest
again as his heart raced. He took his hands from his pockets

and looked ahead. Holding his hands open at his sides, he assumed they would realise he had no weapons. The real weapon was hidden. The weapon he would use was the strength of his arms and they could not take that from him. He knew he was slow, sometimes ungainly, but he knew also he had strength and he knew what he had to do.

One third of the way across, he saw the doors of one of the cars more clearly. They opened and five figures emerged, partly obscured by the mist arising from the river drifting across in front of him. He wondered what Madeleine could see through the sight of her rifle but he shrugged away the thought. It was not his business, not his role here this morning.

Halfway across, he stopped. Ahead he identified a figure looking like Von Schwerin. Next to him he could see her. The German held her by the arm and it seemed as if she staggered as the two approached. Two men flanked them as they began walking.

'No soldiers. Remember our agreement, Von Schwerin,' Raoul said, loud enough to be heard across the space separating them.

He heard Von Schwerin say, 'Where is he? I can't see him in this fog.'

'Behind me.'

'Tell him to approach so I can see him.'

'Let her go.'

'No. Not until I have proof Maujean is here.'

Raoul turned and called over his shoulder, peering into the mist, 'Marcel. He wants you closer.'

'I'm here.'

Raoul could see Marcel clearly a few yards behind him. He felt sure Von Schwerin could too. He said, 'You see him?'

'Yes.'

'Let her go… Natalie?'

The two soldiers at the far end knelt and raised their rifles. Raoul shouted. 'Tell them to step back.'

'It is only a precaution. They won't shoot.'

'Tell them to step back.'

Von Schwerin raised his right hand. Turning back to face Raoul, he said, 'And now what? Six giant steps?'

'Let her go,' Raoul said. He felt faint and steadied himself with his right hand stretched out towards the stone railing. 'Let her come to me.'

Von Schwerin released his grip. Natalie staggered forward and a few yards from him stumbled and fell.

'Bastards,' Raoul murmured and stepped forwards. He reached her and leaned forward. 'Natalie, my love. Natalie?'

He helped her to her feet and at once noticed Marcel pass him, hands up as if it was all over.

Then all hell broke loose.

Raoul, as if animated by his passion, drew Natalie up into his arms. With a faster movement than any could expect from a man of his bulk he made a little jump and sat upon the wide, stone railings of the bridge. He rolled and as he and Natalie departed over the edge, he heard the sound of shots and bullets pinging on the brickwork around him. He glimpsed Marcel, knife in hand, run and lunge at Von Schwerin. Then all became a blur. Falling over the railings, his right shoulder struck a horizontal outcropping of stone two yards down.

Then they hit the water.

For moments all was black. Emerging, Raoul spluttered and gasped. He clutched her with his right arm. The current took them under the bridge. The waters around him boiled with bullets, whipping into the river upstream. In a clumsy sidestroke, he swam against the current, trying hard to remain under the bridge. Trying to stay safe.

In the half-light, he made out the stern of the barge. He swam towards it. His chest ached again. The burden became intolerable, but he felt Natalie push him away.

'I'm all right. I can swim,' she screamed, her voice subdued by the rushing waters of the Seine. More shots from above. Then he heard another loud splash and as he gained the stern of the waiting barge, he began to falter. His left arm would not obey him. His right felt weak. For one short moment, he reached out for the rope ladder. He had to make it. He wanted to be with her.

Darkness came. Pinpoints of light came like bubbles underwater. He struggled to breathe. Then he wanted air. He tried to breathe but nothing came. Only an ominous gurgle of thick, muddied water all around, filling his ears and eyes.

Then nothing.

Then blackness.

Raoul felt as if he could see himself, sinking deeper and deeper into the river. He hovered as if, after all of his life as a big heavy man, he became light as a floating feather. Gossamer to the wind and to the current of the Seine, lifeblood of the ancient city. No sounds interrupted his odd, black descent. The pain in his chest escalated until he felt consciousness slipping away.

Devil take you, you murdering bastards. Devil take you.

Fat bastard. It's all you deserve. You, with your big mouth, you who killed and chopped up a man. But at least she's safe. At least they didn't shoot Natalie. Safe, yes. She would live. Better off without me. What use was I? To die having loved was all that matters.

Love.

Yes.

The only one who ever wanted you.

The only one.

Deep, deep inside, he pictured himself reaching for Natalie's hand, pulling her up into a bright sunlit world where birds sang in the background and the air was warm and comfortable.

2

Raoul woke in a small, unfamiliar room. The walls were yellow-painted, smooth and almost square. The ceiling was white, streaked with cobwebs in one corner. Turning his head he noticed a small window where sunshine entered, illuminating a vase on the sill. The shadow of it stretched towards him as if pointing at him.

Lifting his head he realised he lay in a wide cot-bed, covered by a clean sheet and no blanket, which seemed sensible to his confused mind. The room felt hot. Above him on the ceiling a rotating ventilator moved enough air to prevent the heat inside from building up. There was a thin wooden door separating the room from somewhere beyond but he could not understand where he might be, so he did not puzzle over what lay beyond the door, though he could hear the faint sound of voices.

On a table beside the bed stood a cut-glass bottle containing what he thought must be water. Raoul noted how an inverted glass sat atop it, etched in a similar pattern to the bottle. It looked expensive and it looked neat.

A suntanned man, perhaps in his fifties, came into the room. He was small and round and wore a camel suit, despite the heat. His head was almost bereft of hair and the polished pate reflected the light of the window as if he had rubbed it with beeswax. The grey curly hair above and behind his ears was short and trimmed.

The man placed his hands together in front of his chest, rubbing the palms together and said, 'You are awake. At last, awake.'

He spoke in an accent Raoul recognised as Spanish, though it was faint and the man's French was good.

'Where am I?' Raoul tried to push himself up but he felt weak and his arms would not support him. He said, 'How long have I been here?'

'You came here two days ago. You were in a sorry state. You will take a long time to recover. You have been very ill.'

'Where... Where is this?'

'You are in Odieta near Pamplona, in a small farmhouse where no one asks questions and no one will ask for a passport. You need to rest.'

'Where are... Where are the others?'

'Others?'

'Yes, the people I was with. What day is it?'

291

'Friday.'

'Friday? The rescue was five days ago.'

'I don't know about that, but you, my friend have been here for two days and two nights. Your heart is in a very poor state.'

'My heart? What about Natalie?'

'The woman who brought you?'

'I don't remember who brought me. What was wrong with my heart? Are you a doctor?'

'Of course. I am Doctor José Montoya. You have had a severe case of heart strain. It would have been a serious heart attack had you not been so cold when it happened. Your friends said you fell into a river.'

'River. Yes. I did. Where is Natalie?'

'The woman? She is outside. She has hardly slept while I have been in attendance. She has strong feelings for you, I think.'

'Can I see her?'

'Of course, just let me examine you first.'

The doctor helped him into a sitting position and sounded his chest at the back. He listened to Raoul's breathing with a conical, bell-ended stethoscope. He clucked with his tongue as he recorded the pulse at Raoul's wrist.

'Better,' he said. 'Better. Why you did not get real pneumonia, I have no idea. You are a strong man I think.'

'Can I see her now?'

The door opened and there she stood. She looked a vision in a deep-blue dress embroidered with white flowers, her dark-brown hair held up by a comb at the back. A feeling came over Raoul as if everything in the world was calm and healing.

It was as if no war existed and there were no Nazis in the world.

The doctor stepped back.

'I need to talk to you Señor Verney. It is good that this young lady is present. I need her to support me in what I have to say.'

Raoul looked from the smiling face of his lover to the serious, frowning face of the doctor. Natalie crossed to her man and kissed him on the forehead, then holding his hand sat upon the bed. Raoul clutched her hand like a lifeline.

'I am passionate about my job. I care for the health of my patients and have sworn an oath to heal and do no harm. I am in this way an *aficionado*. You understand what that is?'

'No. My Spanish is rudimentary,' Raoul mumbled.

'You are a great chef, this lady tells me.'

'I am a chef. As to whether I am great only others can judge.'

'You are passionate about your food?'

'Naturally, there is no love as pure as the love of food, is it not so?'

'You understand the word *aficion*?'

'No, I'm afraid my Spanish...'

'Another word in your language would be passion. I understand you, you see. You have a passion for food and a passion for cooking and I have a passion for healing the sick, is it not so?'

'Yes, I suppose so.'

'Then, like me you are an aficionado in your way. Your problem has been that you have an *aficion* for eating as well as cooking, is this not correct?'

'I enjoy my food, yes. But a man of my size must eat more than others. I am happy when I eat.'

'Then in a year or so, you will die a happy man and everyone will be happy for you. Yes?'

'A year?' Natalie said, shock lining her voice.

'Yes. Correct.'

Raoul said, 'You mean I only have a year to live?'

'If you keep eating like you do, a year is optimistic. Your heart cannot stand the strain and has been damaged already by the abuse you have ladled upon it.'

'But if I don't eat?'

'You must eat, but be sensible. Never leave the table with a full stomach. Never. Exercise every day. Walking is good exercise for a man of your size. If you recover from this without pneumonia, then you have a chance.'

'Doctor,' Natalie said, 'I will make sure he controls his eating.'

She turned to Raoul. Her eyes held a look Raoul had never seen before. He thought it was somewhere between determination and anger.

'Well,' Montoya said, 'I will bring you a diet sheet tomorrow and you will have to stick to it. Until then, nothing but pork broth. Good day.'

'Pork broth? But I'm hungry.'

Turning back to Raoul, the doctor said, 'That hunger will kill you. Move your legs around in bed, and take deep breaths whenever you think about it and in two days you may get up. I have other people to care for, people who have not made themselves ill.'

Raoul glared at the doctor's back as he left.

'The man's mad. A little food can't harm me.'

Natalie reached out and smoothed his forehead, her fingers moving in slow and gentle movements. 'He is a good doctor. He is right. From now on you will be a wonderful chef who only tastes, but never eats his own dishes. You avoided me all of your life until it was almost too late. You think I will let you leave me now? I love you and I love you enough to leave you if you don't follow the doctor's orders.'

'What happened on the bridge?'

'Marcel missed Von Schwerin, they struggled and he had to jump from the bridge the way we did. When he saw you were not there... well, we thought you were dead at first. They had to use the winch to lift you onto the barge and Marcel almost died diving in to attach it. In the delay, two of Marcel's men were shot. The others swore at you and called you a fat pig. It took six men to carry you into the truck and all the time I thought you would die. If it wasn't for Marcel they would have left you on the barge. You think it is worth living through that and not changing your ways?'

'I never thought of it that way.'

'Then you will now. I don't want to be alone for the rest of my life. I want to spend it with you. There is one thing though.'

'What?'

'Did you really feed Schiller's body to the Germans at the banquet?'

'I can't say.'

'I want to know.'

'You only think you want to know.'

'I want to know. Did you feed Schiller to those Germans?'

Raoul smiled. 'Yes and no.'

'Yes and no? What is "yes and no"?' She straightened her arms, her hands on his chest and her head to one side. She looked at his face. 'Tell me the truth.'

Raoul inclined his head too. 'Well, it was just a soupçon…'

'You mean they really ate him?'

'Only top table. I couldn't help it—I ran out of marrow-bone. It was a kind of black communion—as if they drank wine and ate the body of their anti-Christ. I hated myself for it at first, but in the end, I resolved my thoughts. It seemed like some kind of poetic justice, Goebbels eating one of his own. I committed a terrible sin. Can you ever forgive me?'

Raoul looked down. He had done it now. Certain she would reject him for the killer and evil man he truly was, he wished he had never told her.

'Me? Yes, I forgive you,' she said. There was a trace of a smile on her lips and the little crow's feet at the corners of her eyes deepened.

'But you must be punished for your crime. You reap as you sow, have you not heard that? Is it not one of your own expressions? Your punishment will be a strict diet for the rest of your life. A kind of life-sentence. A life sentence with me as your *geôlier*—your keeper.'

Raoul reached for her and as their lips met, he had visions of his imminent starvation and weight loss.

Their tongues caressed.

Better than food.

My God, better than anything.

Epilogue

Three o'clock in the morning. The corner of Rue Déchargeurs and Rue Le Plat Detains. A tall man stands waiting in the dark shadow of a doorway. The streets are shiny with rainwater and the overcast sky obscures the moon. Drizzle falls, sloping in the light breeze from the west. His ears are long and the points of them give his face a rabbit-like appearance.

The man is watching a café diagonally opposite. He pulls up the collar of his brown raincoat. He dismisses the thought that he might have had better shelter under the awning that hangs over the café entrance. It would be too close for what he wants to do. A memory of a fat man, a chef, drinking wine in his living room, comes to mind and it brings a smile to the tall man's lips. If only Monsieur Verney could see him now, he would surely be pleased.

A black Renault pulls up outside the café. A German soldier in a green uniform steps out and straightening his tunic, he stands by the vehicle on the side nearest the café. He waits too. The tall man smiles. They are both waiting for the same event, the same person, though their intentions are diametrically opposed.

Within minutes, two men emerge. They stagger a little from the wine and the cognac they have drunk and enjoyed, while the man waits opposite and the car waits by the curb, and the soldier also waits for the two emergent men. The two men are laughing and one slaps the back of the other in gay camaraderie.

The driver salutes. He reaches forward and begins to open the back door of the car as the tall man with the long ears steps forward towards the three men. None of them notices the figure in the raincoat as he draws a Luger from inside his coat. He points the gun first at the driver: he would be sober. He takes him with a head shot, then forgets about him completely, as if he has never existed, never breathed or smiled or driven Von Schwerin around occupied Paris.

With a cool and deliberate aim, the man shoots one of the two men in the chest. The second man, a meerschaum pipe in his right hand, with wide eyes and a look of complete surprise on his face, drops the pipe and reaches for his gun.

Two things happen then at almost the same time. The first is that the rabbit-like man says in a louder voice than was needed, 'Raoul Verney.'

The second is the shot taking Von Schwerin in the face. The exiting bullet blows fragments of bone and blood across the pavement behind him at the same moment as the pipe shatters on the paving stones. Without pausing, the long-eared man squats by the bodies. Taking little time to do so, he removes wallets from all three men and walks with measured tread away across the street to the corner.

Rain begins to fall again as the figure disappears into the darkness, walking along the Rue Le Plat Detains, humming to himself, content he has done a good morning's work.

ALSO BY FREDRIK NATH

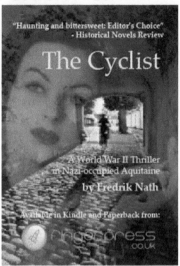

THE CYCLIST

A World War II Drama

by Fredrik Nath

"The story is brilliantly executed... Nath's biggest success is the sustained atmospheric tension that he creates somewhat effortlessly."

-LittleInterpretations.com

"A haunting and bittersweet novel that stays with you long after the final chapter—always the sign of a really well-written and praiseworthy story. It would also make an excellent screenplay."

-Historical Novels Review—Editor's Choice, Feb 2011

www.fingerpress.co.uk/the-cyclist

FAREWELL BERGERAC

A Wartime Tale of Love, Loss and Redemption

by Fredrik Nath

François Dufy, alcoholic and alone, is dragged into the war effort when he rescues a young Jewish girl from the Nazi Security Police.

Then the British drop supplies and a beautiful SOE agent whom Dufy falls in love with. But as the invaders hunt down the partisans in the deep, crisp woodland, nothing works out as Dufy had hoped.

www.fingerpress.co.uk/farewell-bergerac

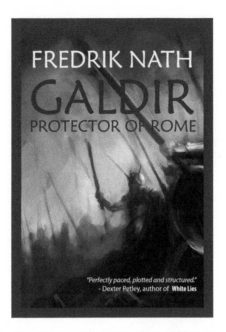

GALDIR: PROTECTOR OF ROME

Barbarian Warlord Saga

by Fredrik Nath

"Beautifully written, perfectly paced, plotted and structured.
It never wavers from its narrative trajectory or its cast-iron
plot... A gripping, thoroughly satisfying novel, genre writing
at its best."

-Dexter Petley, author of **White Lies**

Protector of Rome continues the thrilling saga of Galdir—
slave, warlord and rebel.

www.fingerpress.co.uk/galdir-protector-rome